How To

Escape

The South

By Rey Chambers

I'd like to say that the whole situation was new to me. Then again, I don't want to lie, at least, not to you.

"Well, I'm a Christian. I go to church twice a week. I'm a country girl. I work as a waitress but I'm going to school to be a veterinarian because I love animals so much. I'm a sweetheart but I can be a bitch if you get on my bad side," she says as she takes another drink of her southern comfort.

I find it hard to pay attention when it feels like I've heard this story at least a thousand times in my life. It may be a different girl but it's always the same story. Always a Christian. Always country. Always a bitch. As if that's some sort of compliment on her behalf. It's like if I were to say to her *'well I'm a nice guy but I can be a real dick sometimes'.*

Granted, this girl was prettier than most I've dated. With beautiful short blonde hair just above shoulders length, blue eyes that could stop a man's heart, perfect perky breasts in a typical UT shirt supported by a sexy slim waist just above a tight country ass in blue jeans, she was definitely out of my league, but to call herself a bitch on the first date doesn't leave the best impression.

"What about you?" she says, catching me off guard.

Directing my eyes off her body and up towards her face, I manage to collect myself.

"I'm sorry, what?" I ask.

"Tell me a little about yourself," she replies.

Have you ever heard the saying 'just be yourself'? It's told to nervous men everywhere who are about to go on the first date with a hot girl. He wants to impress her but is too nervous of what she might think of the 'real him'. Meanwhile, everyone around him is telling him to relax and 'just be yourself'. Well, I'm here to tell you that saying is a big steamy pile of horse shit. When a girl ask questions about you the last person you need to be is yourself. The idea is not to tell her the truth but to tell her what she wants to hear.

"Well, I'm a country boy at heart. Jesus and God come first in my life. I absolutely love animals. To be honest, I'm really just looking for a nice, sassy, country girl to settle down with in a house with two dogs while we drink beer, watch Netflix and gain ten pounds," I say as she smiles at the perfect little southern heaven I just painted in her mind.

The next thirty minutes consisted with conversations on topics such as church, animals and football. To tell the truth, I don't actually like football, but I still manage to catch the latest highlights on ESPN in order to hold my own when a girl mentions the sport. Trust me, they will. If there's two things southerners love it's God and football. For me, football is just a way oversized, steroid driven men can give each other brain damage while hiding their homosexuality. I mean, you put ten men in the same shower and tell me they're not gay. Despite my hatred for the sport, I still manage to skim over the scores to strike up a conversation with the ladies. If someone asks who my favorite team is, it all just depends on who's asking. For instance, tonight my favorite team is UT.

After about thirty minutes of chit chat, I finally ask for the check when she looks at me and asks, "Do you wanna go back to my place? I'm not even tired."

I smile and reply with, "Sounds like a plan."

The rest of the night consisted of us going back to her apartment and making out on her couch followed by some heavy petting and finally partaking in my personal favorite past time.

.   .   .

.

"It's a boy!"

The doctor says as he holds the new born baby. After twenty four excruciating hours of labor my stubborn ass was finally born. It was 1991 on a Friday the thirteenth. (It's just my luck.) The doctor looks down at me and then nervously at my father just before handing me over to him. My father, Mark Johnson, with blonde hair, blue eyes and pale skin matched the rest of our family including my mother and sister,

3

I was the exception, born with brown hair, brown eyes and naturally tan skin. He smiles as he walks over to the bed and hands me over to my mother who finally names me, Joshua Allen Johnson.

We lived in a beautiful house in a small town just outside of Nashville, TN. My father worked night shift at a factory making car parts. He was six foot tall with a beard and a muscular build but not the kind you'd get from a gym. He had the kind of rugged muscular build you'd get from working in a factory most of your life. My mother was slim with long blonde hair and wore shirts with bands from the 70's and 80's like a hippie. Because of the money my father made, she was able to be a stay at home mom. My sister, Alexis, was three years older than me and was the perfect cross between our parents. Unlike me who was a scrawny dark haired, brown eyed, tan boy. My sister and I were never particularly close due to her maturity and my immaturity but we still got along for the most part. At a glance we looked like the perfect family portrait, with the exception of me.

I'd like to say that being born in 1991 makes me a nineties kid but I honestly don't remember much from the nineties. While other kids were busy watching cartoons, my attention was elsewhere.

"The beautiful people! The beautiful people!"

The TV screams into my face, not that it had to, I was only two feet away. It was Saturday around noon in 1999 and my father was asleep from working all night while my mother was on the phone gossiping about 'he said she said' bullshit to her friends and my sister was locked in her room. I, on the other hand, was surfing through the channels for whatever offensive, vulgar and obscene thing that cable TV had to offer. I watched men with long hair dressed in all black strum electric guitars as they banged their heads to the heavy, dark noise that is rock.

"That's gonna rot your brain, you know."

I take my attention away from the TV to see my sister making her way into the living room.

"Then again, there's not that much to rot to begin with," She says as I stick my tongue out at her. While my tongue was still out I start to see an image emerge from behind my sister. It's a beautiful young girl around my sister's age with pretty green eyes and silky blonde hair that shines when the sunlight hits it. Her name was Emily. My sister met her at school that year and they became best friends. I've known Emily ever since I could masturbate and still think the two correlate somehow. She leans toward me with her hands on her hips and says, "You plan on putting that tongue back in your head any time soon?"

I was so busy admiring her I didn't even notice my tongue was still out. I pull my tongue back in my mouth and turn red as a stop sign. She crinkles her nose and smiles at me making my little eight year old heart beat faster.

"Mom, can me and Emily go to my friend's house?" My sister ask my mom who's still busy on the phone. She stops talking long enough to say yes, they finally leave, and I direct my attention back to the TV.

.   .   .

.

The next morning I woke up next to the hot, blonde Christian girl. I had barely gotten any sleep that night, not do to the sex, but because I can't sleep in someone else's bed. The girl on the other hand was fast asleep. I tip toe around her room gathering up all my clothes but my shirt. After looking around her room, I finally see it right under one of the ugliest pugs I've ever seen.

"*Gggrrr!*" it growls.

"Ssshhh!" I say to the dog, trying not to wake the sleeping beauty on the bed.

"*Bark! Bark! Bark!*" the dog yells.

"Abraham no! Bad boy!" I look over and it was too late, she was already up and yelling at the dog.

"Abraham?" I ask.

"Yea like the prophet," She replies.

"Well, I think your prophet just pissed on my shirt."

She looks down at my yellow stained shirt and then back up at me.

"Yeah sorry, he likes to claim things as his own."

"Wait, so you're telling me your dog, Abraham, likes to claim things as his own without telling anyone else?" I ask.

She smiles and nods her head. Deep down the irony was killing me but I don't think she was bright enough to get the gist.

"I should probably take him out. C'mon Abraham!"

The dog follows her to the back yard. While they're gone I look down at my yellow, prophet piss stained shirt.

"Abraham can keep it," I say as I make my way out of the front door and into my car.

The ride home was somewhat awkward seeing that every time I stopped at a red light the people in the other lane would stare at me in all my shirtless glory. When I finally pull in my driveway, I see that someone is knocking at my door. It's a taller man, maybe six foot two, with light brown hair combed to the side. He's dressed in a purple button up shirt with a tie to match and tight kakis. When he sees me pull in he smiles big, too big in fact. It's not the kind of smile that's inviting or comforting. It's the kind of smile that might scare young children. This man was too happy, and I didn't like it. So there I was, standing five foot ten with my short brown hair in a mess, wearing sunglasses, black bootcut jeans and no shirt. I looked like the terminators gay cousin as I approached this man who looked like he was into younger boys.

"Hello, sir. I was wondering if I could talk to you for a minute?" he says, extending his hand out for a shake but I ignore it and walk past him to the door.

"Whatever it is, I didn't do it, I didn't break it, I don't want to buy anything and I thought she was eighteen." The man looked confused toward all of my random excuses.

"Actually, I was wondering if you had time to talk about the word of the lord?" he asks.

"Sorry, I'm a Satanist," I say as I juggle with my keys to find the right one for the door. The look on the man's face went quickly from confused to concern.

"Well, in that case you need the word of the lord more than anyone," he says. He's persistent, I'll give him that. I finally manage to open the door when I look into his eyes and say, "Sorry, but I'm happily Satanic. I just love that Satan. Can't wait to get to hell and suck his big red dick." The man's eyes widened at my comment and stayed wide as I shut the door on him.

Once in my house, I walk over to my favorite piece of furniture, my piano. My home was a beautiful, older house just outside of Nashville that I inherited from a dead relative. The house was paid off so with the lack of rent or house payments I was able to pursue my dream of being a writer. There was a two day old glass of scotch on the piano next to an ash tray with one cigarette in it. In front of me was a piece of notebook paper with an unfinished song written in drunken chicken scratch on it. I close my eyes and press down on the keys. A harmonious melody roars from the piano. I strike down vigorously with my fingers as the beautiful sounds travel from my mind down to my hands and the piano screams out a cry of pain, depression and loneliness. I open my mouth but before I can let out one lyric I hear the front door open.

"I told you I'm a Satanist!" I yell.

I turn my head to see a girl standing there. It was a beautiful girl with green eyes and blonde hair that shined when the sunlight hits it. I had grown a custom to Emily walking in my house without knocking. She had stayed the night a handful of times before and felt comfortable enough to barge in at any time.

"Sorry. I thought you were a six foot two pedophile," I say as she looks at me with a combination of confusion and anger.

"You smell like pussy......and what happened to your shirt?" she asks.

"Abraham pissed on it," I reply.

"Abraham pissed on it?"

"Yea," I answer.

"Abraham the prophet?"

"No, Abraham the dog."

She closes her eyes and shakes her head in confusion before replying,

"What the fuck, Josh?"

"I mean, I don't know, the dog may have been a prophet. Who decides these things?" I say as she finally cracks a smile.

"No, fuck face, not the dog. You're supposed to take me to drill practice."

Emily had enlisted in the National Guard that year in order to pay for her to go to college to be a doctor. Personally, I didn't think it was worth it. Leaving the country for years at a time to a dangerous place that hates Americans, but if it pays for school and it's what she wanted, I told her I'd support her. Lucky, she was just a medic but that didn't keep me from worrying. She didn't have a car at the time so I volunteered to take her to and from drill practice.

As she walks over to the kitchen she notices a blinking red light, "You know you have like ten different messages from your mother, right?" she says.

"That's why I got a home phone so I don't have to answer her calls. She keeps changing her number and I can't keep up. Its borderline stalking at this point."

"It's your mother," she says, squinting at me.

"I know, that's what's creepy about it. A mother shouldn't stalk her son like this. Next thing you know I'll be running my own Bates motel and surprising women in the shower," I say as she covers her mouth to try to hide her smile.

She removes her hand from her face and says, "Give her a call? For me?"

Suddenly, she puts on a sad puppy dog face that she knows I hate. She looks down at the ground, then up at me with those big beautiful green eyes while raising her eyebrows and ever so slightly frowning. A late night animal rescue commercial couldn't have looked any sadder. I was waiting for Sarah McLachlan to start playing in the background.

"Ring! Ring!"

At the sound of the phone ringing, Emily quickly goes from sad dog to devious snake.

"Don't you dare answer that phone," I say, but it was too late. She had already picked it up.

"Hello?" she asks into the phone.

"Mother fucker!" an overly happy middle aged man's voice screams from the phone. Finally, I'm blessed with Emily's disappointed face. An image I had become far too familiar with.

"It's for you," She moans, handing me the phone.

"Who is it?" I ask.

"Who else? Your perverted, weird, cokehead manager."

"Hey, that's not true at all……he's my publisher not my manager," I say as she smiles and hands me the phone.

Steve contacted me several years ago when I was in search for a publisher for my songs. He told me he worked for a big name label company in LA and wanted to fly up to talk to me about signing a deal. I said yes and agreed to meet him for dinner to talk it over. He arrived thirty minutes late and blamed the 'hick driver'. He wore all designer clothes and a pair of sunglasses (that cost more than my car at the time) even though it was dark outside. He had an average body with spray tanned skin and a square head topped with obviously bleached hair to cover up the gray and for some reason his teeth were way too white. After an hour of blabbering on about the big named singers he'd worked with and popular songs he'd produced, he finally picks up the check and ask if I'd like to work for him. Like the young idiot I was, I was totally convinced he was the real deal and signed with him. I would later find out that he was actually a complete and total fuck up with a lengthy arrest record. Cocaine possession, reckless endangerment, more cocaine possession, beating up a hooker, cocaine again, all topped with a couple DUIs. Oh, and did I mention the cocaine? His arrest record sounded like the title to an 80's rock star's autobiography. Despite all of his flaws, he did manage to get me paid so I kept him. He may be a weird, perverted, cokehead publisher but he's MY weird, perverted, cokehead publisher.

"Hello?" I say, putting the phone to my ear.

"Well if it isn't my favorite song writer," He says.

"I'm your only song writer, and what do you want?"

"Hey, can't a guy call his friend just to say hi, how ya doing?"

"No," I reply as he laughs.

"Fine then. Look I got this girl down here that I just signed that's got a singing voice that sounds like mother Mary cummin in her panties and I need you to write a song for her."

"I'm pretty sure mother Mary was a virgin."

"So? Doesn't mean the woman can't enjoy some nice quality cunnalingus. I mean, how else you think she stayed a virgin all those years?" he says.

"Ok well, aside from sounding like blasphemous ejaculation, what else is the girl like? I mean, what kinda song is she looking for?" I ask.

"Oh, you know. The typical dark, heartbreak and sorrow shit you like to write."

"Heartbreak and sorrow is my specialty."

"See, now there's my little manic depressant song writer I love. Hey, you know who you remind me of? A young Steven King, that's who."

"Steven King wrote fiction," I say, correcting him.

"Look, whatever man. Can you write a song for this girl or not?" he ask.

"I'll get right to work on it," I reply.

"Ha! See, I knew I could count on you. Hey, I love you man."

"I love you too, Steve," I say, rolling my eyes.

After hanging up the phone I look up to see Emily, arms folded and one eyebrow raised.

"*I love you too Steve,*" she says, mocking me, "next thing you know you'll be sucking each other's dicks."

"Hey, who says I haven't? I mean, how else do you think I got the job?" I say as she laughs at my homoerotic sarcasm.

11

"Haha! Fuck you, Josh!" she replies.

"What have I told you about calling me my writer name?" I ask.

"Chord?" she replies, "do you know how cheesy that sounds?"

"Cheese factor aside, the law says 'Chord' is my name now. You know, legally I could have you arrested," I say as I walk slowly toward her. Once next to her I press my body against hers as I run my hands up her arms, "But I'll settle for just getting you in handcuffs."

She pokes my chest with her index finger and pushes me away, "Chord, I'm gonna be late for drill practice," She says, smiling.

"Right. We should probably leave," I say as I reach for my keys on the counter and make my way toward the door. I stop when I see her still standing there.

"Chord?" she says.

"Yes?" I reply.

"Put a shirt on, please."

.   .   .

.

It was a particularly cloudy day at the lake. Thick clouds blocked out the sun causing a gloomy, somewhat murky atmosphere but it didn't matter. If my sister wanted to have her twelfth birthday party at the lake on a cloudy day with a 70% chance of rain then we were going to have her twelfth birthday party at the lake on a cloudy day with a 70% chance of rain. The beach was surrounded with what seemed like an army of little teenage girls and somewhere in the teenage fray was my sister soaking up the attention and strutting her popularity. My mother was sitting at the picnic tables with the rest of the moms talking about how other mothers, not at the party, had a drinking problem, or were probably cheating on their husbands. Meanwhile, my father was

12

attending the grill alongside the rest of the dads talking about football, taxes and drinking light beer. There I was, an eight year old boy all alone in the sand on a beach filled with intimidating teenage girls. I had been trying my hardest to make a sandcastle by myself but it seemed the wind that day wanted to ruin my fun. I get up and walk past the endless crowds of little girls and toward my father before tugging on his shirt.

"Dad? Can you help me build a sandcastle?" I ask as he looks down at me.

"No. Go play, Josh," he says as he directs his attention back to the conversation between dads.

So, I walked back to my pale and shovel for another try on my own. After several minutes of sand architecture and the wind settling down to a breeze, I finally get a castle going when out of nowhere a horde of running teenagers trip and trample all over it. Without even acknowledging that they had destroyed my kingdom they get up and walk away. I give out a long sigh as I pick up my pale and shovel again.

"You know, that might work better with wet sand, sweetheart."

I look up to see Emily standing there in a two piece bathing suit looking as beautiful as ever. My heart immediately sank in my chest.

"What?" I finally manage to mutter.

"Wet sand usually makes better sandcastles. C'mon, let's move you closer to the water," she says.

We pick up my things and move over to where the water just runs over the sand. Emily sits down next to me and starts piling wet sand into the bucket.

"And where's your moat?" she asks.

"My what?" I reply.

"A moat is like a river that goes around your castle. How else are you supposed to keep your enemies out, silly?" she says, crinkling her

13

nose at me. After only a couple minutes on construction, we finally make the perfect sandcastle, moat and all. I sit back and look at the sandcastle in amazement and then at Emily who's giving me a big smile. Immediately, my eyes go to the ground as I blush bright red. I found it hard to look her in her eyes anymore. I easily suffocated in her beauty. I felt like I was going to melt away every time she looked at me. My little boy emotions were running wild. Love, compassion, confusion and embarrassment all rolled up into one little eight year old body. Lucky my awkwardness was interrupted by the sound of thunder. *"croooosh,"* the sky roars as we both look up only to be hit in the face with a waterfall of rain.

"Emily! Time to go!" her mother yells from across the beach and without even a simple goodbye she gets up and disappears into the crowd of little girls.

Seeing her walk away broke my little heart but I had no time to wallow do to my parents yelling for Alexis and I. So, I pick up my things and walk toward the car trying not to get trampled by the stampede of teens. Once there, I throw my pale and shovel into the trunk and hop in the back seat next to Alexis.

"Everybody here?" my father says in the front seat as he turns his head to see us, "Joshua!" he yells allowed startling my sister and I.

"What?" I reply.

"God damn it, boy! You're covered in sand!" he yells.

I look down and apparently I had forgotten to wash all of the sand off my legs and it was slowly seeping into the seat. He opens his door, gets out and quickly slams it shut. He stomps over to my door and grabs me tightly by the arm just before yanking me out of the seat onto the concrete. After picking me up by my arms he gets right in my face and says through his teeth, "Why don't you ever fucking think, boy!"

Whenever my father was angry with me he had a bad tendency of clinching his teeth together to the point where he could barely speak.

14

Frankly, this scared the shit out of me because I knew something bad was going to happen next. With his grip still tightly on my arm he starts stomping toward the showers across the beach. My feet dragged across the pavement as I try to catch my balance but can't, due to him walking too fast. Once at the showers, he drops me in front of them and turns them on me.

"God damn it, boy! Start using your fucking head!" he yells through his teeth. Between the rain and the water from the showers the only way he could tell I was crying was my pathetically whimpering face, "Quit crying boy! Only babies cry! Are you a baby?!" The only thing I hated more than disappointing my father was crying in front of him.

"No," I mutter through trembling lips. My father stares at me as I fight back tears trying to wash all of the sand off of me. I hate that I disappointed him to the point where he had to hurt me. More than anything in the world, I just wanted him to be happy but every time he yelled at me, every time he lashed out at me, every insult destroyed a part of me inside. Despite his anger, I absolutely loved that man. He was like a superhero to me. I wanted to be everything he was and nothing he wasn't. I wanted all of his time and love but instead all I got was his anger.

.   .   .

.

"Why a Satanist?" she asks, turning over on her side to look at me.

After drill practice Emily came back to my place for a shower and afterwards decided to stay the night. An offer I never refused. After a couple shots of Jack Daniels and fixing her my famous dish of take-out pizza, we finally take our, less than romantic night, back to the bedroom. It was the morning after and the sunlight was hitting her eyes at the perfect angle making them glisten as she stared at me, her sexy blonde hair partially covering her face and a cute little half smile.

"So? Why a Satanist?" she asks.

15

"Well, I wanted to scare him but instead I ended up giving him a massive religious boner," I say and she giggles as I continue, "you should have seen this guy. He had trouble written all over him. He looked like Mr. Rogers became the spokesman for NAMBLA. I imagine he has a hard time getting people to be his neighbor now that he's a registered sex offender."

Her giggle now turned into an out loud laugh, "Oh my God! You're such a fucking liar!" she says, covering her smile.

"In his defense, I wasn't wearing a shirt. I was practically begging to get raped," I say.

"You do look good without a shirt," she says, running her hand over my chest, "Who names their dog Abraham, anyway?"

"That's what I said! The man practically founded Israel. The least you can do is not name an oversized rat after him whose favorite hobby includes licking his butthole. Too bad she didn't name the dog Moses. Then maybe the pee would have split right before getting to my shirt."

"So, what's her name?"

"Who's name?"

"The girl, dummy."

"She had a name?"

"Typical," she says, rolling her eyes at me.

"I didn't know I was keeping track of these things. Should I have written down her social security and driver's license number while I'm at it?" I say, "I can't even remember what I had for breakfast."

"You don't eat breakfast," she says, squinting at me.

"Probably why I don't ever remember it then."

"It's still kinda early. Wanna go get some breakfast?"

"Maybe I just want to have you for breakfast," I say as I post myself over her body and start kissing down her stomach.

"Oh, now you want to eat breakfast?" she laughs as she runs her fingers through my hair.

"What can I say? I might as well put a sign next to your pussy that says *'all you can eat buffet'*." My lips make their way down her stomach then kiss her clit but before I can proceed with making out with her pussy she pushes my head away.

"Wait. Wait. No. No. I have to leave," she says.

"You have to leave?" I ask.

"Yea, I forgot I have plans," she says as she gets out of bed and starts looking for her clothes.

"Plans? What kinda plans?"

"Just...plans."

"Plans with a guy plans?"

"I'm allowed to have plans, Josh," she says, rolling her eyes at me.

"I kinda had a plan too until you interrupted it. It involved my mouth and your pussy. Hey, if you wanna go with *Plan B* you can always hop back in bed. And I mean that figuratively and literally," I say, giving her a wink.

"You know what you can do for me, Josh?" she moves in close and places her hand under my chin pulling me in as she locks my bottom lip between her soft lips, "Finish that song for me."

"Yes, ma'am," I reply.

She walks out of the room but before she leaves the house she screams, "And call your mother!"

"That's not exactly what I want to hear when I have an erection," I say.

When she finally leaves I lay back down and do my best impression of Emily's pussy with my right hand. Don't get me wrong, I love sex, but my favorite part of intercourse is actually the morning after when morning wood has shown its beautiful face and there's still a hint of the woman's natural lubricant resonating on your cock. Which is the perfect concoction for the best masturbating session of your life. Why masturbating, you might ask? Simply put, I've been with numerous amount of women in my lifetime and no matter how experienced or talented they are, they will never know my cock as well as I do. So, after finishing the morning jerk, I finally manage to get out of bed, shower and make my way back to my piano.

.   .   .
                .

As I sit down at my piano, I place my fingers on the keys and close my eyes. Images of my past begin to run through my head like scenes from a movie. I find influence for my lyrics from a combination of my family and past relationships. Thinking of when people hurt, lied, or died in my life help the words to flow out of my mind like water over rocks. Which is probably why most of my songs are about heartbreak.

While it's true that we live in a pop world filled with overly used bass lines and simplistic party lyrics sung by loose bubble gum teens shaking their clits on stage, occasionally people want to be reminded that there's sadness and heartbreak in the world. 'And that's where you come in' Steve would tell me attempting to motivate me into writing yet another four minutes of pain filled, self-pitied smut song that emo girls can sink their little teeth into. So finally, with my eyes closed, I press down on the keys of my piano and speak...

"In this sweet darkness

I found a purpose

But you're in the light and I'm all alone

It's not what I wanted

It's not what was promised

But you're always lost when you don't have a home

But if you still want this

And if it's still worth it

You've got to believe

You've got to believe

I can be broken

And I can be changed

I can be molded

So I can be saved

And if you still hate me

It's all the same

Just don't walk away from what we can be

Some say I'm haunted

Maybe I'm wanted

But the pain goes away

When I'm on my way home

It's not like I'm heartless

Just a little departed

But there's no secrets

When you're never alone

But if you still want this

And if it's still worth it

You've got to believe

You've got to believe

I can be broken

And I can be changed

And I can be molded

So I can be saved

And if you still hate me

It's all the same

Just don't walk away from what we can be"

"RING! RING! RING!"

My singing is interrupted by the sound of the phone. I let out a long sigh as I get up and walk toward the phone dreading what I might see next. When I get to the kitchen, sure enough the phone flashes 'Mother' across its screen. I let it go to voicemail and make my way to the bedroom where I gather up my wardrobe for the day. A leather jacket, tight black shirt, blue jeans and black leather boots with my hair gelled to a tacky mess and aviator glasses. The only way I could've looked more Greaser is if I rolled a pack of Marlboros in my shirt sleeve. When I walk outside, I'm stricken with a sight that shouldn't surprise me at this point. My car is missing. Of course, how else would Emily get too her "plans". She didn't want to ask me to take her to a date but felt perfectly fine stealing my car so she could go. The car is a 69' Dodge charger I purchased after receiving my first paycheck from Steve. Like the young, stupid kid I was, I saw the big check and immediately thought materialistically. So, I ditched my piece of junk car and spent the whole check on a shiny, rebuilt 1969 black Dodge charger, my own penis on wheels. Which made me wonder how these guys feel when she pulls up in a car with bigger balls than them. I reach into my pocket for my cell phone and make a call.

"Hello?" the phone says in a sweet, innocent voice.

"Hey, there's gonna be a change of plans tonight. I need you to come pick me up. A girl I know stole my car."

"Oh my god! You should have her arrested! She should be in handcuffs!"

"Trust me, I tried. Anyways, can you come get me?" I ask.

"Yeah, sure. Sorry about your car," she says.

"Yeah, me too."

Brittany and I had met over social network and after a few pleasantries followed by a couple of my cheesy one liners, we finally decided to meet in person for dinner and a movie. She was a cute little redhead with light blue eyes and beautiful pale skin that seemed to have no flaw. She wore a white sweater and black skirt that went almost to her knees and long white socks that reached over her shins. Her wardrobe was the perfect cross between sexy and conservative, making it somewhat hard to get a read on her, but I can't say I don't love a good challenge. Despite all of her wonderful attributes, my favorite one by far was her voice. She had a soft, sweet but sexy voice that when heard made the inside of my pants tingle. Her voice was so arousing to me that just idle conversation was borderline foreplay. She could read the entire Old Testament to me and manage to give me a full erection.

21

"So, tell me a little about yourself," she says as she takes a drink of her water. The drink was another indication that she might be a little up tight. When the waiter came by I ordered my regular Jack coke n' lime before asking her if she'd be drinking too. She said no and ordered a water. Water, the most bland, tasteless, boring drink in the drink family.

"Soooo?" she continued.

"I'm sorry, what?" I replied.

"Tell me a little about yourself, silly."

I open my mouth but pause just before saying a word and breaking tradition. I usually don't like to talk about myself before letting a woman do so first. It leaves me with nothing to go off of. After all, who 'I am' all depends on what she wants. So instead I just reply with, "ladies first."

"Ok well, I'm a Catholic. The church comes first in my life, obviously. I'm going to school to be a nurse. I'm a country girl. I'm a sweetheart but-"

"-You can be a bitch if someone gets on your bad side?" I interrupt. Suddenly, her face looked like I had just killed her dog.

"I was gonna say, but my friends say I'm too sweet," she says with a slight frown. Figuratively removing my foot from my mouth, I manage to change the subject, "So, you're Catholic?"

"Yeah. My parents were like super strict old school Catholic."

"That must have been really hard on you."

"No, not at all. Why would you think that?" she asks. At this point, I was at loss for words. It wasn't halfway through our date and I managed to call her a bitch and insult her childhood. I quickly found out that the only thing worse than a girl calling herself a bitch on the first date was me calling her a bitch on the first date. Luckily, she interrupted the awkward silence with, "So, your turn. Tell me about yourself."

"Well, I'm a Catholic too. I love God and Jesus. I'm a country boy at heart. The church also comes first in my life. Honestly, I'm just looking for a cute little red head Catholic to settle down with," I say. She smiles and replies with, "What church do you go to?"

Once again, I was at loss for words. After all, I didn't know any Catholic churches. What the fuck was I supposed to say? After skimming every inch of my brain for the word 'Saint', I finally recall a song I had heard years ago and come up with, "Church of Saint...Man...son."

"Saint Manson?" she replies, "I don't think I've ever heard of that saint."

"He was kind of a loner. A bit of an antisocial saint but people still recognized his saintly...ness," a confused look falls across her face as I continue, "He would always talk about the beautiful people. 'What do you see? Something beautiful or something free?' as he would say."

"He sounds like a smart man, I guess," she says.

"Oh yea! He was like your own personal Jesus. Someone to hear your prayers.......someone who cares," I say as her face finally brightens up with a smile.

"That's so sweet. Where was he from?" she asks.

"Where was he from?" I reply.

"Yeah. Your saint, where was he from?"

"......Marilyn," I reply.

"Marilyn?"

"It's somewhere in Italy," I say.

"Well, I'd love to come to Church of Saint Manson of Marilyn with you sometime," She says. Trying my best to wipe the smirk off my face, I manage to reply with, "Sounds like a plan."

"So, what kind of name is Chord?" she asks.

"What kind of name is Brittany?"

"A normal one?" she answers.

"My parents were hippies," I reply.

"Oh, that makes sense. So...." She says as she anxiously leans forward with her elbows on the table and hands below her chin, "What was your last confession?"

"I told a girl she looked fat in skinny jeans," I say as she covers her mouth and laughs. "You know what I mean, silly," she says, "Oh my God. The priest at my church is like ancient but he's actually really cool. I tell him everything."

"Everything?" I ask, raising an eyebrow, "Do tell."

"That's for God to know," she says, imitating my raised eyebrow.

"And for me to find out?" I ask.

"Night is still young, Chord," she replies, biting her lip.

For the rest of the dinner I tried my best to avoid conversations on the topic of church due to the fact that I know very little about Catholicism. So, instead we talked about our past, mostly hers. She told me her parents kept her in catholic school all her life and that she had seen her fair share of corporal punishment which wildly aroused my imagination. After graduating her parents told her to go to college. Any college, in fact. With the combination of her grades and money not being an option, she had her pick of the top institutions but instead she decided to move out, get a job as an assistant and work toward her dream of becoming a nurse.

Once dinner was over, we drove to the movie theater where I quickly picked out the scariest movie they had for us to watch. I don't particularly care for scary movies, but there's just something about a family in a haunted house that makes a girl feel a certain peril and unsafe that she might not want to be home alone tonight. As I sit there watching the helpless teen peek behind corners, slowly open creaky doors and trip over every little nick in the floor, Brittany cringes and latches onto my arm at every horror scene. Finally, I reach over and place my hand on her bare knee. An act in which she looks up and smiles at me for. I lean in next to her ear and say, "I think I have a confession to make."

"What's that?" she replies just before I run my hand across her cheek, wrap my fingers around the back of her neck and pull her into my lips. To my surprise, she was actually an amazing kisser. When our lips finally separate she looks at me and says, "I have a confession too."

"What's that?" I reply. She exhales a long sigh before looking into my eyes and says, "I'm really wet," as she grabs my hand on her bare knee and slowly moves it up to her panties. I look around the theater to see if anyone can see us as she continues to massage her pussy with my hand. Fortunately, everyone's eyes were on the movie until I look to my left to see the couple next to us staring. The woman was giving me a look of shame, while the man behind her was grinning and nodding his head, his girlfriend turns to look at him, to which he quickly changes his complexion to the same shameful glare as his counterpart. I focus my attention back on Brittany. She closes her eyes and leans back into her chair, pressing her pussy into my hand while running my index and middle fingers in circles around the panties covering her clit. I lean in once more and say, "Maybe we can finish this at your place." She finally opens her eyes and let's go of my hand before replying, "Good, cause I'm horny as shit right now."

I spent the rest of the movie with her tongue in my mouth as she pressed my hands into her breast over her sweater. I've never had a woman use my hands to massage and grope herself before, but I must say it is immensely arousing. When the movie was over I stand up only to reveal that my pants were doing a very poor job at concealing my massive erection. As she gets up she looks down at it and then up at me and bites her lip at the sight of the outline of my cock pushing through my jeans.

When we finally get back to her place, she takes me by the hand and leads me to her bedroom. Once inside, she closes the door and shoves me onto the bed before running her hands up my thighs. Her right hand gently grasp my hard dick and starts to slowly stroke it as she leans in and kisses my lips. She stops to pull her sweater over her head and casually throws it against the wall revealing her firm, perky tits in a sexy little black laced bra. She separates my legs to push her tight ass

25

into my crotch as she unbuttons her skirt. I lean forward and remove my shirt, throwing it the floor next to her clothes before she says, "Wait!"

"Wait? Why wait?" I ask.

"I wanna show you something," she says as she makes her way toward the closet. She opens it, searches the top shelf for a second and pulls out a pair of fuzzy pink leopard spotted hand cuffs.

"At least somebody will let me put them in handcuffs," I say smiling.

"They're not for me. They're for you."

"Usually, this is the moment when I'd wonder if you're gonna run away with my wallet, but then again this is YOUR apartment."

"Bend over," she says, pointing to the edge of the bed.

"Wouldn't it be better if I was on top of the bed?"

"No! You've been a bad boy and need to be punished!" she says as she grabs my wrists and handcuffs them to the bedpost.

"I don't recall spanking being in the bible but now I think they should seriously consider a rewrite," I say as she grabs my pants and pulls them down to my ankles, underwear and all.

"One more thing," she says, walking back to the closet.

"What, do you have a hot twin sister in there too? Because honestly, that's the only way this could get any better," I say. She reaches into the closet and pulls out a huge paddle the size of her forearm. It looked like a skateboard with holes in it and a rubber grip.

"Where the fuck did you get that?" I ask.

"I stole it from my old school," she says, smiling and cringing her teeth together, "Now bend over and take your punishment like a bad boy!" she lifts the paddle over her head and...

"WHACK!!"

"Jesus fuck woman!!! Ease up!!!" I yell at her. Apparently, I underestimated how hard the sweet little ginger girl could swing. As my ass throbbed in pain she rears back and yells, "HOW DARE YOU CURSE IN FRONT OF A LADY! BAD BOY!"

"WHACK!!!"

"GOD DAMN! WHAT ARE YOU, BARRY BONS KID?!?!"

"Stop being such a pussy!"

"I think you just turned my asshole into a pussy!" I say.

"You're a bad boy and you need punishment!" she yells.

"And possibly stitches. You psycho bitch!" I yell back.

She gasped just before rearing back again but before she can hit me, I jerk my handcuffs as hard as I can breaking the wooden bed post. I stood there staring at the bed and then at her.

"You broke my bed!" she says.

"I'm sorry. You were going just a little too 'Pamela Vorhees' for me."

"Too what?" she says with a confused look.

"Pamela Vorhees? Mother of Jason Vorhees the retarded serial killer?"

She gasped again at my comment just before raising the behemoth paddle above her head and charging for me. I ran toward the door and managed to get it open before running out of the house. I ran down to the end of the street and looked back to see she wasn't chasing me anymore. I finally stop far enough to where she couldn't see me and manage to catch my breath. So there I was, in the middle of the street on a dark moonlit night with a bright red ass wearing nothing but a pair of fuzzy pink leopard spotted handcuffs.

.   .   .

.

As I walk down the street cupping my dick and balls in both hands, I casually remove one hand to wave at the cars of staring families as they drive by. It only took five cars and two blocks before I saw flashing blue lights behind me. I turn around to see a cop car. When the door opens I was expecting the usual overweight, buzz cut and sunglasses of a man that comes out of blue and white crown vicks but instead I'm blessed with the sight of a woman. She had to be no taller than 5'5, had dark brunette hair in a ponytail, a cute face with baby blue eyes but an expression that screamed 'I'm not to be fucked with'. Despite her petite stature, she looked to have what seemed like plump double D breast but it was hard to tell. Damn bullet proof vest.

"I swear, officer, I'm not concealing any weapons, aside from the nine in my hands of course," I say with an arrogant smirk.

"Looks more like a twenty two," she replies, looking down at my hands.

"Give me a break. It's cold out here."

"Not that cold."

"Ow! My confidence," I say as she reaches for her handcuffs before I interrupt, "No need, officer. I already got some." I raise my hands to show off my fuzzy pink bracelets.

"Oh, my god!" she gasps.

"What?" I ask.

"I just saw your dick," she replies with an insultingly disgusted look.

"Hey, you should feel lucky. Most girls have to buy me a few drinks before seeing me naked."

"I can still detain you, you know?"

"I don't know if I'd be opposed to that," I say, raising an eyebrow but at this point her face had gone from disgusted to repulsive, giving me the impression to back the fuck off. She grabs me by the arm and leads me to the back seat of her car but before I can sit down she looks down at me and says, "Do I even wanna ask why you have red and white polka dots all over your ass?"

"I told Dr. Seuss I was on the pill but he insisted on pulling out," I say. She rolls her eyes before shoving me into the back seat and closing the door.

The ride to the police department was a particularly quiet one do to me running out of cheesy one liners and her not wanting to talk to the naked asshole in the back seat of her car. Can't say that I blame her. Once we got to the jail, all eyes were on me as she escorted my naked ass across a room filled with (what I hope to be) heterosexual inmates. She leads me to a room in the back and practically shoves me inside before slamming the door. The room was empty except for a cushioned bed like you would find at a doctor's office. Florescent lighting gave off a depressingly greyish blue tone but luckily brought out what little muscle that I had. I do my best to flex as I hear the door open and see officer tight panties throw some blue cloths at me before closing the door behind her.

"Put 'em on," she says, pointing to the cloths. I unfold them to reveal they were actually clothes.

"Scrubs? Really? Do you have anything a little more...fashionable?" I ask.

"Says the guy in fuzzy pink handcuffs."

"Fuzzy pink LEOPARD SPOTTED handcuffs," I say, correcting her, "That's high fashion bondage, sweetheart."

"Put the fucking clothes on, asshole," she said sternly.

"Hey, maybe I don't want no scrubs. Scrub is a guy that can't get no love from me," I say, doing my best sassy black girl impression. I wait for a response but instead I get the same menacing stare she'd been giving me all night. I finally break the silence with, "Oh, come on! I'm like the fourth Destiny's child, separated at birth but with the same amazing singing voice and sexy dance moves."

"Do you ever shut your damn mouth?" she asks as I finally manage to get the pants on. She reaches into her pocket and pulls out

29

what looks to be little tiny tools. She grabs my wrist and starts picking at the keyhole. I look into her eyes as she works on the handcuffs like a master thief cracking a safe.

"You know, up close you don't look so......absolutely terrifying. You're actually very beautiful," I say as she finishes unlocking the handcuffs. Without even the tiniest break in her expression she says, "Not even in your dreams, buddy. And by the way, it was TLC that sang 'I don't want no scrubs'."

"Seriously?" I reply.

"Hanging out the passenger side of his best friend's ride trying to holla at me? Yea, I think I know my TLC, asshole," she says as she leaves the room slamming the door behind her.

After only a couple minutes of waiting, I finally hear the door open again. I was expecting a feisty little brunette but instead I see the typical porky the pig in Kevlar. It was a middle aged man with thin brown hair, a round head and a massive beer gut drooping over his utility belt. He points at me and asks, "You the fuzzy pink guy?"

"Fuzzy pink LEOPARD SPOTTED guy," I say, correcting him.

"Whatever. Come with me." He grabs me by the arm and leads me out of my room to a much larger room. Florescent lighting shined down on 30 men sitting on benches aging anywhere from 18 to possibly 300. In the front of the room was another officer behind a counter and a man in raggedy clothing making a phone call. My officer walks me over to a bench and sits me in-between a fat biker in a leather jacket with a white beard going down his chest and a wanna be rapper with scratches all over the right side of his face. Neither one of them looked like they were up for conversation so I direct my attention to the rest of the room. The majority of the men in the room didn't look like your typical jailbirds. Most of them just looked like they were in the wrong place at the wrong time. Possible DUI, domestic violence or drug addicts but nothing serious, aside from the hardcore gangster and possible Hells Angel I was so graciously sat in between. I look to my right to see none other than Mad Max staring right through my skull.

"What's with the scrubs?" the biker asks with a snarl.

"I like the way they bring out my eyes," I say, leaning in and blinking my eyes at him. A jester to which he didn't take too kindly too. He grunts at me, gets up and walks away to the other side of the room when I yell, "Aww don't be like that biker Santa!" Once Honeybuns of Anarchy was gone, I direct my attention to my left to see Scarface staring at me. He was a young black man a little shorter than I with short black hair, brown eyes, scratched face and the athletic muscular build of a lightweight boxer though you could barely tell do to his oversized baggy clothing. He looked like the 'after' picture of a weight loss program.

"Sup, nigga," he says, nodding his head.

"I loved you as the villain in The Lion King," I say.

"Nigga what?" he replies. His face was on the borderline of confused and insulted before I interrupted with, "Never mind. So, what you in for, homie?"

"Shit. Baby mama be trippin, bruh. Bitch tryna say we on a break or some shit. Then she wanna trip cause her friend seen me out with some other bitch."

"Bitches do be trippin," I say in my whitest voice possible.

"Shit, no joke. Let me tell you something, bruh. Never date a black bitch. You can fuck a black bitch but never date one. Ya feel me?"

"Dually noted. My name is Chord," I say, extending my hand out.

"Sup. My name's Murda."

"What kind of name is Murda?"

"What kind of name is Chord," he says, raising an eyebrow.

"Touché," I reply with a smile.

"So, why you here, bruh?" he asks.

"Oh, me? I got sodomized by a Catholic ginger with a telephone pole."

"God damn nigga!"

31

"I guess all bitches are crazy."

"Shit. No joke," he says.

"I take it your girl is the one that went all Mufasa on your face?"

"Shit yea."

"And you?" I ask. He looks down at the ground and his complexion changes to a deep regret.

"Yea, I hit her. That's why I'm here."

"We all make mistakes big guy. Learning from your mistakes is what defines a man," I say, placing a hand on his shoulder. He looks up at me and smiles at my comment.

Our sentimental moment didn't last long though. Before I knew it, he looks up and his eyes light up before saying, "Shit. There go my girl now!" I look toward the counter to see a beautiful young black woman standing there talking to the officer. She was 5'9 on heels with sexy short black hair and big brown eyes. Her lips seemed to shine in the right light, her body did a perfect hourglass impression from her big luscious breast to her thin waist and sexy round ass. The officer points her in our direction and when she looks over I can see bruising under her right eye. Before I can say bye, Murda gets up and walks toward her but not before looking back, pointing to me and yelling, "Ay! Stay real, nigga!"

"You too, nigga!" I reply. I look around to see every black man in the room staring at me, ".......sorry," I say as they all shake their heads and smack their lips. When I direct my attention back to the counter, I see Murda pacing toward her as if he hadn't seen her in years. When they finally meet, she runs into his arms and buries her head into his chest just before breaking out in tears. She looks up into his eyes and mouths the words 'I love you' to him. As I watch them walk away, I can't help but wonder what Emily is doing right now. We've never been in a fight, barely even an argument, I can't ever imagine myself hurting her or vice versa, but for some reason, more than anything in the world, I just wanted her here right now saving me from my own stupidity.

"Chord!" an officer calls out to the room. All eyes were on me as I sat there quietly. An awkward silence falls throughout the room before

I interrupt with, "I didn't know if there was anyone else named Chord here," I say with a smile. The room immediately erupted in off color jeers.

"Man, get yo ass out of here!"

"Fuck wrong with you?"

"Crazy ass white boy!"

I manage to get out of there just as they started throwing pencils and crumbled up paper.

"Someone's here to pick you up," the officer says to me.

"What, No jail time? I was kinda looking forward to the man rape," I say. The officer looks at me with a disgusted expression before replying, "Just keep your clothes on, pervert."

As I walk to the front desk, I imagined Emily standing there with a half smirk and one eyebrow raised as if to say 'what have you done this time'. I would explain to her what happened. She would roll her eyes at me and tease me for running from a 120 pound girl before taking me home where we would lay down in my bed in each other's arms for the rest of the night.

I contemplated this to the point where it became true in my mind and as I approached the front I couldn't wait to see Emily standing there. When I finally get there, I'm stricken with a different sight. It was Brittany. She was standing there talking to an officer, hopefully explaining how this is all her fault. She sees me walking up and her attention immediately goes to me.

"Hey," she says in a sweet, remorseful tone.

"You didn't come to finish me off, did you?" I ask.

"No. I came to take you home."

"Good. Any longer and I would have become the gang leader's bitch to survive."

"I can always circle around the block if you'd like," she says sarcastically.

"No. I've made enough friends for today," I reply.

The ride home was long, quiet and awkward; too much for my comfort. If there's one thing I hate in this world its long awkward pauses, so much in fact that I tend to break them with inappropriate comments. Most of which having to do with sex. This time I thought I'd touch on a different topic. So, as we stare out silently into the open night road lit by street lights of various shades of yellow and white, I finally blurt out with, "At least we have something new to tell our priests now." She rolls her eyes and replies with, "I know you're not Catholic." I wasn't necessarily surprised that she caught on to my lie just surprised that she let me lie for this long.

"What gave me away?"

"Saint Manson of Marilyn?" she asked sarcastically. I finally crack a smile before throwing my hands up in surrender and saying, "Hold the 'S' because I am an aint," I say as we both break out in laughter, "So, why didn't you say anything?"

"I guess, I didn't care. I mean, I like you and you make me feel.........different."

"Different?" I ask.

"I thought maybe I could be myself around you."

"Well, you can. As a matter of fact, I encourage you to be yourself around me. Just maybe dial back a couple notches...........maybe dial back several notches. I don't know if my ass can take much more punishment," I say as she turns red and smiles.

"I imagine you don't want anything to do with me now?" she asks.

"That's not true. I'd like to see what else this little ginger has in her closet."

She smiles once more before pulling into my driveway. I grab my things and start walking towards the door when she yells, "Chord!"

"Yes?" I reply.

"Just……call me. Ok?"

I don't say anything back. Instead, I reply with a wink before turning for the door. As she drives away I can't help but notice my car is still missing. That can only mean one of two things. Either Emily stayed the night with her date or she crashed my car. Honestly, I don't know which I'd prefer at this point. I turn the key to my front door, but pause just before opening it, "…….I hope she's fucking some guy right now," I say, shaking my head. How could I ever wish bad upon my car? When I finally enter my home, I'm blessed with the sight of my beautifully unkempt, somewhat rustic, old house. I walk through the living room where miscellaneous papers lay out on the counter tops. Some being unfinished songs waiting to be completed. Others were random junk mail.

I walk into the kitchen to see the same incessant blinking red light coming from the home phone on the wall. A long sigh leaves my chest before I lean over and press a button on the machine.

"Beep! You have ten new messages. First new message…."

"Hey, Josh. It's your mom. Just calling to say hi, how ya doing. Anyways, call me."

"Second new message……"

"Hey, Josh. It's me again, your mother, the one who gave birth to you and raised you. I miss you. Give me a call sometime."

"Third new message…."

"Hey, Josh. It's me again. I need to borrow some money. I know I still owe you but I can pay you back on Friday. So, just call me."

"Fourth new message…"

"Josh, I really need some money. I promise I can pay you back I just-"

"Beep! Messages deleted."

.   .   .   .   .

.   .

"But the bird, the bird will work."

It was 7am on a Wednesday summer morning. School was out and Alexis, Emily and I were all in Alexis's room watching some Disney movie on her TV. The TV was small and had a huge back to it and a VCR attached. It wasn't the only luxury my parents granted my sister though. After graduating the 5th grade with all A's she asked for a bunk bed for when Emily stayed the night, which she had been doing a lot of lately. My sister and Emily were on the bottom bunk and I was on the top in my favorite wolverine pajamas that were actually just a costume from last Halloween that I refused to get rid of. The sleeves rode up my forearms, the pants were up to my calves and there was a tear just under the right shoulder but I didn't care. I wore them to bed every night and then through as much of the day as I could get away with, without my mother forcing me to put on real clothes. As we sat there watching little animated ants try to outsmart big, mean grasshoppers, I'm blessed with the sound of the front door opening. At 7am on a weekday, the sound of the front door can only mean one thing......dad was home. This was the highlight of my day. Every day after getting home from a long night at work my father and I would sit on the living room couch and watch television together. I would eat sugar covered cereal and he would drink beer as we watched M.A.S.H. I had told him that I loved the show but that actually was a lie. I didn't really care for M.A.S.H very much but it was my father's favorite thing to watch and if it meant even a second of his attention then it was worth it. In fact, there was an entire list of things I pretended to have interest in: old television shows, cars, the rock band KISS, grilling and football (yes, even football). So, I would sit there right next to him waiting for him to laugh so I could imitate the laughter, pretending to understand what was going on in the show, after only a couple of hours he would get tired and head on to bed, then wake up several hours later only to have dinner with us and leave for work. The morning was my time to spend with him. The morning was our time.

As I sit there on the top bunk, my heart leaps in my chest as my father enters the room. He was still in his work clothes which were a dark blue coverall that covered everything but his hands, feet and head. He had his sleeves rolled up to his elbows and his forearms were stained with what looked to be oil or axle grease. His blonde hair was in a mess and he smelled of old warehouse.

"Hi, daddy!" Alexis and I yell.

"Hello, Mr. Johnson," Emily says.

"Hey, guys. You watching a cartoon?" he says with a big smile.

"It's a bugs life," my sister answers.

"Cool. Hey girls, do you mind if I talk to Josh alone real quick?" at my father's demand, Alexis and Emily leave the room leaving him and I alone. I couldn't imagine what he would have to say to me that required us to be alone. Could it be a surprise? Maybe a secret of some sort. At the time I was just enjoying his attention. Once Alexis and Emily left the room the big smile on my father's face quickly left him. The door shut behind him and immediately his complexion changed to an emotionless, stern scowl. As he forced his eyebrows down his face causing the muscles on the side of his head to retract and a wrinkle to form over the bridge of his nose, my heart rapidly went from leaping in my chest to sinking deep down to the point of pain.

"What did I tell you, Josh?" he asked, staring through my little eight year old eyes.

"I don't know," I tremble.

"Josh, what did I tell you?" he repeats.

"I don't know." At a seconds notice he lunges for me with his hands out. I try to quiver to the back of the bed but it was too late. He grabs me tightly by my ankle and quickly jerks me hard to the ground below. My body gives out a deep *"Boom!"* as I crash down on the hard floor.

"I told you to clean up that Goddamn mess in your room, boy!" he yells as I lay motionless holding my sides on the floor, "I told you to have that fucking mess cleaned up by the time I got home, dammit!" he leans in towards me, "Get up! Get the fuck up!" but I didn't get up. In fact, I stayed there laying on the ground holding my sides praying that his sudden outburst of abuse was over. I didn't get up. I couldn't get up. Something was wrong.

.   .   .

.   .

"Fuck face!"

I awaken to see Emily straddled over me, unknowingly resting her butt on my morning erection. There was an empty bottle of vodka next to my pillow and a cigarette that went out on my dresser leaving a trail of ash and a black burn mark along the top of the mahogany. Apparently, not long after deleting my voicemails I had a three-way with my two good friends, liquor and nicotine. The taste of vodka and smoke leaked from my mouth as I yawned. The sun assaulted my eyes with its bright rays. Emily was wearing a British flag t-shirt, a leather jacket and tight blue jeans as she sat comfortably on my crotch.

"Last time I checked, you were American," I say, mocking her attire.

"You smell like liquor and bad decisions," she replies.

"That would explain the liquor and bad decisions I made last night."

"What did you do?"

"Nothing short of getting assaulted by a psycho red head then streaking through a suburban neighborhood," I say as her eyes widen. I was waiting for a response but instead got the same confused stare

38

which I'm used to, "I'll explain later. So, how was your night?" I ask changing the subject.

"Not as good as yours apparently."

"I beg to differ."

"Josh, I have a question," she says pulling the covers completely off my body, "Why are you in scrubs?"

"I thought we could play a little naughty nurse," I reply with a smile, "Excuse me, nurse but I believe I have a growth in my pants I need you to look at," I say, raising an eyebrow.

"You watch way too much porn," she replies.

"Hey, it's not my fault I didn't have parental guidance growing up. I had to learn about the birds and the bees from somewhere else. Luckily for me, the internet became popular right when I hit puberty."

"You say 'luckily for me' but what I think you meant to say was 'I'm a chronic masturbator'."

"At what point does it become chronic?"

"The point where I've walked in on you enough to know that your right hand is stronger than your left," she says.

I stare at my right hand examining it for a few second before replying with, "I guess when you're right you're right." She rolls her eyes and grunts at me before walking out of the room, "Get it? When you're RIGHT you're RIGHT, and I-"

"-Yes, I got it!" she yells from the living room.

As I change out of my silly scrubs and into a more subtle wardrobe then wash the smell of liquor out of my mouth, I can't help but wonder what Emily could be doing in the living room. Often times she'll see my mess of a home and her obsessive compulsive disorder instincts will kick in. Next thing I know she's cleaning every little crevice and crack, dusting every nick and cranny of my old, somewhat rustic house. She would often start cleaning my home without even realizing it, successfully holding an intimate conversation all the while picking up little crumbled pieces of paper, bowls of cereal or various left over hot pocket sleeves. It's not that I'm a slob, per say. I just get into this *writers mode* that causes me to be somewhat messy. Drinking, smoking, eating and throwing things are all a part of the process. I enter the living room to see Emily standing there reading one of the numerous sheets of paper strode out on the countertops. In fact, it wasn't just any sheet of paper.

"Is this it?" she asks.

"If by 'it' you mean my next piece of lyrical desolation that will ultimately be fed to some pop artist who will dismantle it, altering it word for word then calling it their own.........then yes."

"It's beautiful. I love it," she says, staring at me with her big beautiful green eyes.

"It's just a bunch of words jumbled together, sweetheart."

"This one's different though. I can be broken? I can be saved? It's like you're crying out for someone to save you." At this point it felt like those beautiful green eyes were staring right through me. Emily had always been the first to evaluate my work. I couldn't ever consider a song absolute without first letting her read it, but I had never felt this sense of vulnerability in front of her before.

"Or I'm just trying to get into someone's pants," I reply.

She smiles, crumbles up the paper and throws it at me, "You're an asshole!"

"Yeah, but you love this asshole," I say, giving her a wink.

"You sure are confident in yourself, aren't you?"

"Why else would you come to my house every day? Or stay the night every weekend? Why are you there every time I wake up? You're crazy about me," I say with an arrogant smirk.

"Or I'm just trying to get into someone's pants," she replies doing an impression of my smirk, "Besides, I don't see the infamous Chord settling down any time soon...or ever for that matter."

"It's not my fault. I'm emotionally broken. A train wreck of apathy. A dead end road to despair."

"Awww, you poor baby. I got a few tampons in my purse if you need them," she says, mocking me.

"Insulting my manhood? That's not a very good way to get into my pants," I reply, raising an eyebrow. She walks slowly and seductively toward me, placing one foot in front of the other causing her hips to sway alluringly side to side. When she finally reaches me, she runs her hands over the zipper of my jeans, "I guess I'll have to find another way into them," she says as she unzips my pants, slowly reaches down into my boxers and grabs my dick while staring at me with her sexy bright green eyes. She leans in, locks our lips together as she grasp the head of my dick and strokes it with her thumb and index finger. Still enduring the effects of morning wood, I can feel my cock throbbing in her fingers as she plays with it. She takes my tongue in her mouth, sucking on it as she pulls my pants down and my fully erect dick springs up out of my boxers. As she wraps her hand around my rock hard staff, she kisses down my chest before going to her knees, "told you I'd get into your pants," she says just before taking me in her mouth.

"Yes you did," I reply.

.

.   .   .

.   .

"I thought you could heal?" the doctor says with a smile. Apparently, he was waiting for a response. Maybe a laugh or even a snicker but instead I sat there staring at him waiting for the punch line, "You know, cause you're Wolverine?" he points to my costume and puts on an even bigger smile. I don't laugh. Instead, I just look over at my father who had the same blank expression as I did. He was leaned up against the wall with his arms crossed pushing his forearm muscles up and out. He was still in his dirty work suit from this morning and I could tell he was getting tired. After his short outburst in my sister's room he decided to take me to the doctor to see if anything was wrong with my sides. I could tell by his complexion that we were agreeing not to laugh at the doctor's joke. The doctor's office was small and cold. Even colder was the table I was sitting on. It had a soft cushion and paper rolled over it. If there's one thing I hate about doctors' offices it's the damn paper they make you lay on. Constantly crinkling and tearing at your every move making horrible racket in an otherwise silent room. My father hated it more than I. The entire time we waited on the doctor he would snap at me to sit still and stop moving so much. It had felt like we waited an eternity and when the doctor finally arrives he makes a dumb joke about my pajamas. The doctor was an older man with white hair and wrinkles. His teeth were perfectly straight and white which gave me the impression that they were fake and his glasses looked like they could see into space they were so thick.

"Hhhmmm, tough crowd," he says, scratching his head, "Well, I don't think there is any fracture. I'm pretty sure it's just bruised ribs. Why don't you tell me what happened," The doctor asks. I look over to my father who is still leaned against the wall. He looks back and nods giving me permission to speak.

"I was on my sister's top bunk and........I fell. I just fell off," I answer. The doctor raises an eyebrow to my answer as if he possibly didn't believe me. How could a boy just fall off the bed? Why is he so quiet and nervous? I sat there in silence waiting for a response from the doctor when finally he places his hand on my shoulder and says, "Well, I'd recommend some aspirin and a cradle!" he burst out laughing at his own joke while shaking me by my shoulder as if to wake me up to his comedic relief. I look over at my father who was still not laughing so I didn't either.

I don't know why my father had me lie to the doctor and I wasn't going to ask. I was already in enough trouble. He did tell me to clean my room and I did forget. Therefore, I had to be punished. Some punishments are more violent than others; a shove against the wall, pulling my hair and hitting me were all a part of a learning process. I could never predict how much pain I would have to endure in a punishment. I just close my eyes and wait for it to end.

"Ding dong!" The doorbell erupts throughout the house, perfectly matching the vein pounding in the side of my head.

"Ugh!" I grunt.

"Ding dong!"

"Fuck off!" I yell in defense of this assault on my ears.

"Ding dong! Ding dong!" Whoever it was, wasn't giving up. So after finally giving in to this persons will toward waking me up on a Saturday morning, I get out of bed. Without bothering to wipe the morning rust from my eyes, I zombie walk my way to the front door, stepping over various sex toys on the way and nearly tripping over what I assume to be a bondage device of some sort. I look over to see a half empty bottle of Jack on the counter. Even when I'm half unconscious my alcoholic tendencies kick in, so I reach for it then take a drink just before opening the door.

"Good morning, son. I was wondering if......oh my God!" to my surprise it was the old six foot two pedophile himself, "My god, man! Are you wearing women's underwear?" he ask starring at my midsection. I look down to reveal that I, in fact, was wearing women's underwear, and only women's underwear. Stylish ones, in my defense. They were pink with white lace and left very little to the imagination.

"Yeah, you should try it sometime. It's very liberating," I say, squatting down to show their flexibility.

"Oh, dear lord!" he yells out.

"What?" I reply.

"I just saw your ball sack!"

"You're welcome," I say, taking another drink of Jack.

"You smell like whiskey and urine, son."

"Among other bodily fluids," I reply, raising an eyebrow. His face looked like it was on the borderline of vomiting before asking, "I suppose you don't want to talk about the word of the lord, huh?"

"Sorry, but I'm a homosexual," I reply.

"Well, God forgives all sins, my son."

"Not if he knew the gay shit I've done. He'd bitch slap my faggot ass back down to hell." His eyes widened at my comment but still he pressed on.

"Look, I was young and wild one time too."

"Wow, that honestly surprises me."

"That I was wild?"

"No. That you were young." Suddenly, his complexion changed from disgusted to insulted. While I, on the other hand, was trying my best to take another drink of jack while grinning at the same time.

"How old do you think I am?" he asks.

"I just picture everyone walking around in sandals speaking Latin to each other."

"Dang, son! I'm not THAT old."

"What was the revolution like? Are you mad that you had to give up your slaves?"

"What is your problem?" he says insulted.

"Well for one, I'm sober on a Saturday morning. And two, my door is broken."

"Your door is broken?" he asks, examining the hinges.

"Yeah, it swings shut for like no reason. Watch..." I say right before closing the door on him.

Admittedly, I have to admire his persistence, but on the other hand, anything that disturbs my alcohol fueled slumber on a Saturday morning deserves to feel my blasphemous wrath. After getting rid of him, I finally make my way back to bed.

"Who was at the door, baby?" a soft voice echoes from the room.

"Just this Christian guy that comes to my door every week. Possibly a murderer, definitely a rapist. On a separate note......I found your underwear. I was wearing them."

Brittany looks down to see her tight pink panties barely holding in my genitals.

"It's okay. They look better on you anyways," she says, winking at me. She leans in toward me placing her fingers under my chin and pulls me in as she locks our lips together. She pulls back quickly with a face like she just sucked on a lemon, "I immediately regret that," she says repulsively.

"Why? Are we moving too fast for you? Was last night weird? Or is it because you've never kissed a guy in pink panties before?"

"No. It's because you taste like a garbage disposal."

"I know right! It smells like Axle Rose crawled in my mouth and died of alcohol poisoning," I say, making her laugh.

"You should probably wash up. Then we'll get some breakfast," she says.

"Oh, I don't eat breakfast."

"What if I said it's on me?"

"By 'on me' are you implying that you're paying or that I get to eat it off of your body?"

45

"...both?" she replies, biting her lower lip, "but first, you really need a shower."

"I'm gonna go gargle with gasoline and maybe eat a lit match."

As I'm washing off last night's must in the shower, I can only imagine what Brittany could be doing in the rest of the house. This was the first time I had left her alone in my home and as eccentric as she is, the possibilities are literally endless. I grab the bar of soap at my side and start rubbing it against my body vigorously. Apparently, I had done well last night because everything from my stomach to my knees was covered in a thin layer of female ejaculate. Of course, I can't recall anything we did last night due to the traditional alcohol poisoning. Lately my alcohol abuses had escalated from 'the occasional drink' to 'drinking myself to sleep every night'. So much so that the nice Indian man that owns the liquor store down the street from me knows me by name. "At this rate you'll be putting my kids through college," he would jokingly say, attempting to caution me with casual humor. Personally, I don't like the word 'alcoholic'. It gives the impression that I have a problem with my drinking, but I don't. I love drinking. It's a part of my life. The same way the average nine to fiver gets up and has a cup of coffee every morning, or the anxious teen drinks three energy drinks a day, or the old man takes a pill to get his dick erect so he can make love to his ancient, grotesque wife. We all do drugs in one form or another. It's the only way we can get through our short, miserable, and unfulfilling lives. If we didn't do drugs then what would we be? A bunch of Mormons.

When I enter the living room I'm astonished to see that Brittany wasn't trying to start a fire or sacrifice a small adorable animal. Instead, she was going through a composition notebook labeled 'Chord's songs'.

"Is nothing sacred anymore?" I say, walking past her.

"I'm sorry. I didn't know this was private," suddenly she looked like a deer caught in headlights as she quickly closed the book.

46

"No, it's cool. When I spend the night at someone's house I usually go through all of their personal belongings."

"I'm so sorry. I didn't mean to..."

"I'm just kidding. Nothing is private with me. I just wanted to make you feel bad," I say with a smirk.

"You're an asshole!" she replies, smiling and reopening the book, "I never knew you wrote all of these songs. I've heard most of them on the radio. How are you not famous?"

"That's kind of the purpose of being a 'Ghost Writer'. You do all of the work but take none of the credit," I reply.

"But don't you want recognition for your songs?"

"Oh, God no. As antisocial as I am? I would die from overdose of attention. I have only two friends, and that's already pushing my limit for contact with other human beings."

"Two friends?" she asks.

"Steve, my publisher whom I'm financially attached to do to him technically being my boss, and this girl named Emily that occasionally drops by to steal my car."

"And where do I fall into this dysfunctional, reclusive life of yours?"

"Attractive, ginger, nympho, fuck buddy?"

"...yea, that sounds about right," she says.

"What are you reading, anyway?" I ask.

"I don't know the title but it goes '*when I look into your eyes and you look back into mine. You're the best part of my life, you're-*"

"-Wait! Don't read that one!" I quickly grab the book from Brittany's hands.

"Okay, but why?" she asks.

"No reason. It's just...I don't like that song."

"It's really sweet. Whoever you wrote it for, you must really love her." An awkward pause falls between us as I stand there in silence looking at the notebook, "Do you still talk to her?" she ask.

"It's complicated," I reply. I hastily put the folder up in a drawer in the kitchen, away and out of site before looking over at Brittany who is staring at me eagerly waiting for an explanation of some sort. I swiftly change the subject to the first topic I could think of at the time, food.

"Who's ready for breakfast?"

It was cold. Outside it was a comfortable 74 degrees, but for some reason this old timey diner style restaurant decided that the best thing for business was to freeze their customers to the seats. The place was filled with various overweight middle aged couples in flannel shirts and torn hats sporting their favorite football teams on it. The sun was shining through broken blinds revealing settling dust in the air as the jukebox in the corner was playing the best of The Eagles on repeat.

"So, I'm gonna go shopping for a new bed today," Brittany says.

"Why? Your last one seemed pretty nice," I reply.

"My bed WAS nice, until you broke it," she says just as the waitress walks up.

"Hey, Y'all. Can I take your order?" the waitress asks.

"Yeah, I'll have a Jack coke n' lime," I say, closing my eyes and massaging my forehead with my thumb and index finger.

"Sir, its 8am in the morning," she replies.

"Fine, make it a Jack n' orange juice."

The waitress pauses before looking over at me, "Chord, is that you?" she asks. I look up in terror of what I might see next. Rightfully so because it was the Christian girl with the unholy dog. I immediately panic. Mouth wide open, I try my best to form intelligible words but instead I blurt out with, "Hey……Tiffany."

"Sydney!" she snaps, correcting me, "I'm a waitress here. I told you that," she pauses, "and you forgot. Of course. Just like you forgot my name."

"I didn't forget your name. I was just...testing you. To see if you remembered your name. You passed."

"I see you're already breaking other girl's beds," she says.

"You probably overheard our conversation out of context. You see, I broke her bed because-"

"-You don't have to tell me!" she sternly interrupts.

"...she was spanking me too hard," I finish.

"Again, you didn't have to tell me."

"I still have the bruises to prove it. Wanna see?" I get up, turn around and start to pull my pants down before Tiffany...Sydney intrudes.

"Ok! I believe you! I'll go get your Jack n' orange juice," she says, hastily leaving our table. At this moment everyone in the restaurant was staring at us and right before she retreated to the kitchen I yell from across the diner, "And hold the orange juice!" The diner erupted with laughter. I look over to reveal even Brittany was holding her mouth to keep from laughing.

"So, wanna go somewhere else?" I ask her.

With a smile she says, "Yes. Yes I do."

"Do you have any ex boyfriends that work at a Denny's? Maybe we can go there and you can show your ass to everyone," I ask.

"I have a better idea."

After prematurely leaving the restaurant, Brittany and I hopped back into the car to drive around town for a while. I was letting her dictate our every move, turning right or left at her every demand and when I asked where we were going she would say "it's a surprise". We had been driving around town for what seemed like forever and I started to doubt Brittany's navigation skills until finally we pulled up next to a building. I call it a building but really in my eyes it was a castle. It was a beautiful form of architecture that touched the sky with pointed brick towers. It easily dwarfed everything surrounding it and immediately demanded your attention with its enormous walls of old brick and in the center stood a boastfully big steeple.

As we stood in front of this demoted Vatican I look over at Brittany and say, "What are we doing at a church?"

"I'm gonna show you, come on," she says, taking my hand and leading me through two huge wooden doors with metallic ring knobs. When the door shut it gave off a deep roar through the empty hall. There was no one in the entire church. The walls were beige contrasted by stain glass windows with pictures of beautiful angels. The floor was red carpeting covered in floral designs and the ceiling, which seemed to go on forever, held on to bright crystal chandlers. Brittany leads me across the church in the back to a large wooden structure. It stood against the wall and had two doors on each side with mesh screen between them. She leads me through one of the doors and into a small, cramped room.

"Sit down," she demands, pointing to the wooden seat.

"Why?" I ask.

"Oh, you're gonna see why."

Once I sit down, Brittany leans in forward and clasp our lips together as she starts to run her hand up my thighs. Immediately, I feel my dick harden and meet her hand going up my leg. She bites down on my lower lip as she runs her hand over my cock which is now pushing up through my pants. After a couple minutes of teasing, she reaches down, unzips my jeans and pulls them down to the floor. My dick springs up instantly before she grabs it, goes to her knees and takes it in her mouth. As I feel her lips travel up and down, tracing the base of my cock, I lean my head back and enjoy this unholy foreplay. Suddenly, my blasphemous blowjob comes to a screeching halt when I hear the door on the other side swing open. I look down to see Brittany's eyes wide as she stared back at me.

"Well…" a voice from the other side says. The voice sounded like an older man with a slight Irish accent. I look down at Brittany for an answer, who starts to silently mouth words for me to say.

"Forgive me father, I have foreskin. What? No I don't!" I say confused at her choice of words.

"For I have sinned! For I have sinned!" she whispers.

"Oh, for I have sinned."

"And when was your last confession, my son?" the voice replies.

"Oh, you know…a fortnight ago." Suddenly, Brittany looks up at me and mouths 'what the fuck?' I shrug my shoulders at her, expressing my ignorance toward the situation.

"And what have you done in this 'fortnight'?" he asks.

"Just hanging out."

"Well, there is nothing in the bible against just hanging out. How about you tell me your sins, my son."

"But there's so many. Where do I start?"

"Let's focus on the most recent ones and we'll go from there."

I look down and immediately have to bite my lip to keep from bursting out laughing. Brittany looks up at me with a smirk, "Ssshhh," she whispers with my cock in one hand and the index finger of her other hand covering her lips. We were both on the verge of erupting with laughter before the old man interrupts, "I can see you're having trouble

51

opening up to me. It's okay. I have people come to me every day with their personal problems. They can tell me anything. Why, I even had a girl come in and tell me about one of her sexual escapades where she paddled a young man so hard he bled from his butt cheeks," he says snickering. Brittany's expression quickly changed. Now instead of smiling, she looked enraged.

"Father O' Neil! How could you!" she yells.

"Brittany? Is that you?" he asks.

"Yes, it's me! How many people do you tell my confessions too?!?"

"Wait a minute. What are you doing in the confessional?" he asks. A silence falls between the three of us until finally the father says, "Oh, that's sick!"

"Coming from the guy that tells people's confessions. Seriously, you're like the Perez Hilton of priests," I reply

"Get the hell out of my church!" he yells.

"Wow, such language from a man of the cloth. You kiss your altar boy with that mouth?" I ask.

"That's it!" he yells just before swinging open his door.

"Run!" Brittany says as she hastily opens our door and darts to the front of the church. I attempt to keep up with her but quickly realize it was impossible with my pants still at my ankles so I grab them the best I could and shuffled my feet toward the front of the church. Out of nowhere, I feel a hard thump on my back. I ignore it and continue running for the door. After the third thump I look back to see the father hoisting bibles over his head and hurling them at me. I pick one up and run out the door while covering my exposed privates with the Holy Scripture.

Once outside, Brittany and I look around for the car. I look in every direction but instead of finding the car I run into a family of four, walking on the sidewalk on a beautiful Saturday morning. It was a father and his wife with two young boys standing there with eyes as wide as they could get, staring at me with nothing but the good book covering my naked genitals.

"Kids," I say, "This is why you should never do drugs." At that moment the mother covers the two children's eyes and the father takes a step in my direction.

"Hurry the fuck up, Chord!" Brittany screams from across the parking lot as she stands next to my car.

"...or Catholics," I say to the family before making my way to the car.

"What the hell is your problem!" Brittany yells at me as I throw the bible in the car and pull my pants up.

"Me? Nothing. You, on the other hand, have a psychotic priest that throws bibles. Seriously, what kind of priest throws bibles?!"

"A fortnight? Who the hell says a fortnight anymore?" she asks.

"Well, I'm sorry! I don't know how to talk to priest!"

"You talk to them like they're normal people. Cause that's what they are!"

"Pretty sure normal people don't throw bibles."

"Oh, my God! He's going to tell everyone about this. I'm going to get excommunicated."

"Then go to another church."

"It doesn't work like that. You can't just go to another church."

"Is there a pledge involved?"

"What? No! It's not a fraternity. It's spiritual. You have to prove to the priest that you're worthy of being a part of the church."

53

"Not unlike a…"

"IT'S NOT A FRATERNITY!" she interrupts, "You wouldn't understand. You're just an atheist."

"Wow!" I reply.

"What?" she asks.

"I guess you had to say it eventually."

"Well? You're not going to understand religion because you're just an atheist," she says condescendingly.

"At least I don't base my entire life around something I've never even seen before," I reply.

"You don't see God. You feel him. If we all could see him then there would be no need for faith," She says as we both enter the car and drive off.

"What you're 'feeling' is the comfort of thinking that somewhere there is an all-powerful, omnipotent being looking out for you. This 'feeling' you get is just solace knowing that you're protected by something bigger than yourself. But when are you gonna wake up and realize it's not real. It's just a feeling," I say.

"What about love?" she asks.

"What do you mean?"

"People feel love all the time. Does that make it not real?"

"You're confusing abstract with concrete," I say, shaking my head.

"Do you love Emily?"

"What?"

"Do you love Emily? You write songs about her. You spend all of this time with her. She's your best friend. Do you love her?" she asks.

The question struck me by surprise. At first we were debating over religion. Now, I suddenly find myself contemplating about Emily. Not so much as to whether or not I love her, but if I'm even capable of love. In a way, I've always loved Emily. She's been there my entire life. No matter how much success, tragedy or suffering I go through she has always been an object in my life. She is my one true vessel of happiness. Every time I open my door I hoped to see her in my house; eating leftovers from last night, telling me we're out of milk or cleaning up a mess I'd left behind the night before. I always preach about how antisocial I am and how I just want to be left alone, but subconsciously, more than anything in the world, I wanted someone around me. Not just anyone. I wanted Emily. *"Honk! Honk!"* As the car behind me burst out in an obnoxious roar, I suddenly realize that the pause between Brittany and I was far too long for comfort. Luckily, we were almost to her house when I replied, "It's complicated." I could tell my answer upset Brittany. She directed her attention away from me and toward the window, watching silently as the houses went by. The morning sun was shining down on still damp lawns causing them to glisten. Brittany's eyes started to glisten too as water slowly built up in them.

"Maybe you should figure it out," she says, placing her hand on mine and giving me a smile. She was expressing a sense of sympathy that was new from her. This was the first time our conversation ventured away from the traditional kinky sex talk. Usually, after the fourth sentence our clothes are already on the floor. Our relationship was so reliant on sexual tension we forgot that we were both still human. I smile back at her before pulling into her driveway and parking. She opens the door and gets out, but before she can leave I say, "Wait. Are we breaking up?"

"Technically, we were never together. I was just your ginger, nympho, fuck buddy. Remember?" she says with a forced smile then shuts the door and walks away.

The ride back home was filled with more contemplating and self-realization. The question 'do you love Emily?' kept running through my head like a vinyl skipping. So as the white noise of air passing over the car rung through my ears and the vision of clouds in a baby blue sky move over me, I started to think of a life between Emily and I. Maybe I do have the discipline to fall in love. Maybe I could stop sleeping around with random women, whom I can't remember the names of. Maybe I could even drop the bottle and come to terms with my addiction. Is my love for Emily powerful enough to overcome this selfish, arrogant, childish ego I've created? It's not all my fault though. You take a young ignorant man and throw money at him then he is bound to become somewhat destructive. You get a since of invincibility. Like nothing can hurt you. Nothing can go wrong. You're on top of the world. But the reality is everything hurts you, everything is wrong and the weight of the world is crushing you. You start to wonder if this ride ever ends or if you're stuck going down this dark, desolate road for the rest of your short life. The only solace I have is the idea that soon a beautiful blonde haired, green eyed girl will come by and ask if she can stay the night again. Like last night. Like the night before. And the answer is always yes.

Shortly after arriving home to an empty house, I decide to remedy my massive depression the only way I knew how; the devils liquid and music. The sound of ice crackling against the glass wall of my drink was masked only by the guitar resting on my chest as I lie on the living room floor. The D chord is my home, and I would play it over and over. I listen to the deep twiney echo through my house as I watch the smoke tail of my cigarette dance in the air around me. Suddenly, my self-loathing comes to a halt when I hear the front door open. I look up to see none other than the girl responsible for all of my anguish.

"Hey, cry baby," Emily says, walking into the living room. She was wearing tight camouflage cargo pants from the National Guard and a white t-shirt with what I can only assume is a push up bra underneath. Her breast were perky and full with a slight bounce in every step. The sight of her body in tight clothing only furthered my lust for her, "Oh, my God. My day was the longest. First, I had this guy stand me up. Then, drill practice was horrible. Now my whole body is sore," she says, walking to the kitchen. I get up, place the guitar against the wall and follow her as she continued, "I think the Sargent actually works us out too much. Like, I get it we have to be in good shape, but I honestly think he has us doing too much. I mean, does he even want us to fight or are we supposed to die from exhaustion before we even get on the plane," she reaches into the fridge and pulls out an almost empty jug of milk, "Hey, you know you're out of milk?" she asks drinking the last bit. Her comment brought a smile to my face as I watched her stare blatantly at me with an empty jug in her hand, waiting for a response.

"I have to tell you something," I say. At this point my heart was pounding in my chest. My hands were caked in a thin layer of sweat and my body felt like it rose in temperature. Yet still, I stood there with that dumb smile on my face, staring at her like I hadn't seen her in years.

"What's up, crazy boy?" she asks.

"I love you."

.   .   .

.   .

"It's like a mountain."

I hear a voice from behind me. I was so busy staring at this massive stack of presents that I didn't notice her sneak up on me. No wonder, the stack almost reached to the ceiling and was wider than the tree, it was hard not to stare at it. It was Christmas Eve, which meant the entire family (including Emily) was at my grandparents' house eating, drinking and wearing tacky clothes. Zero inches of snow was all we got that Christmas Eve and outside the sun was nowhere to be found. Instead, grey clouds surrounded the sky as the microscopical snowflakes fell down only to melt away on the cold December, Tennessee ground. It had been months since my father had lashed out on me and I felt comfortable in this streak of peace. Comfortable enough to even try to impress him. He was in the kitchen at the time, picking at finger foods with a different drink in his hand every ten minutes. My mother was next to him talking to my grandmother about soap operas and things she had bought on black Friday. My grandparents' house was almost like a hotel there was so many different people coming in and out, bringing various dishes and casseroles. Most of them weren't even related to us. Just people that befriended my grandparents. The door was always unlocked and every soul was welcome to come right in no matter what day of the year. Lunch was at twelve and dinner was at seven, and no matter how many people came to eat there was always leftovers. No one ever left angry and no one ever left hungry. It was a home away from home for anyone who needed one. My grandmother was a smaller women with curly hair and big glasses but despite her small stature she would work harder than any grown man I know. She was always either cooking, cleaning or off tending to her garden; making sure to pick the perfect bright red tomatoes for everyone to enjoy. My grandfather, on the other hand, was a taller man with grey hair and broad shoulders and could always be found in the same place no matter what time of the day. He would always sit on the couch in the living room reading the paper and chewing on some unholy looking tobacco. He was never short of a war story. He may not have had the best short term memory, but he could tell you of his time in war like it happened yesterday.

"Mount present-more!" Emily says, pointing to the stack, "Are those all for Alexis?" she ask. I nod and she continues, "Where are your presents?" I point behind the tree to a small stack of three wrapped boxes, barely noticeable in comparison to the tree or Alexis' tower. Emily looks over at my small pile with a half frown followed by a contemplating stare as if she were devising a plan. She walks over to Alexis' presents, pulls out a marker from her back pocket and proceeds to marking out her name and replacing it with mine. She looks around to make sure no one is watching then quickly throws three newly branded presents over to my stack.

"There! Now you're even," she says, winking at me. Immediately, I look to the ground to hide my red face, but still manage to reply to her wink with a shy smile.

"Thank you," I say.

"That girl has enough stuff as it is," she says before changing the subject, "So, do you have it ready?" she asks. I reach into my pocket and pull out a folded up sheet of paper. Emily holds her hand out and curls her fingers as to say 'hand it over'. She opens it and skims through the words scribbled on the paper, "He's gonna love it," she says with a big smile, "Let's go show him now." I shake my head side to side, but before I can protest she grabs my hand and leads me into the kitchen. This was the first time Emily and I had ever held hands, even if it was only to guide me into the kitchen. My heart was racing as her fingers lapped over mine. I wondered if she could feel how cold, clammy and sweaty my hands were against hers. Maybe she would feel this and decide to never grab my hand again. Or she would realize how nervous I get around her and think I'm weird. I didn't have long to contemplate over this though. Before I knew it, we were standing in front of a crowd of conversing adults eating cheese and meat snacks who probably had far more important things to do than read a little kids poem.

"Emily!" Alexis yells from across the room, "Come on, we're going outside."

"Okay," Emily replies and in a moment's notice she releases my hand before darting to my sister. I watched as her long silky blonde hair waved side to side with every step she took away from me. And just like that, she was out the door. Suddenly, I was left alone in front of a group of intimidating superiors. They were my family so I've known them all my life but right now they felt like strangers as I stood there with a sheet of paper shaking in my hands. I finally muster up the courage to walk over to my father who is engaged in a conversation about football. I tug on his arm to get his attention.

"Not now, Josh!" he says sternly without looking at me. So I abandon my hopes to impress my father and direct my attention elsewhere. My mother was over by the table making herself a drink so I walk over to her, paper in hand, and raise it up to her face so she could see.

"Oh, let me take care of that for you, sweetie," she says before grabbing the paper from my hands and throwing it in the garbage.

"That wasn't trash!" I say hastily. But before she could hear me she was already off to disappear in the large group of adults.

I lean over and start to dig through the trash; pushing aside plastic cups, spoons, forks and paper plates in hopes to find my paper. After a few minutes of fishing, I finally find it hiding under some egg shells.

"You lose something in there, buddy?" a voice from behind me says. I poke my head out of the trash can to see my grandfather standing over me. He had the newspaper in one hand and an egg nog in the other, looking at me with one eyebrow raised probably wondering what the heck I was doing in the trash. I raise up out of the garbage and show him my paper. He grabs it and starts to skim his eyes over the words written on it. Suddenly, his eyes light up and a smile forms on his face, "Did you write this, Josh?" he asks. I nod my head and he continues, "Has your father seen this?" he asks.

"No, but it's okay," I reply.

"Something like this shouldn't go unnoticed," he kneels down and puts his hand on my shoulder, "You got a real knack for this, buddy. Now, you have two options. You can write these artistic poems of yours just to throw them away like yesterday's newspaper, or you can let your voice be heard. Share your talent, Josh. People would want to hear this. So don't just tell someone. Tell everyone! Because even if you only touch one person's heart," he places his hand on my chest, "then it was worth it." I shrug my shoulders and look away. I didn't have the confidence to tell people about my poem. I wasn't brave enough to stand in front of someone and spill my heart out for them. I was too afraid of what they would say. What if they hated it? What if they made fun of me? If it wasn't for Emily pushing me into the kitchen, I probably would have thrown it away myself. No one wants to hear how I feel. No one cares. It was just a waste of time.

At that moment, my grandfather raises up. He had to push down on my shoulder for support and I could hear his knees popping as he stood, but when he did he looked down at me and winked, "Here, let me help you," he says as he reaches for a glass and a spoon on the counter. He taps the spoon on the side of the glass making a high pitched twine a couple of times before saying, "Excuse me! Excuse me, everyone!" immediately everyone looks over at him, "Josh has something he wants to show everyone."

Suddenly, my eyes widen and my face turns pale. I wasn't expecting, nor was I prepared for something like this. I look up to see a room full of towering adult eyes staring down at me as the paper trembles in my sweaty hands.

"Go ahead, Josh. Let us hear," my grandmother says with a smile from the corner of the room. So I lift up the paper and start to read,

"When I hit the ground

And you throw me down

And the terrible sound

I still love you now

I love you now

When I see your face

It all goes away

It's like medicine

I give in

I give in

And I wonder can you walk on clouds

Stop thunder and hold onto sound

With my hero anything is possible

With my hero anything is possible

In the darkest night

I still see your light

Like a shining star

I just want to be where you are

Can you hear me now

As the screams fade out

Let the scars all fade

Fade away

Fade away

And I wonder can you walk on clouds

Stop thunder and hold onto sound

With my hero anything is possible

With my hero anything is possible

When I look into your eyes

And you look back into mine

You're the best part of my life

You're the best part of my life"

.   .   .

.   .

"I guess," she pauses, "in a way, I've always loved you. I mean, you've always been there for me, and I've always been there for you. We care about each other more than anything else and I couldn't imagine my life without you. It only makes sense that we be together," she says, strumming my guitar.

Shortly after confessing my love to Emily, we decided to both lie down on the floor and talk about it. She was leaned up against the wall with my guitar on her lap and I was strode out on the floor with my head resting on her thighs. She wasn't playing any chords, at least not correctly. Instead, she just parked her fingers any random place on the fret board and strummed away with the tips of her nails causing low pitched, flat and nauseating sounds to spew out of the instrument.

"OK, that's enough," I say, taking the guitar from her.

"What?" she asks.

"You playing the guitar sounds like Chubaka having an orgasm," I reply.

"Well, I'm sorry. I'm not the big musician."

"Technically, neither am I," I say with a smirk.

"Oh, yeah. That's right. Mr. Antisocial would simply die if he had a fan base," she says condescendingly. I blow her a kiss and reply with, "All I need is my number one fan."

"But you have no problem telling random girls who you are if it means getting into their pants."

63

"It got me into your pants, didn't it?" I reply then she reaches over and pinches my arm, "Ow! Not the arms. That's how I get the ladies," I say, doing my best to flex what little muscle I had.

"Aww, poor baby," she replies, running her hands across my face, leaning down and kissing my cheek. She raises up and looks into my eyes before asking, "So, do you really think the infamous Chord can settle down?"

"With the right incentive, I think anything is possible," I say, staring up into her bright green eyes. She leans in again and presses her lips to mine while running her finger tips up and down the hair in the back of my head. This sent a slight sensation down my whole body as she continued to immerse her lips with mine. She pulls away for a moment, "I love you, Josh," she says while looking down at me.

"I love you, Emily," I reply.

She leans back into the wall, exhaling and looking out the window. The evening sun shined a deep purple and yellow across her face and her eyes shimmered in the light of the falling star. Suddenly, her hair changed color from a silk blonde to a dark orange to imitate the sun set. We laid there for a few minutes like that, but it seemed like hours. I could've stayed there for days resting my head on her lap with her fingers running over my hair and neck.

"Do you remember," she pauses, "do you remember that one Christmas eve when I made you read that poem to everyone? You told me you didn't want to, but I pushed you into doing it anyway?"

"Yes," I reply.

"I'm so sorry, Josh," with a blink of her eye, a glisten forms below her lashes, "If I knew what was going to happen, I would have never made you do that. I swear." She blinks again and beads of tears run down her face.

"It's not your fault."

"Your dad was such an asshole," she says, wiping her cheeks off.

"Like father like son, huh?" I reply smirking. She lets out a laugh at my comment before wiping the rest of the tears from her face, "Lying, manic depressant, narcissist? Maybe. But asshole? No. You're nothing like him, Josh," she says.

"Thank you." I get up and place the guitar aside before heading to the kitchen. I'm halted by the feeling of Emily tugging on my hand. I look back to see her staring seductively at me. She starts to walk backwards to the room, pulling me along the way and staring at me with those big green eyes through her bangs while biting her lip. When we reach the door I pin her body against it, pressing my crotch between her legs. She wraps one leg around my waist and I could feel my dick rubbing against her thigh as we grind on the door. We lock lips as she reaches down and turns the door knob. She grabs my collar and turns me to push me on the bed but before she can she suddenly stops. Wondering what the delay is, I open my eyes and look up to see Emily, jaw to the floor and eyes wide open staring over my shoulder in shock.

"WHAT THE FUCK, JOSH!" she yells, pushing me away. I turn around to see an entire master bedroom filled with various sex toys from whips, handcuffs, paddles, blindfolds and vibrators all strode out on the floor. It looked like a tornado hit a Spencers as we stared in shock of this BDSM cluster fuck. I look up to see the countertops covered with half empty liquor bottles and lubricants. Apparently, I had completely forgot to clean up after Brittany and I had our little sexual escapade; now Emily had to bear witness to the unholy acts we had committed.

"I knew there was something I was forgetting to do. Hey, you always said I was a procrastinator," I say with a smile while throwing my hands up.

"Oh, my God! Did you do all of this today?" she asks furiously.

"No, of course not," I pause, "it was last night...and some this morning." She gasps at my comment before I continue, "But don't worry. That wasn't here. It was in a church."

"In a church?! Are you serious?!" she asks.

"It's okay cause it was in the confessional. That's like, the place you go to confess sins so I'm pretty sure it was forgiven right then and there."

"What the hell is wrong with you?"

"Would it make you feel any better if I said the priest threw a bible at me?"

"How would that make me feel better?!"

"It made me feel better," I say with a smile, "I mean, a priest literally threw the bible at me. If that doesn't get you into heaven I don't know what does."

"This is not funny, Josh. God! Everything is a fucking joke to you," she yells.

"I mean, you weren't there so I can see how you'd miss the comedy in it."

"Oh! I'm sorry I wasn't there to see your Catholic whore girlfriend fuck you in a confessional," she says sarcastically.

"We didn't fuck in a confessional......it was a blow job," I reply.

"Ugh!" she grunts and shoves me away before darting out of the room, "I can't believe I actually thought you could change. But no, you'll always be the same alcoholic, womanizing, man-child!"

"Emily! Please don't go. I swear I can fix this," I say, following her to the front door. She turns for a moment, looks me in my eyes and says, "How can you fix this, Josh? You can't even fix yourself," then slams the door in my face.

"God damn it!" I yell aloud in my house. I clinch my fist tight, pushing my finger nails deep into my palm before smashing it against the wall.

"Aaaahhh!" I scream, riving in pain at my hand. I lean up against the indention I left on the wall and stare at my shaking hand as it throbbed in pain and slowly started to swell. I didn't care though. Physical pain didn't matter to me now. All that mattered was that the greatest thing to ever happen to my miserable life just walked right out the door.

.   .   .

.

"Ow!" I yell out in pain as the nurse curls my fingers sending a shockwave of agony through my right hand.

"Yep, see how every time I bend your fingers you scream out? It's definitely broken," she says.

"Which begs the question...why are you still doing it?!"

"Every time you look down my shirt, I bend your fingers."

"Really? That many times?" I ask.

"That many times," she confirms just before twisting my hand again.

"Ow! Okay, fine! I'll stop," I reply.

After my assault on my wall and several minutes of appropriate sobbing, I decided I should pay a visit to the doctor's office. The room I was in was exactly what you would picture as your typical doctor's office; small, depressing and fluorescent. The room expressed an unsettling silence with the exception of an incessant clicking noise coming from a rather persistent fly trying its best to concuss itself on the lightbulb above. The nurse, on the other hand, was the exact opposite of her surroundings. She was a beautiful black girl with short dark hair stopping just below her chin. She had smooth dark skin and big light brown eyes wearing a distractingly low cut top holding in her sexy chocolate cleavage. Apparently, my admiration to her bust didn't go unnoticed since she insisted on putting me through agony every time I looked.

"Still worth it," I say before she pushes her thumbs into my palm, "Ow! Jesus! Is this how you treat all the guys that look at you?" I ask.

"Guys don't look at me," she replies, rolling her eyes and finally releasing her grip from my hand. She walks back to a counter and grabs a clipboard and starts to write in it.

"Okay, that can't be true. I mean, I'm having hard time not looking at you. You're like a sexy chocolate cake. I don't know whether to ask you out or put you between two gram crackers and devour you," I say as she finally cracks a smile toward me.

"What's your number?" she asks.

"I must warn you, I did just get out of a bad relationship...that lasted all of two hours."

"It's for the hospital, stud," she replies giggling.

"So, you just pass my number around the hospital to all your sexy single nurse friends? What am I, just a piece of meat to you woman......cause I'm perfectly fine with that," I say. She giggles again and replies with, "Moving on. What's your religion?"

"Why?"

"I told you. It's for the-"

"-I know it's for the hospital but why do you need to know? I mean, do they only give the good drugs to Christians? If I say I'm atheist are you gonna give me Mike n' Ikes and tell me they're Vicodin?"

"No. They ask just in case you die. That way they can get the appropriate priest to bless you and talk with your family."

"In that case, I'm a full blown Pagan. And I demand that upon my death yee praise Thor, Odin son, as I ascend unto Azgard."

68

"Valhalla."

"What?"

"Valhalla. Germanic Pagans believe you go to Valhalla when you die but that's only if you were worthy in battle and judging by your hand, I doubt it," she replies.

"Wow, someone has done their history homework. Are you a Pagan?" I ask.

"No. I just watch a lot of Marvel movies. Thor could hammer me anytime," she answers. A sudden silence falls between the two of us as we sit there looking at each other for a moment.

"So...I don't have a ring on me but I would absolutely marry you right now," I say making her laugh.

"You're cute, but not my type," she replies, crinkling her nose at me.

At that moment, the door behind her burst open and in walks a short man in a long white coat with a horrific comb over and thick glasses holding my X-ray results in his hand. He walks over to me and raises the plastic sheet over the light to get one last glimpse at my bones.

"Well, it doesn't look like you'll need any surgery. Just a cast and some pain meds should do," he says.

"Give it to me straight doctor. Will I ever masturbate again?" I ask in a comically concerned voice. He lets out a long sigh and looks at me as if to express he has better things to do, "Just try not to punch anymore walls, okay?"

"Wow, you can tell I punched a wall just by looking at my X-ray? That's impressive."

"No, I just assumed someone as immature as you would get upset and take his anger out by stupidly throwing his hand at something harder than bone."

"……that's fair," I reply, shrugging my shoulders. He reaches into his jacket pocket and pulls out a bottle of pills before handing them to me, "Take two of these a day and come back in a couple weeks for another x ray."

"Now, do I crush these up and snort them or should I invest in a good spoon and lighter?" I ask.

"How bout oral?" he replies, squinting at me.

"I don't know. I mean, we just met and I'm not really in the mood-"

"-I meant the pills, you jackass!" he yells before stomping over to the door, "and do me a favor Mr. Chord."

"What's that?"

"Get the fuck out of my office!"

As I drive home, tightly gripping the steering wheel with my good hand at twelve instead of the traditional ten and two, I couldn't help but wonder what Emily is doing right now. Could she be waiting at my house to reconcile things? Did she retreat back to her home after realizing how big of a fuck up I am? Or could she have ran to another guy's house to vent about how I hurt her only to fall victim to his false sympathy. Regardless of her whereabouts, I had to find her and somehow fix this. It took my entire life to finally admit that I love her and I couldn't let her go now. If not a relationship, I at least needed her as a friend. I don't know what would happen to my life if I didn't have that blonde haired, green eyed girl barging in my house every other day and demanding entertainment and/or food. As I contemplate this, I look up to see the traffic light turn yellow so I push down hard on the gas pedal. The car lets out a deep roar as I charge for the intersection and quickly the light turns red just as my wheels speed past the line. I let off the pedal and bring the classic muscle car back to a purr, but before I can settle I look in the rearview to see the typical red and blue lights flashing behind me.

For some reason, I've never been particularly proficient when it came to conversing with the boys in blue and didn't think today was any exception. I let out a long sigh as I pull my heterosexual hunk of metal to the side of the road and gather up all the necessary papers; license, registration, proof of insurance and bribe money.

"Hmmm, maybe not the best idea," I say, placing the money back into my wallet.

"*Knock! Knock! Knock!*" I look up to see a middle aged white man in uniform with a short buzz cut, thick mustache and sunglasses knocking at my window.

"And here I thought only porn stars still had mustaches," I say as the officer quickly puts on a scowl.

"License, registration and proof of insurance," he demands and I hand over my hand full of papers (excluding the bribe money), "You know why I pulled you over, son?" he asks.

"You ran out of black people to harass?" I reply. The officer didn't look too pleased with my comment for his scowl grew even stronger.

"You ran that light back there. Wanna tell me where you're headed to in such a hurry?"

"I swear, I didn't see the light officer..." I pause to glance at his badge, "Kowalski? Wow, did you get that when you joined the force or were you actually born with the most generic police name ever?" the officer turned red with anger as veins in his forehead began to bulge. He looked to be on the brink of exploding before pointing over to the dashboard and asking, "What exactly is that?" I look over to see the bible from earlier that day that I had hastily thrown into the car after the incident at the church.

"Oh, that......I'm a bible salesman, sir," I reply. Quickly he regains his color and his face relaxes to its original vapid gaze.

"You a Christian?" he asks.

"Sure am. God bless Jesus, Marry, and Mel Gibson!"

"Uh, yea," he replies slightly confused, "So, is that bible for sale?" he asks.

"Oh, you don't want that bible, officer. It smells like dick."

"EXCUSE ME??" he gasps.

"I said...it's for my friend," I say, correcting myself.

"Oh, well, you must be a good friend then if you're giving the word of the lord to everyone," suddenly he leans in, placing his hands on my door and pushing his face as close to mine as possible without actually touching, "Now," he says softly, "I know a good Christian boy like yourself wouldn't think about breaking the rules of the road again, would you?" Eyes wide, and slightly leaning to my right to avoid physical contact with his face, I manage to reply with, "More than anything, I just want this moment to end."

At my comment, he raises off my door, pulls his pants up and says, "That's what I thought. Now, you have a god blessed day, brother," just before strutting off back to his car. I exhale a deep breath while staring over at the bible resting on the dashboard, "looks like you came in handy after all."

.   .   .

.

The house was quieter than usual. I had just picked up what was left of my little BDSM episode and thrown away the bottles of stale liquor when I started to realize, the site of all of this erotically, experimental monstrosity at once would freak anyone out. At first, I didn't understand how Emily could be so upset. There had always been an unspoken truth to our "relationship" (if that's what you want to call it). She had her guy friends and I had my random females. We knew what we were both doing in our own time. We just didn't care. Whenever I came home and Emily wasn't relaxing on the couch after a long day or in the kitchen eating and drinking what was left of my fridge, I just assumed she was off with another sad sap, giving him false hope toward some sort of stable relationship before running back to my house and venting to me about how they *had bad teeth* or *made her pay half the check*. I wasn't upset about it. In fact, I believe she had the right to stray away from me occasionally. God knows I've had my fill of sexual partners. It's only right that she have hers too but never, not once, did I get mad and walk away. Ever since I admitted to myself that I love her things have changed. Now the thought of her out there with another guy is enough to keep me awake at night. The idea of her being angry, upset or disappointed with me in any way was eating away at my soul from the inside like a cancer. I had spent my entire life not caring what people thought about me but deep down her opinion was essential for my existence. I needed her approval like the air I breathe. Just her believing that I can be a good man gave me reason. I had to find her. I had to fix this. I had to tell her I'm sorry. I'm sorry that I waited all of this time to realize that I love her. I'm sorry I let my sexual appetite and alcoholism consume me. I had to-

"Ring! Ring!"

-I had to answer the phone. As I walk out of the room and into the kitchen, I once again dread what I might see on the caller ID. *"Steve,"* the machine flashes so I let out a long sigh, pick up the phone and say, "Hello?"

"Mother fucker!" he so happily yells.

"What do you want, Steve?" I ask.

"What, you don't like hearing from your favorite manager?"

"You're my publisher," I say, correcting him.

"Really? What's the difference?" he asks.

73

"How do you not know the difference?"

"Shit, all I know is management fees are more."

"Of course," I grunt.

"And right now, I'm fucking rolling in 15 percent of your money. You know why?"

"The price of cocaine went up?"

"No...well, yeah but that's unrelated. I'm talking bout this bitch loves your shit!"

"Am I supposed to know what that means?" I ask.

"It means, mother fucker, that my singer likes this 'I can be broken, I can be saved' shit. Hell, I could smell that sweet pussy getting moist as she was reading it. You could drown a fucking lemur in her panties with lyrics like that."

"Why the hell would I do that?...and why a lemur?!"

"Look, she wants another song pronto from her favorite song writer, The Infamous Chord," he says.

"I'm not really feeling up to it," I reply.

"Well, you need to take some fucking Midol and get up to it. You got a job to do, baby. What have I told you? What have I always told you?" he asks.

"You only have to tell them you have it if it's inflamed at the time?" I answer.

"What?! No! Never leave money on the table! That's what I always tell you. Especially with hookers in the house. They will snatch that shit up like Angelina Jolie at an African preschool."

"I'm having some girl problems at the moment," I tell him.

"What the hell is the problem? Ya fuck 'em then ya leave 'em. Problem solved."

"It's the leaving part that I'm having trouble with."

"If you need some pussy, I can get you some pussy. I got an Asian girl down here that can lick your balls while sucking your cock. Her name is Ming...or Ling...one of those Crouching Tiger Hidden Dragon names. Look, the point is you always card 'em cause they all look like twelve year olds anyway," he says.

"It's not the pussy. It's the woman attached to them I'm having trouble understanding."

"Look man, that's why you need to move out here. You can't throw a rock without hitting some top shelf, premium pussy."

"Why would I throw a rock at a pussy?"

"Can you write this damn song or what?!?" he yells and I laugh before replying with, "I'll see what I can do."

"There's just one thing. She wants a love song this time," he says.

"I thought the last one was a love song," I reply.

"No. It was more of an 'I wanna kill myself I'm so fucking sad' song. She wants lovey dovey, fuck my hubby kinda song. Something to get the dicks hard."

"I'm not really good at getting dicks hard......at least, I hope not."

"Well, you better start listening to some One D. or Justin B. cause this bitch wants a love song," he says.

"I'll get on it," I reply.

"See, that's why I love you, man," he says.

"I love you too, Steve. I love you too," I say before hanging up the phone. After our brief and somewhat disturbing conversation, I

75

decide to mend my broken heart and hand by tossing a couple pills down my mouth and head to bed.

.   .   .

.

"It's all about being yourself and not being ashamed of being different or thinking different. I try to take everybody's ideals, common morals, flip them around and make people look at them differently; question them so you're not always taking things for granted," the man on the TV says. It was a younger man covered in white makeup heavily contrasted by his black clothes and pitch black hair. His eyes looked like that of a ghost and his bright teeth hid behind dark black lipstick. I had seen him before while watching music videos on TV but this was the first time I'd seen him in an interview. I had a hard time telling the difference between his videos and a horror movie meant to frighten people to death. There were always people dressed as monsters or people in contraptions being tortured. A lot of violence and gore but despite how odd the videos were, I still enjoyed watching him and found it very interesting.

It was the morning after Christmas and my mother along with Alexis and Emily were out grocery shopping while my father was in his room fast asleep. I decided to enjoy some unsupervised television while waiting on my father to wake so we could possibly spend the day together. Whether it be going to his favorite BBQ place to get a bite to eat, working on the car or just staying home and watching one of the old prime time shows from his childhood. Any time spent with him was good time.

"Josh!" I hear him yell from the other side of the house and I immediately jump up, turn the TV off and run for his room. When I got there, I open the door to reveal him standing in his room, wide awake and holding a piece of paper. Not just any piece of paper, it was my poem from yesterday.

"Do you like it?" I ask anxiously with a big smile, as his eyes run back and forth over the paper.

"When I hit the ground and you throw me down?" he says, "WHEN I HIT THE GROUND AND YOU THROW ME DOWN!" at that moment he throws the paper at my face and lunges with his hands out in my direction. My body quickly tenses up as he grabs me tight by my little arms and says through his clinched teeth, "I told you not to tell anyone! And what do you do?" he starts to viciously shake me back and forth and my neck snaps with every violent jerk, "YOU WRITE A FUCKING SONG ABOUT IT!" he yells, pressing his top teeth down hard on his bottom.

"Im sorry," I reply and tears start to poor down my face as I shake and quiver in his grasp.

"Stop fucking crying! What did I tell you about that fucking crying, boy!" he screams just before lifting me up by my arms and throwing me on the bed. I try to run away but before I can he straddles over me, holding me down. He forces his hands down on my neck and begins to crush my throat with his strength, "STOP CRYING! JUST STOP CRYING! I'M SO SICK OF YOUR CRYING!" he screams as I start to choke and cough through his tightening fingers around my eight year old neck. Suddenly, the pain starts to fade, sound becomes silence and I see dots form out of the corner of my vision. The black, blue and purple dots grow in number as the sight of my father bearing his weight down on my throat grows dimmer and dimmer. He hastily lets off of my body and jolts back. Eyes wide, he stares in shock at my motionless body on the bed. The dots blocking my sight start to twirl and dance out of my vision as I start to regain feeling in my arms and legs. My face pale and masked in tears, I sit up to look back at him, waiting on his next assault. He quickly comes forward with his hands out and I cringe preparing myself for an attack, but instead he just runs his hands up and down my arms and looks at me, not with anger, but with remorse.

"Are you okay, buddy?" he asks in a soft and concerned voice. I manage to regain my composer enough to nod my head, "Look, you can never tell anyone about this. You understand me? Promise me you'll never tell anyone," he says but before I can answer he quickly tightens his grip on my arms and jerks me again, "PROMISE ME!" he demands.

"I promise," I reply trembling. Finally, he lets go and wraps his arms around me, "I'm so sorry, Josh. I'm so sorry," he says. I could feel him shaking with me as he held me tight. I cried there in his arms, hoping that it was over.

I felt horrible. Not because of the punishment I had endured but because I had let him down. For months I enjoyed peace between my father and I only to have me ruin it by writing some stupid poem. I told him I wouldn't tell anyone about what happened in Alexi's room, but then I had to go and write that damn poem. I hate it! It's just a bunch of words jumbled together on paper and it caused all of this. No! I caused all of this. I let him down. I disappointed him. I made him do this to me. But this time will be different. No one will ever hear about what happened today. Not by me telling them or by some stupid song or poem. No one can ever know. Maybe then he'll be happy again. Maybe then I can have more than just a couple of months of him not hurting me. I can't take anymore of him hurting me. I'm so scared all of the time. I don't want to be scared anymore. All I want in this world is for us to be happy again.

.   .   .

"Knock! Knock! Knock!"

"I'm coming," a voice from inside the house yells, "just a minute."

When the door opens, I'm blessed with the sight of a sweet, older woman in an apron. She was slightly overweight with short curly blonde hair, bright green eyes and a welcoming smile.

"Joshua! Come in. Come in," she demands as she leads me into the kitchen, "How have you been?"

"I've been better, to be honest," I reply.

"My dear! What happened to your hand?" she asks as she continues her previous task of washing dishes. I walk over, grab a towel and start to dry them off for her before answering, "You should see the other guy."

"Oh! Now, who would want to hurt you?" she asked concerned.

"Pedophilic pastors, homophobic doctors, obnoxious officers...just to name a few," I reply as she shakes her head at me in confusion.

"What are you talking about?"

"Um, nothing. I actually came by to see if Emily was here."

"Oh, she just left."

"She did? Do you know where she went?"

"She left with some nice boy. I think his name was-"

"-IT WAS A NIGGER!" a voice from across the house yells.

"Oh, Charles. Hush!" she replies.

"What? I'm just saying it was a nigger!" the voice continues. I start to walk in the direction of the racial slurs to a den in the back, "Did this guy have a name? Or would you rather I ask his plantation owner first?" I say as I enter the room.

"Don't be a smartass, boy!" he replies sternly. It was an older man with grey hair, thick glasses and a more or less permanent frown. I could barely hear him over the sound of football analyst blasting out of the TV as the smell of cigarette smoke and stale beer stained my senses.

"It's okay for them to call me a cracker, but I can't use the N word?" he asks.

"When? When were you called a cracker? Cause that phrase hasn't been used in like twenty years," I say and he waves me off with a snarl before directing his attention back to his football, "Do you happen to know where they went?" I ask.

"How the hell should I know?"

"Well, she is your daughter," I reply.

"They went to Ray's Bar!" the woman in the kitchen yells.

"What!?!" the man yells back.

"Ray's Bar!" she answers.

"What the hell are they doing at a gay bar?" he asks.

"No! Ray's Bar! It's downtown," she corrects him.

"That's another thing I can't stand," he says looking back towards me, "You know they made it where these faggots can get married now?"

"I know. How dare they pursue happiness," I reply sarcastically.

"What, you're pro-gay marriage now?" he asks.

"Technically, I'm against all marriage. But hey, anything that pisses off God, I say."

"It was Adam and Eve! Not Adam and Steve!" he says sternly.

"Oh, I totally agree. It was Lot and his daughter. Not Lot and his son. I mean, that would just be weird," I reply and he waves me off once more with a heavy grunt.

At that moment, I decided that I had agitated him enough and made my way out the door. I knew exactly where Ray's Bar was, just never was a fan. I always preferred drinking at home. Largely due to the fact that when I drink I usually don't stop until I'm unconscious; often in an area that's not my bed.

"Hey, buddy...buddy...hey, buddy!" the bartender yells and I finally break my strain of concentration to reply to him.

"Yes?"

"You gonna order something or what?" he asks.

"Jack coke n' lime, and hold the attitude," I reply and he squint his eyes at me before making my drink.

After our unpleasant first impression, I go back to scouting the place for Emily. Which I would find to be more difficult than I thought. The bar had very dim lighting contrasted by various colored beer lamps on the wall with everything from the tables, stools and floors made of the same mahogany which was covered in scrapes, scratches and possibly knife marks. The entire place was filled with frat boys in polo shirts talking way too loudly and getting excited over the overpriced liquor they were chugging down (and in some cases back up). The bartender was the only one that didn't necessarily fit the scenery. He was a taller white man with a slick bald head, ear rings in both ears and a torn sleeveless shirt. The only females around were helplessly surrounded by walking testosterone-mobiles. It was obvious there was an internal contest between the drunken savages to see who can walk away with one of the few girls there. Yet, inside all of this social revulsion there was no sign of Emily.

"Here's your drink," the bartender says, plopping the glass down on the already bruised countertops.

"Well, there goes your tip," I reply as he grunts and walks away.

"There's two people in this world you never piss off," I hear a voice behind me say, "People who serve your food and police officers."

I look over to see none other than the feisty little cop that arrested me after my involuntary streaking incident. She was wearing a purple top that perfectly complemented her bust, tight jeans and her silky brunette hair reached down her back and curled at the tips.

"Officer Tight Panties?" I say then she lets out a deep sigh and replies with, "And on that note, I'm leaving."

"No, wait!...don't you wanna reject some of my corny pick-up lines before you dart off?" I ask.

"Hmmm. Sure, why not. Give me your best," she says, crossing her arms. I sit there for a moment trying to think of something clever to say that will keep her here but instead I blurt out with, "...I've got nothing. How was your day?"

"Better than yours, apparently," she replies, staring down at my right hand.

"Hey, you should see the other guy."

"Would that other guy happen to be a little red head girl?"

"You heard about that, huh?" I ask.

"Oh, everyone at the station heard about your little escapade."

"Well, I'm glad I could entertain you all. Maybe one day I'll use that toward my community service."

"I don't think that's how it works," she says with a smile.

"Ha!" I say, "I got ya!"

"What?" she ask, raising an eyebrow.

"I just made you smile. That means you have to stay."

She stares at me for a second with her eyebrow still raised and a half grin before answering with, "Fine. But you're buying."

"Bartender! Two whiskeys! And maybe don't drop it this time? It's a whiskey glass, not your hopes and dreams," I say to the bartender and he growls under his breath as he prepares our drinks.

"So..." she says.

"So, what?"

"How did you really break your hand?"

"I got into a fight with a wall," I pause, "Not my proudest moment."

"Looks like the wall won," she says.

"I'd call it a no-contest," I reply, "Were you waiting for someone?"

"I was..."

"Boyfriend?"

"Husband, actually," she answers and I pick up my glass, chug the rest of it and I call out, "Check please!"

She laughs at my sarcastic gesture and says, "You're an asshole!" and we share a smile before she continues, "No, we were separated, and this was supposed to be his chance at redemption but he obviously doesn't care enough to even show up."

"Redemption?"

"Yeah," she replies and suddenly she removes her smile and stares down at the floor.

"Cheating?" I ask.

"Shit, I could handle cheating," she exhales, "I found out he had an entire other life with the girl. An apartment, a car and...plans."

"Plans?"

"Plans to leave me for her."

"And what happened?"

"Hell, she was using him more than he was using me. She left his ass for someone with more money and less baggage."

"So, why give him another chance?" I ask then she reaches into her purse and pulls out a photo and hands it to me. It was three children. Two boys and a girl ranging from toddler to teen, the girl being the eldest. They had dark hair and her eyes, but were tall for their age. The only trait that they didn't share with their mother.

"That right there is the only, and I mean only reason I get up in the morning," she says.

"They're beautiful," I say and at that moment her smile came back, but not the smile she had granted me before. This was a grin of pride. I hand the photo back to her and say, "Well, Mr. Tight Panties is missing out because the girl I see here before me," I say, looking her up and down, "I wouldn't skip out on this for any amount of premium pussy in the world."

"You're sweet, in a perverted kinda way," she replies giggling. Suddenly, her laughter was quickly interrupted by the bartender.

"Here's your drinks," he mumbles before slamming the glasses down on the counter causing the sweet liquid to splash and spill all over me and...I forgot to ask for her name.

"Hey! Watch it!" she yells.

"What the hell is your problem? It's not our fault you made bad life decisions," I say and he turns bright red as I continue, "You look like Moby on steroids."

He points at me and yells, "look here, asshole-"

"-You look like a giant penis with ear rings," she interrupts.

"That's a good one," I say, laughing before directing my attention back to the enraged bartender, "You look like Mr. Clean and Doctor Evil had a baby...and that baby became a cage fighter. But didn't grow up and become a cage fighter just right out of the womb, slapped on a pair of fingerless gloves and started breaking nurse's arms."

At that moment a group of college kids were calling him for more drinks. Luckily for me, because it looked like he was on the verge of jumping over the bar and choking me out.

"You don't like it? Go to another bar!" he yells and walks over to the drunken frat boys.

"Maybe we will!" she replies.

"We should probably go before he goes all Die Hard 4 on us," I say.

"Wait, why not Die Hard 1 through 3?"

"Well, no. Because Die Hard 4 is when Bruce shaved his head and the bartender is all-"

"-Bald. Got ya. Yeah, you're right," she says as she grabs her things and begins to walk away.

"But first..." I say and quickly glance over to make sure the bartender was properly occupied with college kids before leaning over the bar, grabbing a bottle of Jack and not so discreetly hide it under my arm.

"What the hell are you doing!" she says as we make our way out of the bar.

"What? He owes us for the drinks he ruined," I reply.

We start to casually make our way through the bar and I began to think that my crime would go unnoticed until, "Hey!

Somebody stop them!" the bartender screams and I look back to see him pointing directly to me and a bar full of drunk white teens staring dead at me. Suddenly, I had the entire cast of Jersey Shore coming at me as our fast pace walk quickly became a sprint to the door.

We finally burst through the door and run for the parking lot, but are suddenly halted, sliding and almost slipping on the gravel below our feet by the terrifying sound of a gunshot. *"Pow!"* We slowly look back to see him pointing a shotgun in our direction. Luckily for us, he fired off a warning shot into the sky that echoed through the dead air. It seemed as if my luck had run out though, seeing that the barrel of the gun was pointed directly at my head now. We raise our hands in the air in surrender and I yell out, "Wait! Before you shoot me...can I at least finish the bottle?" I ask.

"Oh, I'll give ya a shot," he says, cocking the gun. Chest tight, hands shaking vigorously and knees weak I close my eyes and dread what might come next.

"Drop the gun, dirt bag! I'm a police officer!" I hear her yell and I open on eye to see her standing there, badge in hand, waving it over her head.

"You're a cop? Why the hell are you stealin' from me, then?" the bartender ask.

"I was just showing the new guy the ropes," she says, nodding to me, "It's his first day on the force and I was putting him through a little initiation. So, just put the gun down and go back inside. Or do I need to tell the station that you're firing a weapon into a crowded public area?"

"No! No! I'm sorry, lady," he says lowering his gun, "I didn't know you were cops. Keep the whiskey, just leave. Please!"

"Thank god," I pause looking over at her, "He let me keep the whiskey."

Her eyes widen at my blatant disregard to the sincerity of the situation, "We should probably do what he says," she replies.

"Right. Let's get out of here," I say and we finally make our way to our cars.

"Wait, seriously?" I ask.

"Yes! Why is that so hard to believe?" she replies.

"I mean, I thought everyone has done drugs at some point in their life. The only people who don't do drugs are Mormons and Robert Downy Jr. You know, after Iron Man when he got all boring."

"Well, not me either. I'm a good girl," she says with a grin.

"Says the girl that just stole a bottle of Jack Daniels."

She gasps and replies with, "You stole it!"

"And who was my accomplice?"

"......Shit! I did steal it," she admits before covering her mouth to hide a smile.

"God, I gotta stop stealing stuff," I say.

"Wait, what else have you stolen?"

"Just a bible. But don't worry, it wasn't for reading. It was for covering my genitals."

"What?!?" she yells before I change the subject.

"Uh, nothing. Anyways, it's your turn."

"Oh, right," she says then hands the bottle over to me, "I've never......sat on a police car with my arm around a cop while drinking a stolen bottle of whiskey and staring up at the stars."

"Do you even know how this game works?" I reply as I take a drink.

After almost being shot outside of Ray's Bar, we decided to drive somewhere quiet and finish the bottle of whiskey, and since going to either of our houses was out of the question (Due to her kids being home with a baby sitter and my house looking like the set to a CSI episode) we drove to a beautiful cliff just outside of town and watched as the dawning sky turned black lit by millions of distant diamonds. The city below us shined a deep yellow as the veins of street lights grew stronger to the dimming sun while the designated sound of silence was masked by pulses of cricket calls.

"Speaking of bibles, what religion are you?" I ask.

"You don't know my name yet but you want to know my religion?"

"Shit, I forgot to ask for your name..."

To which she laughs and replies with, "It's Veronica, and I'm an atheist."

"Oh, thank God!...or, you know, someone who actually exists."

"I take it you're an atheist too?"

"Is the pope Catholic?...and possibly a pedophile."

"Spoken like a true atheist."

"So, what about your kids? Are they atheist too?"

"Oh, no. They're Christian. I take them to church every Sunday."

"So, you're an atheist but you raise your kids Christian?"

"Yeah, what's wrong with that?"

88

"It's just kinda weird. If you say you don't believe in God but then take your kids to church as some sort of insurance toward the possibility of there being a God then that means subconsciously in your mind you do believe in God," I say.

"I don't know. I guess, I just want what is best for them and if that means they have to believe that some omnipotent being is watching over them, then so be it. If you ever have kids, you'll understand," she says.

"...so, what you're saying is, I'll never understand," I reply with a smirk.

"What's so bad about having kids?" she ask.

"Oh, nothing. I love giving up my hopes and dreams to wipe up snot and shit for the rest of my life."

"It's not the REST of your life," she corrects me.

"Just the good part, right?"

"Look, it's not all bad. Think of it this way. Every day that I go home, I have these little people that I made waiting for me and no matter what, I know they're gonna love me unconditionally."

"Okay. You've convinced me. Let's have a kid," I say to which she laughs and replies with, "I think you're just looking for an excuse to get in my pants."

"Is it working?"

"I don't know. I mean," she says, looking at the ground then back up at me, "You said you wouldn't pass me up, right?"

"That I did," I reply and at that moment she leans in and locks her lips with mine. I reach my hand over to push her off, but before I can she pushes on my shoulders pinning me down on the hood of her car. Suddenly, she straddles over me while taking my tongue in her mouth; grinding her waist back and forth on my crotch. I could feel her jeans

89

pressing and rubbing against my quickly growing cock. I try to bring my hands up to feel the curves of her body but she continues to bare down on my shoulders as she sucked on my tongue, running it in and out of her vigorous lips. I found this sense of vulnerability wildly arousing as my dick began to bulge out of my pants, pressing and rubbing against her ever grinding thigh. Finally, I manage to push off her hips, spin her around and pin her down on the car. She tries to regain control, but I grab her wrist and force them above her head, pressing them down causing indentions on the hood. For a moment, I worried I was hurting her but when I looked into her eyes all I saw was the lust of a woman crying out for more. I force my crotch down between her legs, pinning her hips to the car before leaning down and placing my lips on her slender neck. Her feet locked behind me and clasped my body down harder between her legs. My lips start to make their way down her neck, glowing in the moonlight but before I can taste the flesh of her breast...

"Ring! Ring!"

"Shit!"

"Ring! Ring!"

"I gotta get that," she says.

"No, please. I beg of you, woman," I plead.

"It's probably the babysitter," she says before sitting up and reaches in her pocket for her phone.

"I'll reimburse you, I swear," I reply with a smile. To which she grins before answering the phone.

"Hey...yeah...I'm on my way. I just got caught up with something...okay, bye," she hangs up then looks up at me with her big, sexy, blue eyes, "I'm sorry."

"You're sorry? Look what I have to go home to," I say while looking down at my dick which is now throbbing and reaching down my leg.

90

"It is nice," she replies, staring and raising an eyebrow.

"Such a waist of a good erection should be a crime."

"Cop pun? Really?"

"It was either that or let me show you my 'Penal' code."

"...yeah, I like the first one better."

"Enough to stay for a minute?" I ask and she leans up running her hands across each side of my face, pulling me into her lips before replying, "Baby, I'll need more than a minute."

"So, call me?"

"Oh, yes. This right here is not near from over," she says, stepping off the hood and making her way to the front door but before she can I stop her, "Wait!"

"What?" she asks and I reach up and casually place both hands on her breast, "Really?" she ask.

"I need this," I answer and she stares at me with a sexy, little half grin as I continue to fill her up, "What are these? 32D?"

"Thirty four," she corrects me.

"If I wasn't atheist, I'd say these were forged by God himself."

"Had enough?"

"Yes. Thank you for that."

"Anytime," she answers.

"Wait, literally?"

"Well, no. Not anytime, but definitely next time," she says while winking, "Are you okay to drive home?"

"Yeah, why wouldn't I be?"

"Well, you've been taking pain meds and you just finished half a bottle of Jack."

"Yeah, so...why wouldn't I be?"

"Ugh!" she grunts

"You wildly underestimate my body's ability to tolerate drugs."

"Just call me when you get home, okay?"

"I'll be far too busy pleasuring myself," I explain then she bites down on her bottom lip and replies, "So?"

Finally, I'm forced to watch as she gets in the police car and drives off into the night.

.   .   .
                    .

I don't even like peas. It's not that I didn't like vegetables. In fact, I love eating vegetables from carrots, potatoes, broccoli, corn and even celery. Anything but these bland, tasteless, light green spheres. Not only was the taste basically undetectable, but the texture was nauseating too. Gooey inside encased in an even less appetizing soft skin; truly offensive to the human senses.

"Remember what your father said. You can't leave the table until you've finished everything on your plate," my mother says as I twirl my fork in circles around the remaining puke balls, hoping that soon her will gives in and she releases me from this culinary prison. Hell, she let Alexis go without finishing her plate, while I'm stuck here drowning in apathy. All because my father insisted that I HAVE to finish my plate even long after he's gone to work.

"But I don't like peas," I plead to my mother.

"Take one more bite, okay?" she says before turning back to finish washing the dishes, and once I was out of her sight, I scoop up a big pile of peas and casually toss them under the table cloth just before smooshing them down for good measure.

"All done," I lie.

"That's my guy! Now bring me your dish," she says. I walk over to the sink and place my dish in it. I start to dart off to the living room where I plan on sitting in front of the TV until bedtime but am halted by my mother.

"Sweetie, what happened to your neck?" she ask.

"What do you mean?" I reply. She walks toward me and places her hand on my chin, pushing up on my head to reveal my throat.

"There's marks all over it," she says. Suddenly, my heart stops. My eyes widen at her question as I stood there frozen in fear. I had no idea dad had left marks on me. If I had known I would have tried to hide them better. Worn a jacket, hoodie, even a scarf, anything to conceal any evidence of my father's abuse. My entire body shook just thinking of the possible consequences of what I had done. I had to hide the truth at all cost.

"I don't know," I reply. Shit, that's not enough. I have to think of something better than that. Think Josh! Think!

"Josh, did someone hurt you?" she asks. At that moment her voice changed from curious to concerned.

"No," I answer while looking off in the distance. I couldn't force myself to look at my mother while I lie to her so for some reason my eyes wander off to the ceiling as I attempt to deceive her.

"If someone is bullying you, you can tell me, sweetie," she presses on. Finally, I cracked under the pressure of her interrogation and in a fit of rage I slap her hand away from my face and yell, "I said I don't know! Now leave me alone!" I sprint off through the house, stomping with every step until I finally reach my room. I grab the door knob and force it open hard causing it to bounce off the wall before slamming it shut. Once in the security of my room, I run to the closet, open it and hide inside. I curl up to the corner, pushing my knees up to hide my face as I begin to cry. I can hear my mother's footsteps making their way to my room as I sit there fighting back tears. I press my fingertips hard into my legs trying to hold back these drops of emotion from falling down my face but there was no use. By the time my mother had opened my bedroom door, my cheeks were covered in the embarrassment. I don't know why I thought I could hide from her in my closet. I just wanted somewhere to go where no one could get me. I wanted a place where no one could see me or hear me or even knew I existed. I wanted to disappear in this dark serenity. At that moment, I hear the doorknob to the closet shake and turn. I dread what will happen when my mother sees me covered in tears and curled up in the corner like a scared, little child. Would she hurt me too? Would she tell dad and have him punish me again? My contemplating comes to a halt as the door swings open and my mother stares down at me quivering behind the clothes hung up in my closet. She doesn't say anything. She just stares at me for a moment in an unsettling, unnerving silence. Then, she leans up against the doorway, slides down to sit across from me, pushes her knees up to her chest to imitate me and says, "I love you, Josh. I want you to know, you can tell me anything. Absolutely anything. If you're being bullied at school you have to tell me. You're not in trouble. I can't let someone hurt you," she says, looking down at me. With my face drenched and my lips shaking, I finally manage to mutter, "But he said he'd do it again if I told. I'm scared, mom."

"I know you're scared but you can tell me. I swear, I'll protect you from anything," she replies. I could feel my heart pounding in my chest. My legs shook with fear. My hands soaked in sweat and face masked in tears, I inhale on last deep breath and I tell her.

.

"Wait, stop! Stop!" Veronica says, pushing me away.

"Stop? Why stop?" I reply.

"It's just, your dick is really big."

"If I had a nickel for every time I've heard that."

"Really?"

"I might have like...two nickels."

"Oh."

"Yeah, it sounded way better in my head," I say, raising off of her naked body.

"I don't know. Maybe it's because I had three kids and haven't had sex in years," she replies.

"Wait, how long have you been separated?" I ask before looking around for my pants.

"A year, but our sex life ended years ago," she says also looking for her clothes, "Wait, is this your shirt or mine?" I glance over to see her holding up a small black shirt. It was hard to tell whose it was so I grab it and start to put it on, but fail half way due to it hugging me tightly at the ribs, "Yep, this is definitely yours," I reply as I pull the tail of her shirt down my stomach.

"Looks good on you. Really brings out your curves," she says, giggling.

"I'm a bad bitch," I reply.

"Oh, my God! Stop!" she yells as her giggle turns into an out loud laugh.

Not long after forcing myself into a chemically induced coma, I woke up to the sight of a text from a certain zealous officer that read 'we have unfinished business'. She invited me over that night after her kids went to bed. We had a couple drinks and talked about our past (mostly hers due to me being so secretive about mine). She told me she didn't always want to be a police officer. In fact, her dream was to become a criminal justice lawyer. She had met Bob (A.K.A Mr. Officer

95

Tight Panties) in high school and have been sweethearts since junior year. After graduation her plan was to start law school while he would get into the same school with a football scholarship. Unfortunately, their plans were instantly fouled by a positive pregnancy test. They both dropped out of college, got full time jobs and shortly after finding out they had one on the way, he proposed. Nine months later Valerie, the oldest one, was born and they both agreed to become slaves to mediocracy. Still haunted with a passion for criminal justice, veronica decided to join a police academy which she would pass with flying colors. With her in the force and him working forty, sometimes fifty hours a week, gradually the passion in their marriage would deteriorate into a bland, lifeless contractual agreement to raise a child. Over the next ten years they would separate on numerous occasions only to find their way back to each other long enough to have another child.

Once the dust settled, they had three children, a four bedroom house; home that was barely being kept together by the wet, futile glue of hope. At a distance, they looked like the perfect family portrait. But as you get closer and the paint starts to peel, you see a black and white picture of domestic violence, screaming fights at 3am in the night and the occasional adultery. Finally, after finding out about the other girl, Veronica had enough and decided to kick him out.

"I'm gonna get some more wine. Do you want another glass?" she ask as she raises up and makes her way to the kitchen.

"Do you have something stronger? Like, anything stronger? Honestly, I'll take a Nyquil and juice box if ya got it," I say before digging in my pocket and pulling out a couple *feel good pills* then toss them down my throat.

"Should you be drinking and taking those?" she ask.

"What are you, a cop?" I reply and she lets out a long sigh and shakes her head before saying, "Be glad you're cute," then makes her way to the kitchen. Once she was gone, I start to glance around at the various photos hanging from the wall. Picture of family vacations, camping trips and holidays where everyone is happy and smiling were all on display, perfectly camouflaging the metaphorical cracks in a slowly breaking home. As I stare out into this false suburban euphoria, I couldn't help but feel that there was another presence in the room observing me, even though Veronica had already left to the kitchen. A sudden suspicion fell over me that something in there was watching me. The feeling of newly occupied space and the faint sound of breathing were both clues that someone was in the room with me. I look around the room only to find that I, in fact, was the only one in it. I look to my left; nothing there. I look to my right and quickly jump to the sight of a small toddler sitting on his knees just inches away from me. It was Taylor, the youngest of the three. He was wearing SpongeBob pajamas and sucking profusely on a pacifier as he stared dead into my eyes. He had short brown hair, blue eyes and freckles like his father. I sit there for a moment staring back at him in silence, waiting for a response but finally manage to break the stillness with, "Hey, buddy. What's up?"

"Bassa wassa wuppa whalla," he mutters.

"Um, what?" I reply.

"Haaaa!" he yells and within a moment's notice he takes his hands, slaps them to both sides of my face, pulls me in and runs his wet, slimy tongue across my cheek.

"Aww! Gross! What the hell!" I yell.

"Haaa!" he laughs.

"Did he lick you?" Veronica's voice echoes from the kitchen.

"Is that normal?" I ask.

"Yeah, he does that sometimes," she answers as she enters the living room, "Taylor! What have I told you about licking people," pointing her finger at him. To which he replies by staring at me with eyes wide and yelling, "Haaa!" before darting off back to his room.

"I should probably put him to bed," she says to me.

"I should probably go germ-x my face."

"He's not dirty. He's just...weird," she sighs while rolling her eyes.

"So, until next time?" I ask.

"I'm sorry. I know this is getting frustrating to you."

"Hey, frustrating is my middle name," I reply with a smirk, "I'm just kidding. I don't have a middle name. I'm like Jesus."

"Just in the sense that you don't have a middle name?" she asks.

"Well, that and also who doesn't like a good whipping?" I say, winking at her.

"If I believed in hell, I would say that you're definitely gonna end up there."

"That's fine. I like warm climates better anyways," I reply as I gather my things.

"Well, good luck with trying to find that girl of yours," she says.

"I'm gonna need it. That girl is harder to find than Sasquatch riding a unicorn while drinking from the Holy Grail."

"Hmmm, maybe I can help," she says while sporting a look of contemplation.

"Thanks but unless you have some sort of tracking device on her, I don't think you can do much. Emily has always been the rolling stone type," I say and just then Veronica reaches into her pocket, pulls out her phone and proceeds to make a call.

"This is Officer Veronica Tate. I need a trace on a number, immediately," she says into the phone before directing her attention back toward me, "What's her number?" I tell her and within a matter of seconds she replies back with, "Apparently, she's back at Ray's Bar tonight."

"*Where ever he laid his hat was his home,*" I sing.

"Look, Ray's Bar is all the way downtown and it closes-"

"*-And when he died!*" I interrupt.

"Chord!" she yells.

"What?"

"Pay attention! It closes in a couple of hours," she finishes.

"Plus, she'll probably be gone by the time I get there, anyways," I say.

"If you take your car, then yes. But I have an idea..." she says glancing over at the keys to her cruiser and then granting me a devious stare. I don't say anything. I just reply with the biggest smile that's ever crossed my face.

.   .   .
                    .

"Still nothing?" the bartender ask, whose name is coincidentally Ray.

"Still nothing," I confirm, finishing off my Jack coke n' lime.

"Well, just keep trying. She'll show up eventually. Here, this one's on me, Officer," he says, finally setting (and not dropping) the whiskey glass down on the wet, crumb covered countertop.

"Says the bartender that charges eight bucks a drink. Seriously, how do you sleep at night? I'm picturing a futon or possibly a slightly torn air mattress," I say before taking a drink.

"Actually, I live here in the bar."

"......keep making your parents proud, Ray," I reply while rolling my eyes.

"Oh, my parents are dead," he sighs, looking down at the ground.

"What'd they die of, embarrassment?"

"No, they died on 9/11," he answers.

"Oh," I pause, "Well, I'm sorry for your loss," I say.

"Yep, I just can't believe it's been a year since they passed," he replies and I stop for a moment to contemplate what I had just heard.

"Wait, you said they died on 9/11!"

"Yep, September eleventh of last year."

"Then why would you phrase it as 9/11?!"

"I mean, it wasn't THE 9/11......just A 9/11," he says and I sit there for a moment staring blankly at him, trying to conceive how someone can be this dense before replying, "Yeah, I think I hear some college kid throwing up in the corner."

"Damn it! I told them to use the puke bucket," he says as he darts off into the fray of drunken youth.

"...and why is there a puke bucket?!" I yell but he had already disappeared into the social wasteland.

Once alone, I finish off my last drink, gather my things, admit defeat and start to wonder if I'd ever see Emily again. I get up and push my chair in then get ready to leave but before I can I am suddenly halted by a voice from behind me.

"My nigga!" the voice said and I quickly turn around to reveal it was none other than my jail buddy Murda.

"Murda! My brotha from anotha mutha! What's up?" I say as he walks over to me.

"Shit, nothin. Just chillin. I'm here wit this fine ass white bitch, tryna get my drink on. You?" he replies with a smile.

100

"Oh, I was actually waiting for someone but it doesn't look like they're gonna show, so I'm gonna wave the white flag and retreat home."

"Hey, fuck that noise, nigga. You stayin here with me and my bitch, and we 'bout to get tipsy, bruh."

"I wish I could but I probably should be going home."

"Hey, nigga! What happened to yo hand?" he asks looking down at my cast.

"You should see the other guy," I reply raising a cocky eyebrow.

"Hell yeah! That's what I'm talkin bout," he says, nodding and bouncing his fist off of his chest.

"Well, have fun with your white bitch," I tell him as I push in my chair and get ready to leave.

"Awe shit. Here she come now," he says, tugging on my arm but I ignore him and continue with my task of abandoning him. It's not that I didn't like the guy, I just wasn't in the mood to stay and converse in my current condition of alcohol fueled, self-pitying, manic depressant bender.

As I leave though, I am stopped dead in my tracks by a voice. A voice that I had heard throughout my entire life. Like heaven to my ears, the one precious sound I had been searching for this whole time. A sweet voice that would simultaneously strike fear and arousal in me, all while invigorating my every sense.

"Josh!" she says eyes wide.

"Chord, I want you to meet my girl, Emily," Murda says to me as he places his arm around her.

"Josh!" she yells in shock.

"Josh?" Murda asks.

"Ugh! Chord!" she answers pointing at me.

"Oh, Chord," he replies.

"Emily!" I yell back.

"Emily??? Wait, you know this bitch?" Murda asks.

"Bitch?!?" Emily snaps.

"Wait, you're with this asshole?" I ask Emily.

"Asshole?!?" Murda replies.

"Wait, wait, wait...what happened to your hand?" she says, looking down at my cast.

"You should see the other guy, right?" Murda answers while pointing to me and smiling.

"You got into a fight???" Emily snaps.

"No, I didn't get into a fight," I explain.

"Wait, you said you got into a fight, nigga," Murda presses.

"I didn't say that," I reply and at that moment Ray the bartender walks up and says, "Hey, if you guys are gonna fight you gotta take it outside."

"WE'RE NOT FIGHTING!" the three of us shout.

"Don't you have some puke to clean up?" I ask him.

"No! Luckily, they got it in the puke bucket!" he replies with a big relieved smile.

"Wait, why is there a puke bucket??" Emily asks.

"I mean, obviously for this very reason," I answer as she glares at me.

"Yeah, and sometimes I wash the bar towels in it," Rays says.

"Why do people come to this bar!" I snap.

"It's like the only bar in a 30 mile radius," he answers.

"Well, that's just a good business decision," I admit.

"Besides, you come here all the time, Officer Johnson," Ray says.

"Officer??? Hey, nigga! You never said you was a cop!" Murda says, taking a step back and throwing his hands up in surrender, "Wait! If you a cop, why the fuck was you at the police station naked and shit?"

"Why the fuck were you at the police station naked, Chord!" Emily chimes in.

"I was......undercover," I answer.

"Hey nigga, you gotta warn a nigga if you a undercover cop, bruh," Murda says.

"Wouldn't that defeat the purpose of being an UNDERCOVER cop?" I ask.

"No, he's right. If he asks, you gotta admit to being a cop," Ray replies.

"Let's all take legal advice from the bartender who shot at me!" I yell.

"Wait, you shot at him!?!" Emily yells at Ray.

"I didn't know he was a cop," Ray explains.

"HE'S NOT A COP!" she screams.

"Wait, how do you know? Do you two know each other?" Murda asks us.

"Wait, how do you two know each other?" I reply to Emily.

"I could ask you guys the same thing," she says to Murda and I.

"I know all of you," Ray says with a big, idiotic smile.

103

"SHUT UP!" the three of us yell at him.

"And why is yo shirt so tight, nigga?" Murda asks me.

"Oh, shit," I mutter, looking down at my torso and quickly realizing that I forgot to change shirts before leaving Veronica's house and still had hers on.

"Hey, yea! Why is your shirt so tight?" Emily presses.

"It's seriously not that tight," I answer.

"I'm surprised you can breathe in that thing," Ray chimes in.

"It's not that tight!" I yell.

"Looks like your gonna crack rib," Ray continues.

"Hold up! Is that a girl's shirt, nigga?" Murda asks, covering his mouth as he laughs.

"Of course, it's a girl's shirt," Emily sighs as she rolls her eyes.

"That shirt is so tight I can see the outline of what you had for breakfast in it," Ray says laughing and pointing at me.

"Really? You can see your mother's pussy in my shirt?" I reply.

"Hey! I told you my parents are dead!" he yells and quickly puts on a hard snarl.

"And I told you I don't care!" I yell back.

"NO, YOU DIDN'T!" he screams at me.

"I THOUGHT IT WAS IMPLIED!" I finish and just then Ray balls his fist up, raises it and launches it right toward my face. Luckily, I manage to duck and dodge out of the way of his punch just in time. Unluckily, the punch continues on with its trajectory and lands smack clean on Murda's face.

"HEY, NIGGA!" Murda screams then lunges toward Ray with his hands out, grabs him by the shirt and slams him on the edge of the bar. Ray then goes for a half ass attempt of a takedown and instead ends up in a front head lock by Murda. He didn't look like he was letting go until a group of jocks in white and pink polo shirts see the scuffle and dart toward the action; most likely to help the one that cleans up their puke every night. I look over at Emily who is watching, wide eyed and in shock at this lack luster bout between a wanna be thug and the world's worst bartender. It looked like a bad WWF wrestling match from the 90's. I reach over, grab her by her arm and say, "Let's get out of here!" and we make our way toward the door just as the herd of gym rats grab Murda and Ray.

.   .   .

.

Outside the air was thick and cold. A dense fog gathered around us reflecting white from the flickering streetlight above us. The midnight silence was hidden behind the abrupt racket of scuffling in the bar next to us, and as I stood there holding Emily's hands in this less than romantic atmosphere, I stare into her eyes that seemed to shimmer under the light, "Emily, I'm sorry," I say to her.

"It's not your fault. That bartender was a jerk," she replies, staring back at the bar. I pull her hands closer, bringing her attention back, "No, I'm sorry about everything. That I can't get my life together. That I'm addicted to just about everything you can be addicted to. That I pulled you into this hollow shell that is my life. I'm sorry I made you bear witness to my self-inflicted suffering. But most of all, I'm sorry I waited this long to tell you that I love you."

Silence fell between us as I stared into her glistening green eyes. I waited for what seemed like an eternity inside this quiet ambiance until Emily finally spoke, "Wait, are you writing a song right now?" she asks.

"I don't know. I mean, it sounded pretty good. Think I could pass it off as a gushy, pop song?" I reply with a smirk.

"You're such a fucking drama queen," she says with a smile.

"I doubt Mr. Murda could do any better," I say, "What are you doing with that guy?" she sighs and replies with, "We've been seeing each other for a couple weeks now but nothing really serious until..."

"Until what?"

"Well, until you decided to showcase your sex-life in front of me," she answers, rolling her eyes.

"I'm sorry. I should have broken it off a long time ago. That would have quite literally saved the skin off my ass."

"I mean, I knew you had your female friends. Just, seeing it was really hard for me. Specially seeing that I had just confessed my love to you," she says, grinning and playfully shoving me.

"So, have you unconfessed your love to me?" I ask while walking slowly toward her, pressing my body next to hers and running my hands up her arms.

"Hmmm, I guess not," she answers, staring up at me with her big green eyes and I pull her in, grasp her lips with mine and kiss her like I hadn't seen her in centuries. Just the taste of her lips ignited serenity within me. I had been longing for the simple feeling of her lips secured with mine, the sweet assurance that I had finally got my girl back.

"So, have you unconfessed you love to me, Mr. Chord?" she asks.

"......I'll have to think about it."

"YOU ARE SUCH AN ASSHOLE!" she yells before smiling and playfully pushing me again. I smile back and say, "What about your nominee for worst rap artist in there?"

"He seems pretty occupied," she replies.

106

"Let's say you and I go home," I ask.

"Sounds like a plan," she answers and with her wrapped in my arm we make our way back to my car. As we walk through the parking lot, Emily safely tucked away under my arm, her head resting on the curvature between my neck and chest as her arm reaches across my lower back tugging me in closely, I feel a sense of absolution that I hadn't felt since we first admitted our love. I wanted to stay inside this flawlessness forever. I embraced her presence as if it was essential to life, and in a way, maybe it was. Without her, I deteriorate. I crumble to the ground like an unkempt tower bent on implosion. Just the sound of her voice, the feel of her touch, the smell of her hair brought me to life and permitted me to exist longer. When she was not around I was vacant inside. Without her, home is just a fantasy, but I finally belonged somewhere and that was wrapped in this feisty, little, military girls arms.

I contemplated this as we walked through the dark parking lot approaching my car. Then suddenly, I feel Emily's head spring from my chest and her arm release from my back. I glance over to see a look of sincerity possessing her. The smile was gone. The lust had faded and all that remained was confusion.

"Josh!" she says sternly as she stared in front of us.

"Yes?" I hesitate.

"Where did you get a cop car?" she asks and I turn my head and look to reveal I had completely forgotten that I drove Veronica's cruiser here.

"Wait!" she yells, "Are you seriously an undercover cop???"

"You've known me since I was eight. I would have to be the greatest undercover cop in the world to get it passed you."

"Then where the hell did you get a cop car!" she demands.

"It's not what you think......unless you think I got it from the same girl I got this shirt from."

107

"Oh, my God! You're fucking a cop now?"

"No! I swear we didn't fuck," I exclaim, "We couldn't, my dick was too big."

"UGH!" she grunts before turning around and stomping back toward the bar.

"What? I took it as a compliment," I reply as I begin to chase after her, "Wait! Emily! I'm sorry, okay? I'll break it off with her just as soon as I return the cruiser. Hey, maybe we could go for a little joyride in it, ya know, like we could-" I'm suddenly stopped in my poor attempt when Emily turns to face me. Her eyes were red and quickly drowning in tears. Her hands were shaking and she looked to be on the brink of collapsing she was so distraught.

"Please," she says, staring at me with her soaked eyes and tears streaming down her cheeks, "Just go, Josh. Please." Then she turns her back to me and walks back into the bar.

I've upset Emily numerous amount of times in the past. I've let her down. I've caused her to yell and scream at me. I've disappointed her to the point of giving up, but she has never, in all the years I've known her, begged me to stay away. The fact that I couldn't chase after her and rectify this and was forced to watch as she ran away into another man's arms at my own fault, broke me. Maybe I did need to stay away. I had done so much damage to that girl, the only responsible thing to do was to relieve her of the constant burden that is my love. Maybe it was time to let her go. She had been submerged in my despair for too long and had finally suffocated under my own debt.

When I finally come back to reality, I'm standing in a cold, dark parking lot, shaking and all alone next to a police car. I reach into my pocket, pull out my bottle of pills and drink a few like a shot of whiskey. I've lost count of how many that is at this point. But the bottle keeps getting lighter.

"I think he's dead," a boy's voice says.

"He's not dead," a girl's voice says.

"Babba da doo," a baby's voice?

"Hey, yeah, he's right, let's poke him with a stick."

"Ow! Fuck off!" I yell as I swat away what might be the sharpest stick ever.

"Aww, you said a bad word," she whines.

"He said a stick not a finely sharpened spear!" I reply, finally opening my eyes and very quickly regretting it, "Jesus! Why did God make the sun so damn bright.....wait! Shit! Why am I outside!"

"You say a lot of curse words," the boy says.

"Yeah, it's called being an adult. Now, get off my lawn," I demand.

"Dappa woop."

"What do you mean it's not my lawn?!?" I reply and rub my eyes then look around to reveal it, in fact, wasn't my lawn.

"You smell like daddy's liquor cabinet!" the girl says.

"Oh, thank God!....there's a liquor cabinet," I reply, "Wait, I have an idea," I say, pushing the youngest kid over a few feet until he completely blocks out the suns piercing rays from my eyes, "Good, now just stay like that for two...three...eh, let's make it four hours."

"Babba doo doo."

"I know! The sun moves as the Earth rotates on its axis throughout the day! So, you're gonna have to periodically step over about an inch every hour, okay?" I ask.

"Kids!" a woman's voice calls from the front door, "Hurry up or you'll miss the bus!" and on that demand the boy and girl dart off to the street, leaving the baby there standing right next to me, still blocking the sun.

"Didn't you hear your mom? You're gonna miss the bus," I say.

"Bassa do wap."

"Well, how was I supposed to know how old you are? I mean, look at me. Does it look like I have any kids?" I ask.

"Baba doo," he replies.

"No, not because of my age. Because of my immaturity."

"Chord!" I look over to see Veronica calling for me from the porch, "Can you get inside before the neighbors see you?" she pleads.

"We should probably do what she says," I admit to the baby. I finally push off the ground and raise up to my feet. The sun bore down on me with relentless rays as I make my way to the front door, feeling the grass between my toes, "Wait! Where the hell are my shoes?!" I yell.

"Ba ba ba?"

"If I knew where I saw them last then they wouldn't be lost, now would they?"

"Da doo."

"This is no time for shoe puns!" I say, "Oh, wait. Unless, you mean 'retrace my steps' like 'try to remember what I did last night'."

"Ba!"

"Sorry for that," I reply, "Well, I remember leaving the bar. Then it's all kinda blurry."

110

"Whooooooooh! Let's go swimming!" I scream as I fumble around trying my best to take off my clothes while stumbling to the pool.

It was the middle of the night and slightly too cold for swimming but for some odd and intoxicated reason I decided to jump the fence of a public pool and take a dip. I raced across the dancing blue and white reflecting lines on the ground until I got to the pool, where I stumble as I try to take off my shoes, "What idiot invented laces! It's like, just make every shoe where you can take them off and put them on whenever you want!" I yell as I struggle to pin point which of the three luminous shoe strings appearing and then disappearing were the real one. Once I managed to master the art of untying my shoes while completely wasted, I start to take off the rest of my clothes, starting with my shirt.

"Jesus! Why is this shirt so tight....oh, yea," I say.

"What in the hell do you think you're doin!" a strong country voice yells from across the yard. I glance over and see a middle aged man in pajama pants and tank top quickly stomping in my direction.

"Other than questioning my widely liberal wardrobe decisions, I was gonna take a dip in the pool," I reply.

"You can't do that!" he shouts.

"Oh, come on! I know it's closed but it's a public pool. These things should be open 24/7."

"This isn't a public pool! You're in my back yard, asshole!" he says, pointing a finger at me.

"Then be a good host and go in there and make me a sandwich. Preferably turkey but definitely not bologna. I might be dressed like a hobo, but it doesn't mean I have to eat like one," I slur as I start to undo my pants.

"My daughter is inside!" he screams.

"Oh...is she hot?" I ask while raising an eyebrow.

"She's sixteen!"

"Well, I didn't invent the age of consent, now did I!?!?.....although, if I did, it'd still be pretty high. I mean, even I'm not that fucked up."

"I'm calling the cops!" he says before stomping back to his house.

"I am a cop! Officer Joshua Johnson! I've been undercover since I was eight. Just ask my best friend and love of my life. Who doesn't even love me anymore cause I'm a pathetic peace of shit," I whimper before pressing my hands into my face to hide the tears falling down my cheek.

"Oh, my God!......I really want a sandwich now," I say as I walk through the door.

"Looks like you had one hell of a night," Veronica says, standing there with her hands on her hips, "Any luck with your girl?"

"If by luck you mean I almost got into a fight, ruined any chance of getting back with the love of my life, got shit faced on whiskey and pills and...oh, shit!" I pause, quickly reaching into my pocket to feel the bottle still there, "Oh, thank God."

112

"Seriously?" she sighs.

"Well, maybe not God but, ya know, thank someone," I say, "Anyways, where was I?"

"Uh, you were at the part where you almost overdosed on pain killers and alcohol."

"Please!" I reply laughing, "It takes more than a few shots of whiskey and three, maybe four pain killers to kill me. But, apparently, that's the exact amount it takes to get me wasted enough to go skinny dipping in your neighbors pool in the middle of the night," I say.

"He has a daughter! She's only-"

"-Sixteen! I know! But don't worry. I'm almost certain she didn't see me," I reply.

"Chord!" she snaps disgracefully.

"What? I said almost certain! Although, I'm almost even more certain that he called the cops. How did you not hear about that?" I ask.

"First off, I wasn't on call last night. Second, even if I was, I wouldn't have heard it because you were out with my cruiser with a combination of liquor and pills in your system," she answers.

"A cruiser, to which, you LET me have," I reply.

"Borrow," she corrects me, "and I didn't tell you to drive it high and drunk!"

"Well, you didn't NOT tell me to drive it high and drunk."

"Which, I will never make that mistake again," she says, exhaling a sigh of relief.

"Awww," I whine, looking at the ground.

"Hey, at least you got to ride it once," she says.

"I hope that's not the only thing I get to ride," I say, looking up at her while raising an eyebrow.

"You know," she says exhaling again, "You make it really hard to stay mad at you."

"I know," I laugh, "It's like a curse."

"Anyways, you hungry? I was gonna make some breakfast," she asks while making her way to the kitchen.

"Oh, my God. Do you have any sandwich meat?" I request as I follow her into the kitchen.

"We have bologna," she answers.

"What do I look like to you, a hobo?"

"Actually..." she replies, looking me up and down.

"Oh, yeah. I forgot I don't have shoes."

"And how long are you gonna wear my shirt for?" she asks.

"Until you take it off of me," I reply, winking.

"Not in front of the kid," she says, winking back.

"The what?" I look down to see the baby standing at my feet, "Oh, I forgot you existed."

"Doo doo daa."

"Give me a break. I almost died last night," I say to him.

"I'll make you some scrambled eggs," Veronica says.

"The perfect hangover food," I utter as I start to pull out a chair from the table but am halted by the feeling of a baby tugging on my pants. He was standing next to me holding his arms out and whimpering under his breath.

114

"Trust me," I say to him, "You don't want me to hold you right now. I'm barely holding myself up as it is."

"He wants you to put him in his high chair," Veronica tells me as she shuffles through the cabinets. I pick him up and place him in his chair then look up to see him giving me the biggest smile. His blue eyes lit up and his cheeks grew twice as big as he grinned ear to ear at me. Such an appreciation for something as simple as putting him in a chair, or was it that this kid was starting to really like me. Somehow, in the two times we've met he decided that I'm a good person and he likes having me around even if it's to pick him up or use him as a sun visor. It didn't take him long to come to the conclusion that I'm a good person underneath and my presence is of some worth to this kid. I contemplate this as the morning sun reaches out and touches his baby blue eyes causing them to glow as he stared at me.

"Eh, whatever," I reply apathetically as I sit down.

"Ya know," Veronica says as she starts cracking eggs, "I could probably find that girls address if you want."

"I already know her address."

"Then why don't you-"

"-I did. She wasn't there. That's what led me to Rays bar in the first place. Jesus! Is that not the worst bar ever?" I ask.

"Then why don't you go back?" she presses.

"Where do I start; the drinks are outrageously overpriced, everyone there either wants to beat me up or shoot me and...oh, my God! I forgot about the puke bucket!"

"Not Rays bar! I meant, why don't you go back to her house?"

"I think at this point its best if I give her some space. Plus, she's probably too busy banging Chris Brown."

"Wow," Veronica gasps in shock, "Racist much?"

"No, seriously. The guy she's dating was arrested for domestic violence. How did you not hear about that?" I ask.

"Again, just because I'm a cop, doesn't mean I hear about all crimes that happen."

"Oh, but you make sure to tell the whole station about my arrest??"

"I didn't have to. You came in completely naked!"

"Hey, I wasn't COMPLETELY naked," I correct her.

"Oh, I forgot about the fuzzy, pink, leopard spotted handcuffs," she says.

"Da doo da?" the baby asks me.

"Don't worry about why they were fuzzy, pink and leopard spotted!" I say to him.

"Doo da doo."

"Ugh," I grunt before continuing, "When a mommy and a daddy love each other very much, sometimes, the mommy handcuffs the daddy to a bed post," I tell him.

"Chord!" Veronica yells at me.

"Or the daddy handcuffs the mommy. Jesus, you conservatives and your gender roles!" I reply.

"Why are you telling him this?!" she asks.

"Oh, yea. I forgot you're a baby," I say.

"Boo daa!" he snaps.

"Toddler! Whatever!" I say correcting myself.

"Will you shut up and enjoy these eggs," Veronica says, shaking her head with a big smile while placing a plate in front of me.

"Enjoy, might be a little premature," I reply.

"Hey!" she says insulted, "I'm a great cook!"

"No, I'm not denying your cooking ability. It's just I'm pretty sure I'm still partially drunk."

"I'll make you some coffee," she sighs while rolling her eyes.

"Irish?" I ask.

"You said you're still drunk!"

"Partially drunk," I correct her, "I have to taper down or else I'll have a massive, splitting headache."

"Well, you're out of luck. Cause all I have is wine."

"I recall hearing about a liquor cabinet?" I ask.

"Not here. Probably at their fathers," she answers.

"Well then, now this is happening," I say reaching into my pocket for the pills. I pop open the bottle and down two little white miracle workers into my mouth.

"Really?" she asks, "In front of the kid?"

"What?" I say, shrugging my shoulders, "the bottle is child proof...I think."

"If you can get into it, then obviously it isn't," she mocks me with a smirk.

.   .   .

.   .

"Snap snap snap!"

117

"Almost over, buddy," the officer assures me as he presses his fingers into my chin to reveal my neck.

"*Snap snap snap!*"

"The flash is hurting my eyes," I plead.

"You're doing great, pal," the other officer says as he takes pictures of my exposed throat.

The past few days have felt like years, so much has happened. After telling my mother about what dad did to me, for some reason, she decided to pack some of our stuff and stay at grandma and grandpas for a few days. It was early morning and I was still in my pjs/Halloween costume (yes, the wolverine one). Last night I had slept on the floor in the living room with mom while my sister stayed in her room. She has always had her own room at grandmas and grandpas ever since I can remember. Every time we'd come over to visit I would sleep on the floor and she would retreat to the luxury of her room. Inside, she had her own TV, computer, bookshelf stocked with books and king size bed, while I, had the living room floor. I'd sit there on the floor for hours, sometimes playing with toys, as I listen to grandpa tell me about all the different countries he's been too and how different they are from us while he chews tobacco and flips through the newspaper. Other times, I'd be in the kitchen coloring at the table as grandma cooks some of my favorite food, while telling me stories about my mother when she was a child. Usually, I loved visiting here but this time was different. I didn't like this. It felt weird, different and wrong. So many questions ran through my head. When were we going back home? Where was dad and is he okay? Why were they taking pictures of me? With just one sentence, I felt like I changed the entire universe around me. It's going to take a lot to fix this, and if anyone can fix it, it was dad. He could fix anything.

"Alright," the officer says, releasing his finger tips from my chin, "We're all done."

"See," the other officer continues with a smile, "It wasn't that bad, was it?" before he directs his attention to mom, "Mrs. Johnson, can I speak with you alone?"

"Sure," she replies looking down at me, "Josh, why don't you go play in your sisters room," she suggests and I look to the ground and scoot my feet across the floor to her room.

I didn't know what they were going to talk about, and I didn't care. Any excuse to get away from those police officers was a good enough for me. Then again, whenever police show up that usually means someone is in trouble. The question was, who? Could it be me for causing such a mess, for forcing half of my family to leave the house away from my father, or for causing so much trouble that dad couldn't take it anymore? Suddenly, my heart sank in my chest. What have I done? Can we ever go back to normal? Are we ever going home again? I thought about this as I scooted my feet across the hardwood floor down the hallway. A peeve that my father continuously told me not to do in the past so I pick up my feet and heel-toe the rest of the way.

As I practically stomped down the hallway, my vision is assaulted by an endless array of family photos plastered across the wall. From ceiling to floor, every inch was covered in pictures of the three of them (dad, mom and Alexis) at camping trips, Disney World and birthday parties. I finally get to the end where I expected to see pictures of me but instead I'm bombarded with more photos of Alexis as baby. As if I don't exist. I was born and they thought, "Let's just start over and remember the good times we had with the girl." I let out a painful cloud of air trapped in my chest as my shoulders sink down and my eyes go back to the floor where they belong. I walk up to the door and reach for the knob, but before I can I turn it, I am interrupted by the sound of weeping. It's coming from inside the room. The faint sound of a little girl crying into a pillow seeped from the cracks as I opened the door. When I look inside, I see Alexis sitting on her bed, face buried in her pillow. She removes the pillow from her face to reveal her cheeks are soaked with tears. I didn't know what to say. I've never seen her this way; so sad, so heartbroken, so...vulnerable. She had always been the powerhouse of

119

the family. Barking orders, shouting demands and getting everything she desired was her way of life, but here she was, covered in tears and crying profusely like a wounded animal right in front me. The moment didn't last long, though. Once she collected herself, her complexion quickly changed from sorrow to anger.

"What the fuck do you want!" she yelled and my body jumped in shock. I had never heard her curse before. I opened my mouth but struggled with my explanation, "Mom...mom...mom told me..." I attempt but am quickly cut off.

"Mom...mom...mom," she replies, mocking me with a crude impression, "You're such a fucking baby. All you ever do is play the victim. That's why no one even likes you. Why do you have to ruin everything?"

I didn't answer. I just stood there shaking, waiting her to dictate what I do next.

"This family was perfect before you were born. Then you had to mess everything up. I hate you!" she screams, wiping the remaining tears from her eyes, "What the fuck do you want? Why are you even here!?!"

She rolls her eyes and grunts before slamming her feet to the floor and darting toward me, knocks me to the wall as she sprinted past me and down the hallway. Once she was gone, I entered the room and closed the door behind me. I walked over to the bed and stared down at the tear soaked pillow for moment. Suddenly, the blood rushed in my body. My veins flexed through my skin as I clinch my fist forcing my fingers nails into my palm harder and harder trying to pierce the skin. My chest shook with rage until finally I reach up and plunge my fist into my face. After striking myself, I look down at my fist. It felt good, really good, so I do it again and again. Clashing my hard knuckles into the soft flesh of my cheek, then my nose, then my lips just above the teeth. The force wasn't enough so I begin to jerk my head into the strike, head-butting my fist over and over until...

"What the hell are you doing?!?!" I hear a voice behind me. My heart sank deep and painfully in my chest with embarrassment. Someone had caught me. I slowly turn around to see it was the last person I'd want seeing me in such a psychotic state. It was Emily.

"Sweetie, why are you hitting yourself?" she asks as she runs to me and grabs my hand. She starts to examine it and then my face to see if I had broken the skin. Out of nowhere, my body settled. My heart rested in my chest, my arms no longer quaked and I felt no pain. All I could feel now was Emily's hands running over my cheeks. For some reason she decided to leave her hands resting between my chin and neck with her fingers spanned out and reaching around the back of my head.

"What did you do that for? You could've hurt yourself," she pleads as she stared into my eyes.

"I don't know. I just…"

"You just what?"

"I deserve it. I deserve to be hurt."

"Why would you say that?" she asks and I start to feel her thumbs swipe back and forth just under my ears.

"Because, I broke the family. I made everyone split up. It was cause I told mom what dad did," I answer as the flood gates of my eyes break and a waterfall streams down my face, "If I didn't say anything, we would all be home right now and everyone wouldn't hate me and I wouldn't be in trouble."

"Sweetie," she stops me as she looks into my moist eyes, "Listen to me very carefully. This is not your fault. You did nothing wrong."

The tears stopped. I didn't reply, though. I just stood there in her hands staring at her as she stared back. It felt like an eternity next to her in silence and I would have stayed here forever, but then I see her vision go from my eyes and travel down to my newly bruised and slightly swollen lips. For a split second she glanced at my mouth, then back up to my eyes, then back down to my mouth and within a moment's notice she leans in, presses her soft lips to mine and kisses me.

"Umm..." she pauses, "You okay?"

"Sorry, this has never happened before. It's just..."

"The pills?" she finishes for me.

"The pills," I confirm.

"I mean, I could give you more head if you'd like," Veronica insisted.

"I don't think it would do anything at this point. My dick is like the arm you slept on all night," I say, "Seriously, I'm so high right now you could perform open heart surgery on me and I probably wouldn't even notice."

"Ugh!" she grunts as she raises off of me, "Okay, but you owe me."

"Of course, I'll make up for it next time," I reply.

"And no pills next time," she demands.

"I don't like to make promises I know I won't keep."

"What?!? I'm not worth it?" she asks.

"Oh, you're worth it. It's just, when I tend to make promises, I tend to almost always break them," I reply.

"Well," she says as she rolls out of bed then begins to search for her clothes, "You'd better not break this promise because I'm not even close to through with you Mr. Chord."

"I love that I don't get off that easy," I say as Veronica shuffles around, looking for her clothes then seems to be shocked to hear the front door open and close.

"It's too early for the baby sitter to be here," she says as she frantically throws her clothes on then marches over to the window to peak through the blinds, "Shit!"

"What is it?" I ask.

"Umm, nothing. Just stay here, okay?" she pleads.

"What is it, your husband?" I ask jokingly, "...Oh, it is your husband."

"He's not supposed to be here," she says as she quickly pulls her pants up.

"Babe?!?!" a man's voice calls throughout the house.

"One second!" she yells back before directing her attention back to me, "Just stay here, okay?"

"You already said that," I reply.

"And trust me, I meant it," she assures before taking a deep breath and leaving the room.

Luckily for me, even when I'm higher than Willy Nelson in an air balloon, my primal male instincts still kick in and right now they were telling me to get the hell out of here. So, I jump out of bed and hastily throw my clothes on.

"Damn," I say as I realize that I still have no idea where my original shirt is......or my boots for that matter. I comb my eyes over the entirety of the floor only to see Veronica's shirt I had been sporting. I pick it up and stare at it for a moment, "No, no, no. I'm not gonna put

123

myself through that again. I've learned my lesson...Jesus, I never thought I'd say that," I say and suddenly I'm stricken by the sound of yelling from the living room. I rush to the dresser and open up the top drawer. Still, just Veronica's clothes.

"Seriously, no matter how much you tempt me, I'm not wearing women's clothes again," I speak before looking over to the closet, "Worth a try," I run over to it, open it up and see men's shirts neatly hung up and organized.

"Holy crap! I gotta get a wife. I mean, most the time I just throw my clothes in a pile on the bed. This is like having your own personal maid that you can bang. This must be what Arnold Swartzinager feels like all the time," I say as I hear the yelling travel down the hallway. I shuffle through the shirts, trying to find the perfect one that no one would notice if it was gone. I finally come across an old, torn, stained orange shirt that looked as if it'd been scribbled on with a marker or something, "Who's gonna miss an orange shirt?" I ask myself, "I'm practically doing him a favor," I quickly put the shirt on and run for the window, pushing it open. The doorknob starts to turn right as I fall to the ground outside.

"Ahhh!" I cry, "Hello, Mr. Sun. I see you're as bright as ever, you ruthless bastard. I mean, why can't it just always be night. I feel like that would somehow fix our global warming problem," I contemplate as I approach my car but am quickly halted by the most horrific sight ever to cross my eyes. Nothing could prepare me for the horrendous scene that was assaulting my every innocence. The one vision that could destroy my soul from inside like a cancer.

"That asshole keyed my car!" I scream as I stare down at a white scar traveling from the fender to the rear door, "God damn it! How could this day get any worse!" I yell at the top of my lungs to the sky, "......and that's not an invitation to actually make my day worse either!" I shout to the heavens.

"Who the hell are you talking to?" a voice to my side says. I glance over to see that it was the neighbor from last night baring witness to my celestial assault.

"Uhhh, nobody," I say as an awkward silence falls between us, "Hey, you haven't happen to see some boots lying around...perhaps, near your pool?" at my question, the man gives me a hard snarl and flexes his arm as he points across the lawn to a Rottweiler. The dog was casually resting in the grass enjoying the morning sun and right under his paws were two newly chewed up boots.

"Hey there, buddy," I say gently to the dog as I attempt to very passively approach him, "Mind if I take those from you?"

"*Grrr!*" he growls, showing his sharp pearly whites and I quickly retract my attempt.

"Fine! I hope you choke on a lace!" I yell back at him and make my way back to my disfigured car.

"You can't talk to my dog like that!" the man screams at me.

"You can't feed your dog my wardrobe!"

"You left your boots in my yard! What did you think was gonna happen?"

"I DON'T THINK WHEN I'M DRUNK!!"

"You're a disgrace to the force," he says, shaking his head.

"What?? I'm not a cop......Oh, yeah. God, I gotta stop lying about that," I say to myself, "I mean, there's gotta be some kind of impersonation law I'm violating."

"It's called impersonating an officer," he says correcting me.

"That was an A...Umm, I guess A-A conversation, so C your way out!"

"That doesn't make any sense! You can't skip B!"

"I'll skip whatever letter I want to, old man!"

"I'm only thirty eight!"

"Thank you for proving my point," I mutter, rolling my eyes and suddenly yet another awkward silence makes its way between us, "on a side note," I say breaking the silence, "Do you think it would help global warming if it was always night time?"

"GET THE HELL OUT OF HERE!!" he yells one more time.

"Fine! God, I guess some people don't care about the environment," I reply, finally getting in my car.

There's nothing like a long, hung over, post-adulterated, early morning ride to make you seriously examine your life decisions. So far, I'm out one pair of boots, one expensive paint job, one love of my life and I should probably consider being out one horny and married cop. I mean, literally only bad things can come from this. On the other hand, I do owe her for my case of the oxi-dick...no, no, no! I've got to start thinking with the head on my shoulders and not the one in my pants. Veronica and I had fun and the one kid I spent time with is moderately cool, but I've got to move on. Now, on to how the hell am I going to get Emily to talk to me again? I could go to her house again, but I imagine she's already told her parents not to let me in. Also, after the scuffle that I kind of caused, I can only assume Ray doesn't want me anywhere near his bar. Which, I can't say is entirely a bad thing. On the other hand, it might be best to give her some space after the tornado of damage I've caused. But how much space is enough space? Too much space and she might run away with the Notorious B-I-T-C-H. Not enough space and she will resent me forever. I wish I had a friend to go to for advice, but Emily has always been that friend. Whenever I was feeling more depressed than usual, whenever I was suffering from severe case of writer's block or when I just needed a drinking buddy, she was always there for me. Without her, I literally have no one. I scoured my mind looking for someone I could go to for help but ultimately came up blank. Steve would just tell me to forget about her and then offer me a hopefully legal aged, Chinese hooker. Mom, she would just be happy to hear from me before prawning me for any money I have. Alexis...ugh, I give up. I don't know how to fix this and I don't know anyone who can tell me how to fix this. I'm so emotionally impaired. I'm obliviously apathetic to everyone around me. All I do is break things. The only thing I'm good at is....wait! That's it! I know how to fix this! I know how I can make everything right again with Emily.

"I am gonna write her a song!......Wow, that sounded terrible out loud," I say as I pull into my driveway, "What was I thinking? I can't fix everything with a song."

I finally approach my door and prepare myself for a day of wallowing, licking my wounds, probably shopping online for a new pair of boots and of course the recently traditional pills. I start to turn the key when I'm once again interrupted by a familiar voice.

"Good morning, neighbor," the man's voice says. Without even turning around to acknowledge him, I reply with a hard sigh followed by, "God damn it."

"Oh," he gasp, "I don't know if I like that kinda language," he says politely as I turn to face him.

"Sawdy," I say with a Mexican accent, "No habla Espanol."

"Wait, did you just say you don't speak Spanish...in Spanish?" he ask.

"Shit," I snap.

"Did you mean, *no habla inlges?*"

"Yeah, that one, no habla ingles. Adios!" I answer.

"So, last time you were a homosexual. Now you're a Mexican?"

"I can be both. Haven't you ever heard of Ricky Martin?"

"Puerto Rican," he says.

127

"What?"

"Ricky Martin is Puerto Rican."

"What's the difference?"

"Well, one's Mexico and one's Puerto Rico," he answers.

"Potato, pa-homo," I reply while waving him off.

"Look," he says with a smile, "I know you probably don't want to talk about our lord and savior-"

"-About as much as I want a pedophile showing up at my door every week," I interrupt.

"-But I wrote down some passages that I thought you might enjoy," he finishes as he reaches into his pocket and pulls out sheets of paper with bible verses printed out on them.

"That's fine, I already have plenty of toilet paper," I reply and he rolls his eyes with a smirk before replying.

"Look, you don't have to read them. Just take the papers and maybe one day, in your darkest hour, when you've hit rock bottom, when all hope seems lost then you'll find these papers and Jesus can help you."

"Cause what I really need is a thirty year old virgin that still does magic tricks," I say finally taking the papers to shut him up.

"So," he says, raising an eyebrow, "I have a question."

"I'm well over eighteen, Sandusky," I reply.

"That's not what I was gonna ask! And don't call me Sandusky!" he snaps, trying to hold back his frustration.

"Then, what do you want, Jared?"

"Jared??"

"Yeah, you know, like the pedophile from sub-"

"-I KNOW WHAT YOU MEANT!" he interrupts.

"Then, why did you ask?" I reply laughing.

"Ugh!" he grunts before taking a deep breath and asking, "What happened to your car?"

"Ugh," I grunt myself, "Don't ask."

"Looks like somebody keyed it pretty bad."

"Tune in next time to the adventures of Sherlock Holmes," I say in an old timey radio host voice mocking him.

"Why does it not surprise me that you tick someone off so bad that they keyed your car?" he asks.

"Okay, first off, I didn't tick him off. I slept with his wife-"

"-and you didn't think that would tick him off?"

"-Secondly!...actually, I don't think I had a secondly."

"Secondly," he says, finishing my rant, "Premarital sex is a mortal sin."

"It wasn't premarital......she is married."

"That's not what I meant!" he snaps, "Every time I see you, you're either talking about sex, half naked or wasted off your butt."

"I fail to see the downside to all of that."

"Son," he says while calming himself, "a life filled with random, meaningless, pointless, premarital sex is only going to lead you down a path of pain and misery."

"Duh! That's what the alcohol and drugs are for."

"Oh, dear lord!" he sighs, throwing his hands in the air in surrender.

129

"I mean, come on, It's not premarital if I never plan on getting married," I say with a pretentious smile.

"You can't 'loop hole' the bible, son."

"Says the guy who cuts the sides of his hair while wearing a polyester shirt and downing some hotdogs."

"It's actually one hundred percent cotton," he tells me, grabbing his shirt.

"It's ACTUALLY hypocritical of a Christian to judge others, knowing that they break just as many Old Testament rules as non-believers, homosexuals or premarital sex...havers! When in that same passage it states that we can't even eat shrimp!"

"Actually," he corrects me, "Those rules were set in place by Moses through God strictly for the Hebrew people," he adds with a smug smile.

"AND DO I LOOK HEBREW TO YOU?!?!" I press on, raising my voice. He pauses for minute contemplating this before replying, "I guess, I never thought of it that way."

"Exactly! So, while you stand there, questioning and subconsciously regretting your life decision to become a Christian, I, on the other hand, have to go inside, sober up enough to confidently get back on the road so I can buy an entire new wardrobe and hopefully find a shop that's open so they can paint my disfigured car because I had the once in a lifetime opportunity to fulfill my fantasy of sleeping with a cop!" I yell, hoping that my volume would offend him enough that he would leave.

"......she was a cop?"

"Yes! She was a God damn cop!" I could tell that my selective cursing was beginning to really bother him by the look in his face. Still, he managed to collect himself only to attempt to continue our conversation.

130

"Speaking of wardrobes," he says looking at my shirt with wide eyes.

"Oh, my God! I'm not into men!" I reply while rolling my eyes.

"That's not what I was gonna ask!" he snaps, "I was gonna ask if you were gonna watch the game tonight?"

"The game?"

"College football. I just assumed cause-"

"-If you assumed," I say, cutting him off, "That I'm some sort of inbred, ignorant redneck that enjoys watching grown men on steroids give each other brain damage in between rape convictions, then no. You assumed wrong," I finish before attempting to shut the door on him.

"Wait! Wait! Just one more thing," he presses.

"What? God damn it!" he sighs and grunts at my choice of words.

"I mean, at this point it's like you're doing it on purpose," he implies.

I laugh and reply with, "I so am."

"I was gonna ask, what happened to your hand?"

"Oh, this," I say, raising my cast, "I broke it fisting your mother."

His face quickly turned red, "My mother is dead!" he says sternly.

"I mean, who could have lived through a fisting like that?" I reply before finally slamming the door in his face.

Once I got rid of him, I let a long and much needed sigh of relief before dragging my feet across the floor through my house. As always, the house was as empty as it was messy and as I turned the corner to the kitchen, I remind myself not to expect a cute, little, blonde tomboy in army pants to be sitting on my counter asking why I'm out of food, "Maybe I'm out of food because you keep eating it," I say to myself,

131

grunting but quickly correcting myself. At this point I would buy all the food in the world just to see her again. I would fill ten houses with milk, chips, sodas and those horrible sandwich cookies she likes, "She doesn't even eat them. She just breaks them in half and licks the frosting off," I speak as I enter the kitchen. I had to stop, though. Just thinking about her was putting me through unbearable pain. Even mentioning the little infuriating things she does that seem to creep and crawl under my skin was forcing tears to my eyes. The times when she would irritate me to the brink of insanity now seemed like heaven compared to this hollow and silent solitary I call a home. Suddenly, in the midst of all my wallowing, I notice out of the corner of my eye that the answering machine was flashing again so I pull and drag my feet to it with my shoulders sunk down as if I were carrying a large weight. My back crashes against the wall as I hit the button on the machine to play me the inevitable charity case.

"Beep! You have one unheard message. First unheard message..."

"Hey, Josh. It's your mother. I was just wondering-"

"-Beep! Message deleted."

.   .   .

.   .

"Seriously, it could work!"

"Nope," he said, shaking his head.

"What?!? Why not?"

"Because, if it was always night time here, then that would mean it's always daytime on the other side of the planet. Like China n' stuff," he explains.

"Damn, I always forget about China," I reply.

132

"Also, global warming isn't caused by the sun actually getting hotter," he says.

"What?!? Yes it is!"

"Nope. It's caused by greenhouse gasses getting caught in the Earth's atmosphere and heated by solar rays."

"......damn," I replied as I sat there, stunned by his immense knowledge of the world.

"Yep."

"Hey, how do you know all of this?" I ask, "Aren't you like, five?"

"I'm eight!" he snaps, correcting me, "and, I don't know, I just really like science."

"I wish I was as smart as you when I was that age," I say.

"You're not as smart as me now," he replies while staring off into the distance. I wanted to get mad, but he was probably right. After spending almost all day with this kid, I can honestly say he was the most intelligent five...or eight year old kid I had ever met. His name was Benjamin and he was a scrawny little boy with brown hair and blue eyes like his mother. He got straight A's without even trying, doesn't enjoy sports very much but absolutely loves everything to do with science. I could barely keep up with this kid on how much he knows about space, physics and chemistry. I learned more conversing with him in a few hours then all my years in school. Mostly, because all of my years in school were spent staring at girls.

While I was enjoying my custom 'sleeping in until the sun goes down' Veronica decided to call me. Then, call again and again until I finally gave in and answered the phone and agreed to go with her and her kids to the park for Valory's cheer practice. I had been keeping Ben company while Valory practiced with her team and Taylor, the youngest and oddest one, stayed glued to his mother's side, who was sitting on the bleachers watching the girls twist and twirl to choreographed

133

cheers. Ben and I, on the other hand, were sitting over on the swings, rocking back and forth while contemplating whether or not a child's play thing can support a grown man's weight. Then, quickly realizing that it wouldn't matter, because I'm way too high to feel pain anyways. Speaking of...

"How many of those are you gonna take?" he asks as I shuffle through my pocket for a little bottle of magic.

"As many as it takes until the pain goes away," I answer before popping the bottle open and letting a few white pills fall in my mouth.

"Dude, you broke your hand like, weeks ago," he says, rolling his eyes.

"Yeah, *DUDE*," I reply mocking his slang choice of words, "and it still hurts. So, I have to take these."

"It says take like, three a day."

"It didn't say how many times a day I should take three," I reply with a smirk, but he wasn't entertained. To my remark, he just rolls his eyes again and glances back toward the cheerleaders before I continue, "Besides, I'm dealing with some internal pain also. And if these doctors would stop prescribing me refills maybe I'd have some incentive to quit. Jesus, they're like legal drug dealers. I mean, the system is so......hey! Are you listening?" I ask as I look over to see his eyes still fixed on the girls dancing, "Ohhh," I say, "So, that's what you're looking at."

"What?!" he gasps, hastily directing his attention back to me, "No! I was just-"

"-which one?" I ask, interrupting him.

"Which what?"

"Which one of the girls do you like? Don't lie." He pauses for a moment, contemplating whether or not to tell me when I start to lightly shove him, causing him to rock back and forth in the swing.

"Alright, alright," he says with a smile, "the girl on the right."

"Well, why don't you go talk to her?"

"I can't just 'go talk to her'."

"And why the hell not?"

"I don't know. What would I say? I mean, you're obviously good with girls."

"Actually, I'm TERRIBLE with girls. I mean, yeah, I got a certain boyish charm about me that women find cute, but when it comes to actually speaking to them, I'm a nervous wreck."

"You are?"

I pause for a moment, reminding myself of my traditional strategy of lying to women right to their face. Telling them what they want to hear instead of the truth then temporarily altering myself to meet their standards only to fuck them, then dismiss them as if they don't even exist. Obviously this hasn't worked out for me lately. If there was ever a morally accurate time to be honest it was now. So, I let out a long sigh, look down at him and say, "I have no idea what to say to women when I'm in front of them, so I just be myself. I know it sounds corny but women respect honesty. Trust me, there is no 'one liner' you can think of that they haven't heard already. And if you pretend to be something you're not, and it ends up working, then you have to continue acting like that person you were pretending to be. Because, that's who she fell for, not the real you. So, just tell her how you feel, and if you embarrass yourself, so what! Who gives a fu....crap. We all embarrass ourselves at one point or another," I explain.

"Even you?" he asks, looking up at me.

"I've embarrassed myself more than anyone. I mean, the first time I met your mother I was naked and handcuffed."

"Wait! What?!" he yells.

"Oh, uhhh, pretend I didn't say that," I say while shaking my head, "Look, the point is, if you're wondering what to say to a girl that you like, the last people you should ask is men. Because, no matter how 'George Clooney' they think they are, we don't know what the hell women want. But, if you ask any woman, they'll all say the same thing. Just be yourself."

"I just have one question," he says with a raised eyebrow.

"A Catholic girl took my clothes off, handcuffed me to a bed and spanked me till I bled out of my ass," I answer.

"WHAT?!?! NO!!" he yells again.

"Oh, my bad. Then, what was your question?"

"Who is George Clooney?" he asks and suddenly a dead silence falls between us as I sit there staring at him with disappointment.

"I don't even know how to answer that," I reply, squinting my eyes at him when at that moment I hear a voice ring throughout the park.

"Chord! Ben!" it was Veronica calling us over, "It's time to go," she shouts and on her demand we both raise from our swings and make our way toward her.

"Wait," I stop to reach in my pocket, "You go ahead. I gotta do something real quick."

"Another one?!?" he replies in shock, "Dude, you just took three!"

"DUDE!" I say mocking him again, "That's not what I'm doing," I answer as I pull out a pack of cigarettes.

"Ohhhh, that's waaaay better," he replies sarcastically.

"Just go to your mom. I'll be there in a minute," I order him with a smirk on my face. Once alone with my cancer stick, I inhale the toxic aroma until the tip flares up as I stare out into the hordes of happy

136

families around the park; mothers, fathers, sons and daughters all holding hands in synchronized harmony. All of them smiling and so perfectly placed with one another like puzzle pieces linked together in flawless absolution. The most talented painter couldn't imitate this vision of American dream marveling in front of me. And then there was me. An alcoholic, drug addict and (let's be honest) sex addict with no one. In the perfect puzzle of happiness I was I broken piece. An extra fragment with nothing to connect to so the only other option is to discard it in the trash and accept its expendable worthlessness. I didn't even know what I was doing here. I mean, I enjoyed spending time with Veronica, and her kids were really starting to grow on me. Ben is cool as hell and smarter than most adults on this planet. Valory is a little firecracker and has no problem speaking her mind without any regards of others feelings. Taylor is...kinda weird, but for some reason he looks at this 5'10 stack of human failure and decides that he actually enjoys having me around. But what exactly am I doing here?

"That's bad for you!" I hear from behind me. I turn around to see a little girl pointing in judgement.

"Contemplating my place in life?" I ask.

"What?" she replies, cocking her head to the side in confusion.

"Uh, nothing. What do you want, little girl?" I ask as I take another puff of my cigarette.

"Smoking is bad for you!" she screams while pointing and glaring at me with contempt.

"So is talking to a registered pedophile. Now get lost!" I demand her, attempting to scare her away as I take my last puff.

"What's a pedo...pedo..." she struggles.

"It's uh...it's something you get to make your toenails pretty," I answer and at that moment I see her parents approaching.

"Sweetie," the mother says, "There you are. I've been looking all over for you."

"Mommy!" she replies back while looking at me, "I want a pedophile!"

"Excuse me?!" the mother gasp in shock and on that note the father rushes to the girl's side while snarling and staring a hole through me.

"Have you been talking to my daughter!" he presses as he takes a step in my direction. He reaches over, grabs me by the collar and begins to raise his fist. My body tenses up and I close my eyes and prepare myself to get punched in the face before the little girl interrupts, "I just wanna make my toenails pretty," she mutters under her breath.

"Oh, my goodness," the mother exhales in relief, "Sweetie, you meant a pedicure not a pedophile," she says, looking over at the father giving him the gesture to let me go. He releases me before dusting me off and doing his best to hide his embarrassment, "My bad, buddy," he says, stepping away from me.

"You know, not every single guy at the park is a creep," I reply fixing my ruffled shirt, "then again, there was that time two boys saw me naked outside of a church."

"What?!?" the father yells, quickly turning from embarrassed to enraged again.

"No! No! It's not what you think! It was the naughty, Catholic girl. Just ask Ben. He's the little eight year old boy over there. He knows all about it," I poorly explain.

"There's something seriously wrong with people like you!" he screams in my face.

"No! You got me all wrong! I actually totally agree with you. I mean, I have a pedophile at my house, like every week," I say while throwing my hands up in surrender.

"Let's get the hell away from this guy!" he yells one last time before rushing his family away.

"Oh! Not like that! I meant..." but they had already retreated far enough that they couldn't hear me.

"Well," I say, shrugging my shoulders, "That's one way to get rid of an annoying kid."

"Chord!" Veronica calls from across the park.

"On my way!" I reply, waving then sucking what little nicotine my cigarette had left.

As I try to shake off what had just happened to me, I begin to make my way to them and I start to see a crowd gathering around them. All filled with the typical mother, father and kids scene that I had been tolerating for my entire visit to the park. I pause for a moment, asking myself if I really want to enter this crowd of good ol' all American dream, then quickly deciding that I've had my fill of Brady Bunch impersonators, so instead I just hang back, awkwardly standing around with my hands in my pockets waiting for the mass of mediocrity to thin out.

"You smell really bad," I hear a voice from behind me say. I turn around to see Valory standing there in her cheerleading outfit eating an ice cream cup.

"I smell bad?"

"You smell like a house fire got caught in a forest fire."

"That's not stank. That's the smell of tobacco granting me the will to put up with little annoying children."

"Well, whatever it is, it stinks."

"Wait a minute, when did we get ice cream?" I ask.

"I got ice cream," she says, correcting me, "The squad always has ice cream after practice."

"The squad?"

"Cheerleading," she answers.

"Jesus, I need to become a cheerleader," I say.

"You're a boy! Boys can't be cheerleaders!" she snaps before taking another bite of ice cream.

"Oh, yeah? Tell that to George Bush!"

"Who is George Bush?"

"I swear to God if you kids keep making me feel old-"

"-Uh, you are old," she snarkingly replies.

"Well, tell Emily that," I quietly mutter under my breath but apparently not quietly enough.

"Who is Emily?" she asks.

"It's my girlfr....It's my friend."

"You have a girlfriend and you're dating my mom?!?!" she yells.

"Yeah, say it a little louder. I don't think the entire park heard you," I sarcastically whisper.

Suddenly, she stares blankly at me before sporting a devious smirk then inhaling until her lungs were completely full, "YOU HAVE A GIRLFRIEND AND-" she screams at the top of her lungs before I run over a hastily place my hand over her mouth.

"First off," I whisper, "I'm not dating your mom. Secondly, I don't have a girlfriend. And thirdly, if you promise to keep your mouth shut, I'll buy you whatever kids are recklessly throwing their parents

140

hard earned money at these days." At that moment her eyes light up as she mutters, "a mmmhhh uhhh ehhhh!"

"What??? I can't understand you," I whisper then she raises an eyebrow and glances down at my hand that was still covering her mouth, "Oh, right. My bad," I reply, moving my hand away.

"A new iPhone!" she shouts.

"Whatever your little materialistic heart desires. Just, please stop yelling," I plead while rolling my eyes.

"You pinky promise?" she asks, sporting a stern expression and extending her hand, pinky finger out toward me.

"I don't like making promises I know I won't......actually, yes, I pinky promise," I reply with a smirk and lock pinky fingers with her.

"I promise," She routinely spouts out as our hands move up and down, "You have to say it!"

"Oh, my bad. I promise," I repeat.

"So, if this Emily girl is not your girlfriend then why do you call her that?"

"Call it wishful thinking."

"So, do you not like my mom?"

"I do. I really do. I mean, she's fun, beautiful, intelligent and not to mention the sex is amazing."

"What!?"

"Oh, uh. Pretend I didn't say that."

"I will!" she grunts, "Anyways, if you like her that much then why don't you date her? Dad obviously isn't coming back."

"It is far more complicated than that. Besides, your dad might come back, you never know."

141

"Nope. I've heard them arguing. Mom says she never wants him back."

"Eh, adults say things they don't mean all the time."

"Dad's too busy with his new girlfriend. Mom says she's like half her age."

"Trust me, once daddy realizes his new girlfriend is so immature that it gets under his skin, then he'll come crawling back to your mom."

"How do you know," she ask as the rest of the family breaks away from the group and starts walking in our direction.

"Let's just say, I've been on the other end of that scenario," I answer before Veronica approaches us. I could tell by her body language that she wanted to show some sort of physical affection to me; a hug, a kiss, maybe even a nice slap on the ass cheek but she quickly prevents herself from showing any attraction for fear of other people seeing it. So, instead she just stands in front of me, smiles and exhales while looking me up and down.

"You ready to go?" she asks.

"I was ready to go before I even got here," I reply with a smile.

"Oh, hush! You and Ben have been talking the whole time. And then, I come over here to see you talking to Valory."

"I don't know if I'd consider it talking as much as tolerating."

At that remark Valory squints her eyes at me, "Yeah, ME tolerating YOU! And the fact that you smell like a trash can," she says.

"Do you smell?" Veronica asks before leaning in to sniff me, "Oh! She's right. You smell like a wet dog gave birth to an even wetter dog."

"You smell like the act of dying," Ben says before everyone (except for me) burst into laughter at my expense.

142

"Oh, come on! Not you too!" I say to Ben.

"Yassa babba doo," Taylor says jokingly.

"Okay, that one was pretty funny," I finally admit with a smile and on that note we all start to walk to the car.

"Wait, he didn't say anything," Veronica says to me.

"What are you talking about? That was the best joke out of all of them," I reply.

"But-" she says but is suddenly interrupted by a voice behind us.

"-Well, look who it is," the voice says as the entire family stops and stares at me.

"Well," Veronica presses, "Aren't you gonna turn around?"

"Honestly, I've had enough bad luck with people sneaking up on me today," I answer.

"How are the sales coming?" the voice says to me.

"Wait......Kowalski?" I reply, finally turning around to see none other than the retired porn star turned cop himself.

"How do you guys know each other?" Veronica asks us.

"Wait, how do YOU GUYS know each other?" Kowalski asks Veronica.

"Seriously guys, the last time I played this game I almost got jumped by a bartender, a bunch of frat boys and a black man," I tell both of them.

"WAIT, WHAT?!?!" Veronica snaps at me.

"Oh, sorry. AFRICAN AMERICAN man," I correct myself.

"No, you almost got jumped??" she asks.

143

"So, that was you that started the Rays Bar Brawl," Kowalski says.

"It has a name?" I ask.

"There was a brawl at Ray's Bar?" she asks.

"Seriously, you're a cop, how do you not know these things?" I say to her.

"BECAUSE YOU WERE OUT WITH MY CRUISER!" she yells.

"Wait, you let him drive your cruiser?" Kowalski says.

"It's cool, I'm a cop," I explain to him.

"YOU'RE NOT A COP!" she yells again.

"Oh, yeah. God damn, I gotta stop lying about that."

"Hey! You're a man of God. Watch your language, brother," Kowalski says to me.

"Man of God?" Veronica ask, scowling at me.

"I sell bibles," I say while shrugging my shoulders and smiling.

"Since when do you sell bibles?"

"Since I got pulled over by some dumb Christian cop and I needed a way to get out of a ticket," I answer.

"A WHAT???" Kowalski snaps.

"Oh, not you. I was talking about another Burt Reynolds Doppelganger," I reply.

"That's it!" he yells, "You're under arrest!"

"For what? Being smarter than you? Jesus, you might as well arrest everyone here...including the kids...and pets," I say.

"CHORD!" Veronica screams at me.

144

"I think I saw a dog eating cat shit over by the concession stand, even he knew I don't sell bibles," I say with a smart ass smile before he grabs me by the wrist and starts twisting my arm behind my back and tells me, "How about running a red light-"

"-A red light that you LET me run."

"Starting a Bar Brawl-"

"-Allegedly."

"Stealing a cop car-"

"-Borrowed."

"And impersonating an officer!"

"Actually, yeah, I really need to stop doing that," I admit.

"Look," Veronica says to him attempting to calm the situation, "Aubrey-"

"-Ha! Your name is Aubrey???" I say laughing.

"Crack!" my wrist goes as he twist it in the wrong direction.

"Hey! That's my bad wrist, asshole! If I wasn't high as shit right now that would really hurt!" I yell at him.

"Oh, so you're high too? Well, that's just more charges on ya," he says.

"Yeah, no shit! I've got a broken hand, genius!"

"And how did you break your hand, tough guy?" he asks.

At that moment, a dead silence took over as everyone stopped and stood there waiting on my response. A battle was forging in my brain on what to say as his grip tightened around my broken hand. Should I do the responsible thing and tell him the truth about how I broke my hand? Should I sincerely apologize for lying to him, taking Veronicas cop car, causing an entire bar full of people to fight,

145

impersonating an officer of the law this whole time and just finally admit that I have a serious problem with drugs, alcohol and sexual addiction but mask it with immature humor to the point where everyone thinks that I'm fine and it's all one big joke when in reality I should just succumb to the ultimate truth that I need help?

"......God damnit, I broke it fisting your mom," I say regretfully.

"Crack!"

"Ahhhh!" I cry out as he cranks my wrist again until Veronica intervenes, "Please, Aubrey-"

"Ha!" I laugh.

"Crack!"

"Ahhh!" I scream.

"CHORD! SHUT UP!" she yells at me.

"Seriously, I don't think I have any more bones in my hand," I reply.

"Then stop laughing at my damn name!" he demands me.

"Listen, Aubrey," she says to him, "This is just one big misunderstanding. You did LET him get away with running a red light. I let him borrow the cop car for an emergency. He was gone before the brawl even started. He was just joking about being a cop and he has a prescription for all the drugs he's on because of his broken hand," she explains.

"Well, what about pretending to be a bible salesmen?" he presses.

"Technically, that's not against the law," she says to him.

"Oh, yeah," he admits.

"But what is against the law is police brutality. And I'm pretty sure my family and I just watched you break his wrist in about ten

146

different places, so I'd recommend you let him go before I decide to call this in and he uses his one phone call to contact his lawyer who would be more than happy to sue the station because some idiotic cop decided to abuse his power all cause he got his feelings hurt."

"I actually don't have a lawyer," I intervene.

"CHORD! SHUT UP!" she orders me.

"Yeah, you're right," Aubrey says, releasing his grip on my now shattered wrist, "Listen, buddy. I'm sorry about losing my temper like that. Look, if you agree to look the other way about your wrist, I agree to look the other way about literally all the laws you broke."

"Deal," I say, stepping back and collecting myself, "I'd uh, shake your hand but I'm pretty sure my bones are dust now."

"Chord," Veronica sighs as the children gather around in shock at what they just saw, "Let's go home."

"Agreed," I reply as we go back to walking to the cars and Aubrey begins to retreat.

"Hey, you!" I hear from behind me and we all freeze in shock. With wide eyes Veronica slowly looks over at me.

"Seriously, I'm not turning around this time!" I say to her.

"What did you do this time?" she asks.

"That guy told my daughter he's a registered pedophile!" the voice yells.

"He's a what??" Aubrey asks.

"Yeah! He likes to show his wiener to little boys outside of a church!" he says to Aubrey and suddenly he turns bright red as he snarls at me.

"I can explain. That guy set me up!" I say, pointing behind Aubrey.

147

"Who?" he asks, turning around to reveal there was no one there. Then, turning back around to see me darting to my car, "You son of a bitch!" he screams before sprinting off toward me.

"That's why you never turn around, asshole!" I yell back as I quickly approach my car, jump in the driver's seat, rev up the engine and burn rubber down the parking lot.

As I practically drag race through the lot, I look back to see Aubrey still chasing after me on foot. When I look forward again I see, casually resting on the dashboard, the bible that started it all. I immediately slam on the breaks. My tires squeal and screech as my car comes to a halt. I reach over, grab the bible, roll the window down and stand on the seat so that my entire body was outside of the car excluding my legs and yell, "HEY, AUBREY! I GOT A BIBLE FOR SELL! IT'S ON DISCOUNT CAUSE IT SMELLS LIKE MY DICK!" I scream then throw the good book in his direction. Once back inside my car, I floor it as I drive off down the road.

"Well," I say calmly, "this was the worst day of my life......and that's not an invitation to make my day worse, either!"

.   .   .

        .   .

"Jesus! What happened?!" the doctor asks in shock.

"Uh, I broke my hand. Don't you remember?"

"Yea, but not this bad!"

"Don't ever tell a cop that you fisted his mother."

"You fisted a cop's mother?!" he gasps.

"No! I told him I fisted his mother. A pastor too."

"So, you told a cop and a pastor that you fisted both of their mothers?"

148

"Also a bartender......oh, wait. Or did I just laugh at him for having dead parents?"

"What the hell is wrong with you!?" he yells.

"They died on 9/11."

"How does that make it better?"

"No! Not THE 9/11. Just A 9/11."

"That still doesn't make it right!"

"I know! You don't say 9/11 unless it like, happened on THE 9/11."

"THAT'S NOT WHAT I MEANT!"

"Jesus, calm down. Maybe you should be the one asking for painkillers."

"Yeah," he pauses, scratching his head while examining the new x rays of my hand, "Usually, when people come in asking for more pain meds, I just assume they are *pill seekers* but I honestly don't know how you're not in excruciating pain right now."

"It doesn't hurt that I'm partially drunk right now."

"Wait, how did you get here?" he presses.

"*Golle gee, President Cleveland! There's a new invention called an automobile. We aint gotta ride on horseback no more!*" I say in an old timey voice.

"Ugh," he grunts and rolls his eyes, "look, you're definitely going to need surgery this time, and I'll write you a new prescription. You obviously can handle a higher dose."

"Legal drug dealers," I mutter to myself.

"What?"

149

"Nothing," I quickly reply, changing the subject, "So, this surgery? It's optional, right?" I ask.

"Mandatory," he answers.

"Right, but if I really didn't want to do it, I don't have to?" I request.

"Mr. Chord," he sighs while crossing his arms, "I honestly don't care what you do-"

"-My point exactly."

"But if you don't have surgery you may never be able to use that hand again," he warns, suddenly scowling at me.

"So, that means..."

"Yes, Mr. Chord!" he interrupts, "No more masturbation."

"Well, when you say it like that. Yeah, we definitely have to do the surgery," I reply with a smirk.

"Ugh!" he grunts again before continuing, "I will schedule the surgery for next Saturday. Is that fine with you?"

"I actually planned to sit around, get drunk and order a pizza that day but I'm sure I can push that back. I just hope there aren't any scheduling conflicts between me and Pizza Hut."

"You absolutely can not drink Saturday-"

"-Then again, there's always Little Caesars."

"Or eat-"

"-Talkin bout that Hot N' Ready!"

"And you should try to get plenty of sleep-"

"-Then again, every time you get there it's like they're already out of them."

"MR. CHORD!"

"They shouldn't call it Hot N' Ready. They should call it Cold and...wait, what's the opposite of punctual?"

"QUIET!"

"How is that the opposite of punctual?"

"No! I'm telling you to be quiet! Now, are you done talking?"

"......Belated! Okay, I'm done," I say calmly.

"Next Saturday. Don't eat. Don't drink. Get plenty of sleep. And above all, shut the hell up."

"Is that really a surgical procedure?"

"GET THE HELL OUT OF MY OFFICE!" he yells at me and I take the warning and dart out of the room toward the hallway.

Once in the hallway and at a safe distance from Mr. Hyde, I glance around to study the atmosphere. The walls were painted a calming baby blue reaching down to a white carpet covered in floral designs. There were various photos of waterfalls in the rainforest and close ups of exotic animals, while the air complemented your senses with an aroma of lavender and pine. I've never understood why doctor's offices try so hard to enhance their décor. As if a couple pictures of monkeys and a waterfall on the other side of the planet along with a few glade plug-ins are going to make me forget that I'm stuck in a tiny strip mall office in the middle of country ass nowhere with a broken hand.

"There's a Dollar General next door, for Christ sake," I say as I stare at a zebra drinking from a watering hole.

"You got a problem with Dollar General?" I hear a voice down the hall say. I walk down the rest of the hallway, dodging clouds of air freshener, when I see none other than the beautiful, busty nurse from last time sitting behind a desk in the typical scrubs swinging back and forth in an office chair while twirling a pen in her fingers.

151

"Nurse Chocolate cake!" I say with delight.

"Please tell me that's not what you've been calling me," she asks, quickly putting on a stern face.

"How could I call you without your number?"

"Smooth," she admits, cracking a smile.

"So, the love life?" I press on.

"The love life?" she asks.

"How is it?"

"Same as always," she sighs, "Single and not ready to mingle," she reaches over to shuffle through some papers.

"That's too bad. I'm great at mingling."

"Don't you remember last time? How you're not my type?" she asks, grinning at me.

"Well, how would I know if I don't know you're type? I might not be dark and tall but I'd like to think I got the handsome down."

"Yeah, you're cute. I'll give you that."

"Is that all you'll give me?" I ask, raising an eyebrow. She pauses for a moment to look at me in silence before exhaling and saying, "Look, you're good looking and you're actually kinda funny-"

"-Funny is scarce these days."

"-Yes it is," she agrees, "but you come in here, you clearly don't know how to dress properly, you're young, immature, you piss everyone off and you broke your hand punching a wall."

"Actually," I say, correcting her, "this time I didn't break it punching a wall."

"How did you break it this time?!"

"A cop twisted my wrist until my bones were basically gravel."

"Why did he do that?!"

"......because I pissed him off."

"Of course," she says while rolling her eyes then hands me some papers and a bottle of pills, "Your surgery is scheduled for next Saturday. Here's your new prescription. Wow! That is a high dose. You sure you can handle that?"

"Honestly, they should probably just give me horse tranquilizer at this point."

"Because you're a horse?" she asks sarcastically.

"Well, everything from the waist down," I reply with a cocky smirk.

"Wow! And here I was about to give you the benefit of the doubt," she says before getting up and walking away while shaking her head.

"Oh, come on! I meant because of my leg stamina. Seriously, you should see me gallop," I reply with a smile as she walks into another room.

After scaring off another potential ex Mrs. Chord, I decide to retreat for the door and leave this false display of serenity. You could practically see the cloud of air freshener escape as I opened the door and stepped outside, finally breathing in tolerable air. It was a dreary and dull day with thick clouds blocking out the sun and threatening rain at a moment's notice. I stomp and kick my way through puddles left behind from previous rainfall as I make my way to my car with my hands buried in my pockets and my eyes fixed on the ground, "Jesus, I am immature," I say to myself as I realize only a child would find this much entertainment in disrupting the natural stillness of sitting puddle water. The five year old inside of me leaped for joy every time I slashed my foot through these miniature lakes, trying to see how far I can launch a wave of dirty street water with one good punt, "What the hell is wrong with me?" I ask, refusing to stop. My fun comes to a halt as I hear a horrendous noise of clanking metal.

"What the hell!" I scream as I look up to see a tow truck lifting my car off of its front wheels. I sprint toward the behemoth truck as fast as I could then come to a dead stop when I see a massive blob of overalls exiting the driver door. It was a man well over three hundred pounds covered in every auto fluid known to man with a beard in desperate need of trimming.

"What the hell do you think you're doing?" I yell at him as he wiggles out of the truck causing it to bounce, "there's no time limit on these parking spots. I can be here as long as I want!"

"Sorry, buddy," he moans, "some doctor called and said you were too drunk to drive."

"I'm not...TOO drunk," I plead.

"Really? How bout ya say the alphabet backwards."

"What, are you giving me a sobriety test now? You can't do this! I'm a police office...no, no. I promised myself I'd stop doing that," I say to myself.

"Stop doing what?" he asks confused.

"Nothing! That was an A-A conversation!"

"Look, whatever man. I gotta take this car to the impound. Unless, you can recite the alphabet backwards."

"I can't even do that sober."

"Exactly. So, you can come pick this car up tomorrow but it'll cost ya," he says as he begins to reenter his truck.

"Oh, come on! I bet even you can't recite the alpha-"

"ZYXWVUTSRQPONMLKJIHGFEDCBA," without missing a beat.

154

"Holy shit," I gasp.

"Yep. So like I said, make sure you bring cash cause it's gonna cost ya to get her out."

"Her?"

"The car," he answers.

"I know what you meant. It's just, the car is a boy," I explain, pointing to my beloved machine.

"You call your car a boy?" he asks, raising an eyebrow, "that's kinda gay."

"I'm not gay!......although, there was that time I wore pink panties."

"I don't even wanna know," he mutters while rolling his eyes before continuing the tedious task of mushing himself into a vehicle.

"Wait! Wait! Give me another test," I beg.

"Fine," he stops, "If you can balance on one leg then I'll let you drive out of here."

"Okay, see I would but I'm still kinda loopy from the painkillers," I say but he quickly ignores me and goes back to wiggling himself into the giant hole in the side of the truck called a door.

"Well, why don't you try balancing on one leg, big guy! Exactly! You can't! Because-" and on my demand he hops out of his seat, raises one leg high in the air behind him and perfectly balances there for several seconds with not even a flinch, "Wow," I say marveling.

"Yep. So, like I said, bring cash tomorrow cause it's gonna cost ya to get HER out. And by the way, you shouldn't leave the keys in the ignition of a car this nice," he says in his impressive yoga pose on one foot.

"All three hundred pounds resting on one meek ankle. I'm surprised it doesn't collapse under the sheer weight," I say with wide eyes and immediately he glares at me and places his foot back down on the ground.

"I'm two sixty five, asshole," he snarks at me then launches himself back into the front seat and forces me to watch as he drives off down the road with my beautiful testosterone-mobile.

"That's clearly a boy, I might add!" I yell to no one.

"*Croosh!*" the sky screams as the celestial floodgates open and a waterfall comes crashing down on me.

"Seriously, how could this day get any..." I don't finish. Instead, I just let out the deepest, longest sigh, point my eyes to the ground and start to drag my feet home.

There are times in life when giving up is actually not an option. One by one fate has chipped away at you until you're left with nothing but a hollow shell that you tried so hard to mask. Cars, clothes, money, drugs, alcohol and women were just building blocks upon a fragile foundation that you attempted to conceal from yourself. Now you're forced to confront your own image as the insecurities amplify onto your own discrimination. When I look into my reflection, I start to hate the person staring back at me. I created this invincible super-being that existed in a realm without responsibilities, rules and an endless supply of time. Yet, I'm stuck in a world filled with people who answer to responsibilities, follow rules and have absolutely no time. I began to feel devoured by this person that I created; this accumulation of characteristics that seemed to insight emotional and physical destruction everywhere I go. For years I've been reaping the consequences for my eccentric personality. Yet, change is hopeless. It's too late for change. Every time I try to reach for a shred of potential, I'm stricken down beyond my control and forced to retreat home while licking my wounds. But if I give up now, what exactly am I giving up? I literally have nothing left to forfeit to fate. My only option is to salvage and attempt to recreate structure in my life.

"Honk! Honk!" I hear a car behind me.

I look over to see a white sedan slowly pulling up beside me. It stops on the side of the road right next to me. When the window rolls down, I see nurse chocolate cake sitting in the driver's seat, "Hey, centaur! You need a ride?" she asks with a smile.

"Finally! This whole 'self-realization' thing was getting depressing," I say.

"This what?" she asks confused.

"Um, nothing," I quickly reply as I open the passenger door and get in, "You wouldn't happen to have any Simon and Garfunkel would you?"

"Any what?" she asks even more confused.

"Ugh," I grunt, "never mind."

"Sorry my boss called a tow truck on you."

"What the hell is that guy's problem, ya know, other than me pissing him off every time I see him."

"Hey, he was gonna call the police before I convinced him not to," she says as we take off down the street.

"Which I would have preferred! Jesus, I know a ton of cops."

"You do?"

"Well, two actually."

"One of them being that cop that broke your wrist?"

"Yeah, but we're cool now...oh, wait. I forgot about the bible."

"The bible?"

"I kinda threw a bible at him."

"You threw the bible at him!?"

"Yeah, but not metaphorically. I mean, I literally threw a bible at him," I explain.

"Why did you throw a bible at him?"

"Oh," I say calmly, "did I forget to mention that he broke my wrist?"

"So, you throw a bible at him?"

"That was thrown at me by a priest."

"Wait, a priest threw a bible at you!?"

"Yes! God! What is this, twenty questions? Is he a male? Is he alive now? Is he pissed off cause his car was stolen by a three hundred pound red neck that is surprisingly agile?! Is he me?!" I yell.

"Seriously, dude?" she says with wide eyes.

"Well, no not seriously. He was actually only two sixty five."

"No. I mean, seriously calm down," she pleads.

"Oh, sorry. I've just had a really bad..." I stop myself.

"A bad what?" she presses.

"I actually can't say."

"Why not?"

"It's just this thing I do. Look, never mind. What's important is that I need to get my car back from the guy who stole it."

"Well, he didn't STEAL it," she tries to tell me.

"I don't have a dictionary on me but I'm pretty sure taking something without permission is the definition of stealing," I say back.

"Yeah, but he only took it cause you're drunk-"

"-Partially," I interrupt as I reach into my pocket.

"And you REALLY shouldn't be drinking since we raised the dose on your...holy shit! Did you just take four of those!?" she gasps.

"What are you, a nurse?" I sarcastically ask before swallowing the magic pills.

"Why did you take that many!?"

"Well, I was taking one like you told me, but that stopped working. So, I started taking two, and that stopped working. Now, I believe I've found my sweet spot at four."

"But that's a higher dose!"

"Okay, then I've found my...sweeter spot."

"Oh, my God," she sighs.

"I know, right?" I say with a smile, "I'm like, unbearable."

"You really are!" she agrees as we pull up to a four way stop in the middle of town, "So, where are ya?"

"As of right now? I just had my car stole...taken. All my bones from elbow down are basically Nesquik powder. And I don't acknowledge this enough, but I'm actually pretty heartbroken," I answer.

"I meant where do you live."

"How do you not know where I live? Don't you have all my medical records?" I ask.

"You mean the medical records that you DIDN'T fill out?"

"Exactly. I mean, why do you need to know my life story just so you can give me drugs."

"We don't need your life story. What we do need is info like allergies, which you put 'holy water' and then just 'regular water'. Emergency contact, you put 'trust me if it was an emergency I wouldn't be in this crummy doctor's office'. And blood type, which you just left blank."

"My blood type is...alcohol," I answer.

"Could you be any more immature?" she asks raising her voice.

"I feel like I could if I applied myself but, then again, applying oneself would show maturity so I guess that's a," I pause to think, "I wanna say paradox?"

"WHERE THE HELL DO YOU LIVE!?" she screams.

"Now who needs to calm down? I live that way," I reply, pointing her in the direction.

.   .   .

.   .

"Wait, this can't be where you live," she says as we pull up to a metal fence. Behind the fence was an acre of gravel and dirt with rows and rows of cars neatly parked beside each other and a rusty old trailer in the middle of it all.

"That's because it's not," I reply, getting out of the car, walking up to the fence and putting my fingers through then pulling on it to test its stability.

"You said you were taking me to your house," she says as she gets out and watches me tug on the fence.

"It's this thing I do called lying. I'm actually pretty good at it," I reply before reaching as high as I can with my good hand and pulling myself up the metal links.

"What are you doing!?"

160

"It's called climbing. Jesus, did you not take grammar in school?" I snark as I extend with my bad hand and pull myself higher.

"Doesn't that hurt??"

"It probably should, but I think the pain killers I downed are starting to kick in. Hey, at least we know they work, right?" I laugh.

"Mr. Chord, please!" she begs me.

"Wait," I pause, "are we not on a first name basis by now?"

"That is your first name," she answers, still looking worried about my vandalism.

"Well, what's your name?"

"I'll tell you, just please get down," she pleads.

"I will...when I'm on the other side of the fence," I answer as I continue to scale over.

"Chord! That's barbed wire!" she yells.

"Please," I laugh, "I know how to climb a-" but before I can finish, I slip on the top rail and my body goes smashing into the sharp blades before tumbling over and crashing to the ground on the other side.

"God damn it!" I scream.

"Oh, my God! You're bleeding!" she yells, pointing at my neck.

After a few seconds of groaning, I roll over and push myself to a stance. I place my fingers to the side of my throat only to feel a wide separation in my skin. I pull my hand back and glance at it to see my fingertips covered in red.

"That looks really bad, Chord. We need to go back to the doctor's office," she trembles on the other side of the fence with a look of terror on her face, "You have to get out of there!"

"I'm not leaving without my car!" I raise my voice, "I've lost everything at this point. I have absolutely no control over my life. And one by one, I have to sit back and watch while everything I love is taken from me beyond my control. But one thing I can do is get my fucking car back!" I say sternly then turn around and march my bloody and high carcass into the vehicular wasteland.

"It's just a car, Chord!" she hollers at me.

"It's not just a car," I mutter to myself as I stomp over wet gravel through the rows, "It's a 69 Dodge Charger. And it's a boy."

As I scour my eyes over the rows of cars, vans and busses, I still couldn't seem to pick out my beautiful hunk of metal. I crouch down, ducking below the vehicles and sprint through row after row of cheap sedans and warn down trucks, "Where the hell is it?" I say to myself as I comb my eyes over the entire yard. I look left, nothing. Right, still nothing. I glance behind me and I'm finally blessed with the sight of my big, sexy, black piece of absolute power. I quickly run over to it, dash for the front door and reach for the ignition, "Of course," I sigh, rolling my eyes as I see that the keys are nowhere to be found. Surely, this Duck Dynasty Yoga expert wouldn't leave the keys in the cars, "He keeps them in his trailer," I mutter before walking towards it but am quickly halted and throw myself to the ground when I see none other than the hillbilly whale walk out of the front door.

"Wait......free Hillbilly Willy?" I whisper, "Eh, I've done better. I have lost a lot of blood, after all," I admit then as I lay in the gravel peeking my head under a cars bumper, I reach over into my pocket, push the bottle of pills aside and pull out my phone. After a few seconds of searching on Google maps, I make a call.

"*Ring! Ring! Ring!*" a phone from inside the trailer screams and hastily the man darts inside.

"Hello?" the man says.

"How-dee, partner," I reply in a thick and somewhat insulting country accent, "I jus called ya on muh tell-ee-phone ta tell ya, I dunt seen a boy out dare uh-climbin yur fence out front."

"Climbing my fence!?" he asks.

"Yeppers. Look like he had himself uh cast on his hand. He was in front uh-scalin dat dare fence uh yurs. Sounded like he was tryna recite duh alphabet back-ards," I mumble and within a moment's notice he hangs up, runs out the door and waddles as fast as his stubby legs could waddle toward the front.

"Bingo!" I say then sprint through the cars to the trailer. Once at the back door, I open it up and walk inside, "Wow!" I gasp in shock, "this is actually really nice!" I look around to see fancy furniture, floral wallpaper, expensive tile and granite counter tops with a big pot of spaghetti and meatballs prepared and ready for devouring resting on the eye of the stove, "I gotta get a trailer. I mean, I never knew they looked like this on the inside. You hear 'trailer' and you think meth house, not Whitehouse," I say as I walk through the spotless kitchen to a poster board with keys all hung up nice and neatly in order. I scan over each and every set of keys before finally finding mine.

"GRRR!" I hear from behind me. I slowly turn around in terror to see an enormous bodybuilder pit-bull staring at me while flashing his razor sharp teeth.

"Hey, buddy," I say to him very calmly while attempting to sneak past him, "mind if I-"

"GRRR!!" he snarls, raising his volume at me.

"Ya know what!?!?" I match his volume, "FINE! YOU WANNA GO, BITCH? LET'S GO! YOU AND ME RIGHT NOW! CAUSE I'M NOT FUCKING AROUND ANYMORE!" I scream at the top of my lungs ready to fight this swollen and steroids fed beast, but before I even take a step in his direction, he suddenly whimpers and submits to my random aggression. With his tale tucked between his legs he cowers to the corner and shakes in fear.

"Awww," I say to him, "I'm sorry, buddy. Look, I've just had a really bad...shit, I promised myself I'd stop saying that," then I reach over, grab the pot of well-prepared spaghetti and meatballs and very obnoxiously pour it out all over the floor, "here, it's all yours." The dogs ears leap for joy before he darts over to the five star meal that I so graciously spilled in front of him. I rush to the back door, burst through it and make my way back to my car.

Once at my car, I jump in the front seat, shove the key into the ignition but before I start the monster, I look up to see the man in the front of the yard pacing back and forth around the gate probably looking for me, "Damn it. There's only one way out. Guess we're gonna play a little game of chicken," I say, turning the key, revving the engine and flooring it in his direction. When he sees me, his eyes grow wide and he posts himself confidently in front of the gate as my car shoots toward him, sending dust and gravel flying. He forces his eyebrows down his face and snarls his nose then bends at the knees and places his hands in front of him to get ready for impact. I squint my eyes at him as I force the pedal down and the car roars through the yard getting closer and closer until, "JESUS CHRIST!!!" he shouts before launching his body out of the way and into safety as the front of my charger smashes through his gate, bursting it open and I take off down the road.

"WOOOOOOOHHHHH!" I yell aloud, "THAT'S WHY IT'S A BOY, ASSHOLE! A GIRL CAN'T PENETRATE THAT DAMN GOOD!"

.   .   .

.   .

"Ow! Jesus, woman! Be gentle. That's neck skin not a cheap leather hand bag that you're stitching," I tell her as nurse chocolate cake pierces my throat with a tiny wire.

164

"Oh, hush! You big baby," she replies.

"Easy for you to say. You don't have a wire sticking out of your neck."

"I told you not to climb that fence."

After stealing back my car followed by a brief case of attempted murder, I decided to drive back to my house to assess the damage. When I get home I see that the nurse had followed me. Several minutes of arguing about whether or not I should go to the doctor's later, we came to the agreement on fixing my gash right here in my house.

"At least this time you're not staring at my boobs," she rolls her eyes as she prepares for another stitch.

"......Ow! Shit!" I scream as she purposely stabs me with the wire, "well, if you don't want me to look at your boobs then maybe don't mention them."

"My bad," she giggles.

"By the way, I never got your name."

"Because you climbed the fence anyway!"

"But did I get my car back?"

"Yeah," she admits, "that was actually kinda cool."

"Cool is my middle name," I say, grinning.

"No, it's not. You don't have a middle name. Which is odd. Also, what kind of name is Chord?"

"What kind of name is....see, I still don't know your name."

She laughs and replies with, "It's Janice, stud."

"Oh, and now I'm a stud, huh? Last time I checked, I was an immature man-child that didn't know how to dress."

"Well, you still don't know how to dress," she replies looking at my wardrobe, "but I guess, I was wrong about you."

"All it takes is a quick hop of a fence and possible grand theft auto and all of the sudden you realize I can be your knight in," I pause to look down at my clothes, "not so shiny armor."

"I still can't believe you stole your car back like that," she says with wide eyes and shaking her head.

"So, now it WAS stolen?"

"I've never met someone like you. I mean, you didn't care what happened to you. You're fearless. You're brave. All you cared about was getting your car back. I've never seen someone care that much about anything. To be honest," her attention travels from my neck up to my eyes, "it was kinda hot."

"Oh, come on. I'm sure you got a guy somewhere that would do the same, even more, for you," I reply, staring back into her big brown eyes.

"Please," she moans, "guys don't care that much. At least, not about me. But you're...different. You were so passionate and driven. You were gonna stop at nothing until you got your car back. You must really love that car," she says with a smirk.

"It wasn't about the car," I reply as the smile leaves her face and she stares passionately at me, ready to absorb every word I say, "You WERE wrong about me. You said I was immature. You probably thought I was an apathetic, insensitive, dispassionate jerk who cared about nothing but himself, but it's not true. I guess, I act that way to push people away from me because the truth is, I'm afraid to get close to anyone for fear of getting hurt by them. You called me fearless and brave but in reality, I'm terrified. I'm terrified of losing the things in life I care about the most. And the car? I guess, I just wanted to prove to myself that I had the determination to get back one of the few things in

166

life that I love. Because once I do decide to add something to that short list, I would do anything to get it back."

"Wow," she gasp, "that was the most honest thing I've ever heard you say."

"Well, that and I actually am half horse," I wink at her.

"And we're back," she groans and finishes sewing my throat together, "Alright Mr. Chord, you're stitches are all done."

"How long do I have to leave these in?" I ask, running my fingers over the stitches.

"First off, stop playing with them," she demands as she removes my hand from my throat, "they're not scratch and sniff-"

"-and now I'm wondering why they aren't. Wouldn't that make the whole 'getting stitches' experience way more tolerable?"

"Secondly, you need to leave them in for a few weeks. Then I'll come by to take them out," she says and she stands up and makes her way to the door.

"So, does that mean I'll see you again?"

"Unfortunately," she jokes.

"Well, until then, I'm gonna need a few more of these," I reach into my pocket, pull out the bottle of pills and pop a few in my mouth.

"What the hell!" she turns and yells as she stops on her way to the door, "you literally just took four of those!"

"That was like, hours ago."

"It was thirty minutes ago!"

"Oh, who's keeping count?"

"I am!" she answers sternly then begins to walk toward me. It only took a few steps for her walk to turn seductive as she stares in my

167

eyes and sways her big, sexy hips with every step. Once next to me, she holds her hand out in front of my mouth, "spit em out."

"Spit em out?" I ask with a mouthful.

"The pills, hot stuff," she say while sporting the same sexy smirk she had been blessing me with for her entire stay.

"But I want them," I plead. She pauses for a moment while contemplating her next words. Her attention travels down my bruised and broken body then back up to stare deep into my eyes.

"If you spit them out I'll stay."

"You'll stay?" I ask. She doesn't answer. Instead, she slowly raises an eyebrow to my question before I open my mouth a let the pills slide onto her hand. She places the pills on the counter next to us then wipes her hand up and down my shirt.

"Hey! That's my shirt!" I say and before I can get another word out she grabs me by my collar, pulls me in and wraps her big, sexy, black lips around mine. She forces me against the counter as she consumes my bottom lip. I reach around her neck, lacing her hair in my fingers before forcing her harder into me. She tightens her grip as she aggressively turns me so she can sit on the counter then pulls my body between her legs, wrapping them behind me. I reach up, grab her top and force it down exposing her dark brown nipples as I kiss down her cleavage and taste her tit.

"Bite it," she demands through heavy breath.

"What?"

"Bite my nipple. Roll it in your teeth," she pants while running her fingers through my hair and I grasp her nipple with my teeth then slowly roll it back and forth, "Oh, my God!" she lets out, pushes me off and pulls my shirt off to throw it aside. I quickly move my mouth back to taste her body, kissing down her stomach as I undo her jeans then throw them next to my shirt on the floor. I place my lips on her panties just above her clit, moving my mouth back and forth to stimulate her. She hastily pulls her panties off, spreads her legs again and forces my head between them making me taste her chocolate pussy.

"*Ring! Ring! Ring!*" the phone screams and I pause for a moment to look up at it.

"Ugh! Ignore it!" she orders me before pushing my head back on her wet pussy and I continue sucking her clit while thrusting my fingers inside her. She cocks her head back lets out a loud moan.

"*Beep!*" the phones chimes, "*Mother fucker! It's me, Steve. Ya know, your manager? The one you never call. Look, I need that song sooner than later. You wouldn't believe how impatient these spoiled, little, rich kids can get when it comes to getting their songs out. Oh, or are you still whining over that girlfriend of yours?*" suddenly, Janice pauses my meal time by pushing me off of her and staring at the answering machine.

"*Look, I know you love the bitch and you're all head over heels for her but I'm tellin' ya, you need to forget about these women and focus on gettin' this fucking money, baby. Call me back as soon as you get this.*"

"*Beep!*"

"You didn't tell me you had a girlfriend," Janice says, raising off of the counter.

"Ummm," is all I could manage to mutter.

"Wow!"

"It's not what you think. It's this girl I've had a crush on for my entire life who I've had an *on again off again* sexual relationship with, but here recently have come to realize that I'm actually crazy in love with her and have been trying for weeks to get back in her good graces so I can overcome my addictions and settle down with her."

"Wow!"

169

"You already said that."

"And I meant it. Both times. And now I'm leaving," she snaps as she gathers her clothes and starts to put them on.

"I mean, don't be mad. This happened way before I ever met you. Actually, come to think of it, it happened fairly soon before I met you. Like, right before I met you. Crazy how these things happen, right? It was this whole crazy scene at this really shitty bar where-"

"-Let me stop you there," she interrupts, "I honestly don't care how you know this girl, or what happened at this shitty bar, or why a man is calling you for a song, but Chord," she says, placing her hand under my chin, "you really need to get your life together," then kisses me one last time before marching toward the door.

"Are you still coming back for the stitches?" I holler at her.

"*Slam!*" the door roars and I'm left there, alone in my empty house with a broken-er hand, female lubricant on my face, stitches across my neck, high off my ass with a full, unattended erection.

"Hmm, I guess I can get a boner on painkillers."

.   .   .

.   .

"So there we were, in this old run down restaurant in the middle of Bangkok Thailand," my grandfather reminisces, sitting at the edge of the couch with a newspaper in hand. His glasses were halfway down his nose and he had a lump in the side of his cheek where a glob of tobacco sat and leaked into his mouth. I was sitting on the floor playing with toys in my favorite shrinking pjs while doing my best to reenact his old war stories with my action figures. Batman had just arrived at the restaurant in Bangkok with a few Ninja Turtles and Goku when I look up for the rest of the story, "and I hand the waiter a twenty and he says 'sorry, sir. I can't take this'. So, I look at him and say 'well, why the hell not? Me and

170

my good friends came here, sat down, filled our bellies to the brim and emptied just about half of your bar. Is my money no good here' and I swear, Josh, he looks at me and says 'no, sir. I can't take this cause it's too much money'. That's when I realized the American dollar goes a lot further in Thailand. So, we decided to stay a little longer," he rambles on as I watch and listen in admiration while adjusting the toys accordingly.

It had been three months, two days and almost four hours since I had been home or seen my father. As much as I loved being here, more than anything, I just wanted to go home. The floor was getting cold, hard and difficult to sleep on. The days were getting longer and the nights were getting shorter as I laid awake counting down from the last time I was in my own bed or spent time with dad. I would watch an entire marathon of M.A.S.H. and fake laugh at all of the jokes that I didn't understand if it meant I could see him again. I had grown accustom to the schedule at my house that allowed me a short period every morning of uninterrupted time with him, and being away from that tradition was jading me from the inside. The only thing more frustrating than being away from home was the uncertainty. I had no idea where our future lied or what was next for our family. Questions haunted my conscious to the point where it made me physically sick. Thinking had now become a burden that I tried to avoid for fear of mentally breaking down. There's only one thing that I could occupy my mind with that made me forget about this unpredictable world I had been so unwillingly thrust into...the kiss.

Emily had made me promise that I wouldn't tell anyone that she kissed me just as long as she promised not to tell anyone about my self inflicted assault. Just because I couldn't tell anyone, didn't mean that I couldn't think about it. Every day. Every minute. The kiss ran through my mind in circles causing it to play over and over again like a broken record I never wanted to fix. I could close my eyes and still feel her soft lips pressed against mine. So, at night when I lay there, eyes refusing to close, mind defiant on settling, I would imprison myself in the vivid memory of Emily kissing me until I finally fell asleep.

171

"And the women!" Grandpa says as I snap back to reality, "oh, boy! Let me tell ya about the women in Bangkok."

"Oh, hush," Grandma snaps as she enters the room. She was wearing an apron and smelling of freshly cooked cobbler as she condemned my grandfather who was now giggling under his breath, "He's too young to hear about all of that!"

"Never too young to hear about the ladies, am I right, Josh?" he asked, smiling and showing off his brown, tobacco stained teeth. I grin back at him but before I can indulge in his misogyny, Grandma intervenes, "Come on, Josh. I got some cobbler waiting for ya," and on that demand, I raise up to my feet and practically race to the kitchen.

"Ya know," she says as I sit down at the old, cold metallic table that was painted a tacky yellow, "Your mother used to love cookies, cake, pie and pudding but not cobbler. You're the only kid I know that prefers cobbler. She used to sit at that table there and color and paint while I made her favorites. Then," she sighs while placing a plate in front of me, "she got older and angrier. She used to hang out with a group of boys doing God knows what. Going out, getting into trouble and coming back covered in dirt and scratches was a normal night for her. It seemed harmless at first. Then when she left school, she decided to start traveling around with these musical bands. If you call that music, that is."

"What was she doing with the bands?" I ask with a mouth full of cobbler.

"First off, don't talk with your mouth full. Flies will swoop into your mouth hoping to get a bite of what you're eating and you'll end up eating them," she warns me and I immediately seal my lips in fear, "anyways, I didn't ask what she was doing with those people. There was one band that was actually pretty popular. Even had a few hits on the radio. Traveled all around the country and, where ever they were, your mother was. I'd be sitting at home wondering where my little girl is and if she was okay then, in the middle of the night, I'd get a phone call from

172

some area code I didn't recognize and it'd be her off in some different time zone, telling me that she was fine and just enjoying life," she exhales before continuing, "We're a family of rollin' stones, Josh. It's a blessing as much as it is a curse."

"*Ding! Dong!*" the doorbell interrupts.

"Now, who could that be?" she says.

"Ding! Dong!"

"Everyone we know just walks right in."

"Ding! Dong! Ding! Dong! Ding! Dong!"

"Honey," she calls to my grandfather, "can you see who that is?" I hear the smacking of lips and ruffling of newspaper as he pushes himself off of the couch and his knees give out a load pop. As I shovel another spoon full of cobbler in my mouth and quickly close my lips, making sure to keep them closed, I hear the door open and the faint sound of arguing.

"I can't let you in," Grandpa says. The man replies, but it's too incoherent to recognize as he was slurring his words, "Now, I said you can't come in and I mean it!" Grandpa orders.

"Honey?" Grandma calls out and she leaps up from her chair and makes her way to the front door, "You're drunk! Go home!" she demands followed by an unintelligible reply from the man.

Curiosity had taken over me and I drop my spoon and peak my head around the corner, "Dad!" I yell as I see my father slumped over the edge of the door. His hair was in a mess, he hadn't shaved and his clothes were dirty and wrinkled.

"Hey, buddy," he says softly, "why don't you go get your sister for me?"

"Mark!" I hear from across the room and I look over to see mom standing there pointing and yelling at him while Grandma and Grandpa

173

stood side by side almost barricading him from coming inside, "You are not allowed here!"

"She's my daughter too!!!" he screams as he swings himself off the door but stumbles over to the wall.

"You're drunk! Go and sober up and maybe we'll talk about you seeing her!" mom tells him.

"You can't keep her from me, damn it! She's my child and I want to see her!" he yells before attempting to walk into the house but stops when Grandpa pushes him back, "Don't fucking touch me, old man!" he screams in Grandpa's face, barely keeping himself standing.

"You're a danger to your family. Go home and we'll talk about this later," Grandpa says gently, trying to calm him.

"Dad! I missed you!" I shout as I sprint through the living room but am stopped when mom intercepts me half way and holds me back.

"Go get your sister, boy! Do what I say, now!!!" he screams at me.

"Dad! I'm sorry!" tears force themselves out of my eyes as mom holds me back from running to him, "I'm sorry about everything! Please, forgive me!"

"GO GET YOUR FUCKING SISTER!!!" he yells and at that moment he forces himself through my grandparents, knocking my grandmother's frail body to the hard wood floor.

"YOU SON OF A BITCH!" Grandpa shouts then he slaps his hands down on dad's shoulders and, "*Smack!*" slams his forehead into dad's nose. Dad collapses to the floor holding his face as blood starts to seep through his fingers.

"I'm fine. I'm fine," Grandma calmly assures us as she makes her way to her feet and Grandpa posts himself in between her and dad.

When I look down at my father and he removes his hands from his face, I'm shocked to my core at what I saw. It wasn't the blood pouring out of his nose onto floor, or the flesh just under his eyes quickly swelling and turning black; it was that he was crying. My father was crying. For years he convinced me that crying made you weak. Crying was for pathetic little babies. Boys don't cry and, sure as hell, men don't cry. Yet, there he was lying on the floor covered in blood and tears. But he wasn't crying from the pain of having his nose smashed in; he was crying for my sister.

"Alexis!" he wept as water consumed his eyes.

"Dad!" I call out to him.

"Alexis!!" he shouts again through trembling lips.

"Dad!!!" I call harder as my mother's grip tightens around me.

"Come on, Mark. It's time to go," Grandpa says as he helps him up and guides his bloodied, tear covered body through the door.

"Wait! Dad! Please don't leave me!" I cry to him but it was too late. He was already out of the house.

Three months, two days and almost four hours. It had been three months, two days and almost four hours since I got to see him. And when I finally do get to see him, he just wanted Alexis.

.   .   .

        .   .

"Wow," I gasp in shock at what I was seeing on the computer screen.

"Yep," Veronica confirms as she scrolls up and down the web page.

"That is way worse than I thought."

175

"Two accounts of domestic violence. Three accounts of reckless endangerment. A few DUI's and the cops have been called on him more times than I can count," she explains.

"And this is the guy that's dating Emily?" I ask concerned.

"If she wants to run off with this scum bag, I say let her. She doesn't deserve you, Chord. You're a good guy," she says, looking up at me from her chair.

"I literally just stole a car," I reply while laughing.

"You can't steal your own car," she explains while joining in on my laughter.

"That's what I tried to say!"

"Jesus," she reaches up to feel the stitches, "you really scratched yourself up bad, huh?"

"Not as bad as your husband scratched my door."

"Yeah, but you did take his shirt."

"It's an orange shirt! The damn thing is filthy with scribbling all over it!"

"It's filthy because he never washed it. He never washed it because of the scribbling," she says.

"Was that all supposed to make sense to me?"

"Peyton Manning," she answers.

"Who is 'people I don't know or give a shit about' for five hundred, Alex," I say, mocking her.

"Peyton Manning is a football player. Seriously, you were born and raised in the south and you don't follow football at all?"

"Oh, wait! I have heard that name before. Sorry, it's been a while since I've paid attention to football. I mean, I was only keeping up with it to get into girls'...never mind."

"I know what you do, Chord," she grunts, "Look, that dirty orange shirt was a UT shirt he got signed by Peyton Manning himself."

"Wait, but Peyton Manning plays pro football and UT is a college team."

"Wow," she says, shaking her head, "he didn't start off in the NFL. He started in college football. And guess which team he played for?"

"Shit. UT?"

"Ding! Ding! Daily double!" she mocks me back, "and I can't believe I'm actually describing this to someone that was born in Tennessee."

"Okay, so I stole a car and a red neck aphrodisiac."

"You're not a criminal!" she snaps, "and you're not a bad guy. That's why I really think you should forget about Emily."

"But look at this guy," I point to the computer screen, "he's obviously dangerous. Even if I don't get her back, I can't let her be with him. I'd kill myself if anything ever happened to her. I love her too much to put her in any danger. Even if she ends up hating me, it would be worth it to know she is actually happy and safe."

"Chord, you waste so much time and energy on this girl. You keep trying to track her down, but what has she done for you? How has she shown that she cares about you? You've put yourself through so much trouble and pain just trying to get her back, but if she really loved you, she'd be here for you. What is it about her? Why do you obsess over her? What does she have that I..." she stops herself before finishing the sentence, then directs her eyes back to the computer screen to exit out the page and walk to the bed.

"I'm sorry. I shouldn't have asked you to do this."

"You didn't ask. I offered. I keep helping you try to find this girl, but I honestly don't think she wants to be found," she pleads as she grabs my hands and sits down on the bed, pulling me in slightly.

"I know his address now. She might be there with him and in that case, it means she could get hurt," I explain, staring into her despairing blue eyes.

"Well, it's actually not his address. It's his sister's house. He just stays there," she tells me.

"Guy doesn't even have his own place? Competition just got easier," I say, grinning.

At that moment, Veronica's grip tightens around my fingers as she exhales and struggles with her next words, "Chord, I'm not going to ask you to stay. All I'm going to say is, you deserve better."

The grin leaves me and I look down at the floor and reply, "Please don't ask me to stay, Veronica. I'm afraid I would, and I really need to do this," I plead to her. She doesn't answer back. Instead, she just nods and turns away as my fingers slip through her grasp. I could tell she was fighting herself not to show any emotion, but I couldn't stay there to mend her heart. I had to go to Emily. I had to protect her and let her know that she might be in danger. I had to try. So, I walk away from Veronica who was now curled up in her bed purposely facing away from me. I open the door to her room, walk out and gently close it behind me.

As I walk through the hallway, I try my best not to slip or bump into anything as the lights were off and it was too dark to see anything. It was late at night on a week day and all of the kids were tucked away in bed for school tomorrow. As I tip toe my way through the house, attempting not to creek the floors, I start to see a light at the end of the hallway. It was the kitchen light, and as I approached it I can hear the faint sound of ruffling plastic and clanking glass.

"So, either the father is home or this is the shittiest burglar in the world. Who leaves the light on?" I say as I turn the corner to the kitchen and am delighted to see Ben sitting at the table with a bag of cookies and glass of milk as he chowed down.

"Dude, you say a lot of curse words," he says, looking like a deer in headlights.

"Didn't your mom put you to bed?"

"Yeah, but..." he pauses.

"But you sneak out of your room at night to eat cookies and milk?"

"Yeah," he admits with a look of guilt on his face.

"Well, don't hog them all," I demand and take a seat next to him, grab a cookie and dunk it in the milk, "Please tell me you have something other than sandwich cookies."

"I love sandwich cookies."

"But you eat the whole thing, right? You don't just break them in half and lick the frosting?"

"Duh," he replies, "What are you still doing here?"

"Your mom and I had to...nothing," I stop myself.

"Ewww!"

"Not that!" I snap, "Although, I probably could have got a quickie before I left."

"What's a quickie?"

"Damn it, this is why I try not to talk to kids."

"Whatever, dude. You're really weird, and you curse too much," he says, waving me off before dunking another cookie.

"I guess, I'll try to stop," I say to him.

"I don't know, dude. You're pretty weird."

"I meant cursing!"

"Sure," he laughs, "Whatever you say."

"Besides, you're kinda weird yourself," I reply as I give him a playful shove, "Speaking of social awkwardness, how's that girl?"

"You mean the one that doesn't even know I exist? Oh, she's good," he says sarcastically.

"Well, why the fu...darn doesn't she know you exist? Didn't you talk to her? Show her that big brain of yours that you're always boasting in front of me; making me feel like I need to go back to school or something."

"You do need to go back to school, like, my grade," he laughs.

"Alright, alright, you got me. But seriously, why haven't you talked to her?"

"I can't just go up and talk to her."

"What happened to the whole 'be yourself' speech I gave you?"

"Yeah, I'm sure she would love to hear about my theories on the Big Bang, black holes and other universal anomalies."

"Jesus, now that you mention it, I wanna hear all about all of that. Will you teach me?"

"That depends, do you have an endless amount of time?"

"Jokes on you. I actually do," I laugh.

"Well, could you stay sober long enough to spend time with me?" he presses and suddenly a silence falls between us as I contemplate the question.

"Ya know what, sure. For you, anything."

"Anything?"

"Well, no not literally anything, but most things."

"Cause, I actually wanted to ask you if you'd do something for me," he says putting the cookies down and staring at me.

"Listen, I can't promise that I'll stop sleeping with your mother. I mean, we're both two grown adults and-"

"-WHAT! NO! NOT THAT!" he yells.

"Oh, then forget that I said that," I reply, shaking my head.

"Look," he quickly changes the subject, "there's this thing at school-"

"-I was joking when I said I need to go back to school. I'm pretty sure I'm rich. Then again, I can't remember the last time I even looked at my bank account. Wait, do I have a bank? No, no, I definitely use a card every time I buy stuff. I just thought-"

"-Stop interrupting!" he orders me then lets out a deep breath before continuing, "It's like a 'bring your dad to lunch' thing"

"Then why don't you do just that? Bring your dad."

"He never wants to do stuff like this with me. Every time I ask, he just acts like he has better stuff to do. Mom says he's just busy but I know he's actually with girls."

"Well, lucky for you, I'm terrible with girls. I'll do it, buddy."

"You will?" he asks as his eyes light up.

"How could I pass up a free meal?" I ask, smiling and throwing up my hands.

"There's just one more thing," he says.

"Look, your mom and I-"

"-and if you mention my mom again, I'm going to literally throw this glass at your head!" he snaps grasping the milk glass tightly in his hand. The sincerity didn't last, though. We both burst out into laughter at the comedic relief.

"Fine," I surrender, "what is it?"

"The girl is gonna be there, and I was wondering if you'd be my wing-man."

"Your wing-man?"

"Yeah, ya know, my buddy, my pal, the guy who supervises as I talk to a girl," he smiles and puts his arm around me.

"Sure, pal. I'll be your wing-man."

"Thanks, Chord!"

"Dude, you gotta go to bed. It's getting late," I say as I close the cookies and hand sweep the crumbs on the table to my palm then toss them in my mouth.

"Ew! Dude, those were on the table!" he says disgusted.

"Yea, I have this thing called an immune system. You should know all about it, boy genius," I say before playfully pushing him off to his room.

"Good night, Chord!" he hollers.

"Good night, wing-man."

After sending the little Einstein off to bed, I continue my mission of finding Emily and hopefully winning her back. I make my way through the living room and out the front door. Outside was a typical slightly cold southern night where the fog is almost thick enough to drink and the glowing moon peaked around dense clouds. Wind was basically nonexistent in the south, and on the off chance that you did feel a breeze, chances are a tornado followed, "Maybe I should move to L.A. I'm kinda getting tired of waking up hot and going to bed cold," I mutter as I walk through the grass to my car, "it's like we're all frozen meals living in a microwave."

When I get within a few feet of my car, I'm suddenly stopped dead in my tracks to the sight of someone sitting in the driver's seat. It looked to be a young pale man with a goatee that could have been drawn on with a mechanical pencil it was so thin. He was wearing a large cap tilted to the side and enough fake gold chains to fill a quarter machine at a dollar store.

"HEY!!!" I yell then dart toward my car. The young man's eyes widen when he sees me sprinting for him and, within a moment's notice, he swings the door open and tries to run away but trips over his own pants that were barely holding on to his knees. I grab him by his loose fitted shirt, slam him against the car door, holding him there with my good hand, then raise my fist and scream, "Give me one good reason not to punch you in the face!"

"Ummm," he mumbles in shock, "Because your hand is broken?"

"Oh, that's actually a pretty good reason," I admit as he starts to laugh, "Hey! I will shove this cast up your asshole, K-Fed!"

"What the fuck is a K-Fed, bruh?"

"No! Don't do that! I hate that!"

"Do what, bruh?"

"Don't make me feel old! I'm not old!" I demand as I force him harder against the car.

183

"I mean," he pauses, "you are kinda-"

"-I swear to the God I don't believe in, if you finish that sentence I will kill you."

"You don't believe in God?"

"I'm indifferent!"

"What he fuck does that mean?!" he asked confused and shaking.

"Jesus, could you be any dumber?"

"Man, you shouldn't use the lord's name in vain like dat, bruh," he warns.

"SAYS THE GUY WHO WAS ABOUT TO STEAL MY CAR!"

"He wasn't going to steal it," a girl's voice from behind the trunk says and I look over to see Valory making her way around the car, hands in her pockets, shoulders slouched with a look of complete guilt plastered on her face, "we were just gonna go for a ride," she poorly explains.

"Please, tell me you're not friends with this poor man's Fred Durst. Oh, wait. Or...is Fred Durst a poor man's Fred Durst?" I ask myself.

"Who da fuck is Fred Durst?" the boy ask.

"What did I tell you about doing that!"

"Doing what, bruh?"

"He doesn't like it when people make him feel old," Valory says to him.

"Because I'm not," I tell her.

"I mean..." she snarks.

"I'm not old, God damn it!"

184

"Bruh, Lord's name in vain," he reminds me.

"If I want your advice, it will be on how to properly remove a cast from you're rectal cavity!"

"What is your obsession with anal?" he asks.

"Seriously," Valory chimes in.

"Ask your mother," I tell her.

"Stop doing that!" she orders me.

"Doing what?"

"Talking about how you and mom are having sex!" she answers.

"Wait, you're bangin' her mom?" the boy asks.

"Well, not anymore. I'm actually trying to turn over a new leaf," I explain.

"Wait, you and my mom aren't together anymore?" she asked, concerned.

"Why do you care?" I say pushing off *even Slimmer Shady*, "you hate me."

"I don't hate you. I mean, you're annoying sometimes and pretty lame and you smell like smoke and you're kinda old-"

"-Was there a point you were getting to?" I interrupt.

"I don't know, I guess, I...like you," she admits, rolling her eyes away.

To her sudden forced admiration, I give her a big smile and reply with, "I like you too, Valory."

"Oh, my God! Whatever! You're such a dork!" she smiles.

"Look, guys," Vanilla Ice intervenes, "this is really sweet n' all but are you gonna call the cops on me?"

"News flash, Beasty Boy, her mom is a cop," I say.

"You said we wouldn't get in trouble!" he snaps at Valory.

"Chord," she pleads, "please, just let him go."

I pause for moment, staring at Valory as I get taken over by her remorse. I let out a long and heavy sigh then glare up at the boy, "Alright, Marky Mark, it's about that time to get the hell out of here before I bring forth an ass whoopin," I demand, pointing down the street.

"Bruh, who da fuck are all of these people?" he asks, shaking his head.

"GET THE HELL OUT OF HERE!" I scream and he sprints off down the road, "I wanna see sweat comin out of ya pores, asshole!" I holler as he disappears.

"You're gonna tell mom about this, aren't you?" Valory sighs.

"I guess, I don't see why she needs to know," I groan.

"Thank you so much, Chord!"

"So," I say, looking over at my car, "still wanna drive it?"

"You mean, I can?" she hesitates.

"You gotta learn sooner or later. And who better to teach you than...actually, I'm the worst person to teach you."

"Why do you say that?"

"Well, I've been pulled over more times than I can count, I just got done driving this car through a fence and I often times drive high off my ass. Speaking of..." I say before reaching into my pocket.

"Wait!"

"Wait? Why wait?" I ask, ignoring her and pulling the bottle out.

186

"If we're gonna hang out, should you be downing pills?" she insists.

"So, now we're hanging out?" I ask sporting a big, goofy smile. She exhales and replies with, "Sure, but you can't take any pills!"

"Fine, shit!"

"Or curse!"

"Jesus Christ!"

"And stop using the lord's name in vain!"

"Fine! Fu...God dam...just get in the car!" I yell and she gives me a smirk as she takes my keys and struts to the front door. I make my way around to the passenger side and get in when I look over to see Valory frozen.

"Well..." I press.

"What's the first step?" she asks wide eyed.

"The first step is not hanging out with little Eminem wanna-bes in their mid-twenties......and also, buckle up."

"He's seventeen," she corrects me, fastening her seatbelt.

"That's not better! Why are you hanging out with that guy? And where did you guys meet, Dateline?"

"What's Dateline?"

"Chris Hansen? Why don't you take a seat? Take a seat right there?!"

"What are you talking about?" she shakes her head in confusion.

"Just start the dam...darn car," I say and she laughs at me before turning the key.

"You're so weird," she giggles, "but still kinda cool."

After several excruciating minutes of instructing her about ten and two, treating the gas pedal like an egg shell, not slamming on the brake, looking ahead of you not in front of you, and not turning so sharply, we finally settle down to a reasonable coast. We drive around her neighborhood on a foggy, dreary night (probably not the best idea) and I cringe every time she runs over just about every curb we come across. I grab the wheel a few times to keep her in the middle of the street and keep her from hitting every mailbox in town before...

"Smash!"

"Oh, my God! I'm so sorry!" she begs as she stares at the mailbox lying on the ground. She looks over at me in terror of what I might say, but instead I just laugh, get out of the car, walk over to the metal box on a stick and try my best to fix it.

"What ever happened to just throwing the mail through a slot in the door?" I mutter as I struggle to put it up right.

"Is it broken? Can you fix it? Are we gonna get in trouble?!" Valory stresses.

"Yes, maybe and no. People do this all the time. You just prop it up and apologize," I tell her as I fail to get the wooden plank back in the hole. I quickly stop and look up when a light on the porch turns on and shines right on me in all my vandalizing glory.

"What the hell do you think you're doing?" a man yells from his porch at me.

"Oh, so you get to curse but I can't?"

"What the hell are you doing with my mailbox!"

"I'm...the new mailman," I answer.

"You don't look like no mailman. Also, it's the middle of the damn night!"

"I work night shift."

188

"And since when do they deliver the mail in a beat up dodge charger?"

"Uh, since they started compensating us better. Gotta love that capitalism, am I right?" I say with a smile.

"I'm calling the cops!" he replies before marching back into the house. Immediately, I run back to the passenger seat and yell, "Floor it!"

"You said not to floor it!" Valory yells back.

"That was before, when we weren't possibly going to jail."

"You said this happens all the time!"

"I lied! I have no idea how often this happens. Now, back it up and floor it out of here," I order her and she reverses the monster back into the road and punches it down the street causing the tires to squeal and the stench of burning rubber into our nostrils. Once at a safe distance, I look over and yell, "Brake!"

"Now?!" she ask as we quickly approach the end of the road.

"Yes! Now!"

"Okay," and she lightly taps the brakes and the power-house of a vehicle barely slows.

"Brake harder!" I scream as we get closer to the grass and trees.

"But you said-"

"-I KNOW WHAT I SAID, GOD DAMN IT! NOW, BRAKE HARDER!" and she slams her foot down on the pedal. The wheels screams against the pavement as they're torn of their tread. The car slides over the concrete and jumps into the grass when Valory sharply turns the wheel to avoid the forestry doom.

"NO! DON'T TURN THE WHEEL-" is all I could get out before the car tips over on two tires then violently rolls over on the hood as our bodies are thrown from side to side in our seats. The sound of crashing metal and shattering glass shrieked throughout the car as the nauseating sight of the entire world being turned upside down assaulted my vision. The charger leans over, balancing on the doors for a split second before tipping over and crashing back down on its tires. Valory and I sit there in dead silence, air struggling to enter our lungs, eyes flashing every inch of white in them and attempting to gather ourselves.

"And that," I say calmly, "is why you always buckle up."

"Chord," I look over to see Valory's eyes absolutely soaked in tears, "I'm so sorry."

"Well, at least it rolled back over on its wheels," I reply laughing.

"What have I done!" she cries, forcing her hands into her face.

"Other than the coolest, most awesome and most accurate portrayal of Fast and Furious?"

"Seriously?!"

"Yeah, you're right. I actually don't even like those movies. Let's go with...Die Hard," I say, nodding.

"No, I mean, how are you not furious??"

"I told you, I don't like those movies. I mean, the first one was alright. Basically just point break with cars. The second one sucked. Then, they went to Japan for some reason and after that it's pretty much just a budget project to see how much stuff they can blow up in between possible homoerotic friendships."

"NOT THE FAST AND THE FURIOUS!" she snaps, "I meant, how are you not furious with me?"

"What's important is that you're okay...oh, I forgot to ask if you're okay."

"I am. I just wanna go home," she sighs.

"That makes two of us," we trade places and I, to my own surprise, start the car up and drive us home.

Once safely back home, we quietly retreat back into the house and tip toe our way to her room. She opens her door and walks in but before calling it a night, she turns around and blesses me with a big smile.

"Now, I really don't see any reason to tell your mom about tonight," I say.

"I won't. I promise," she replies.

"You pinky promise?" I ask, extending my hand, pinky finger out.

"Pinky promise," she confirms grabbing my finger with hers and moving our hands up and down.

"I promise," I recite, "You have to say it!" I demand and she giggles before replying, "I promise," then she lets go and starts to close the door but stops half way.

"Chord," she says softly, "I know you're not dating my mom but if you were, I guess, I'd like that," she tells me before granting me one last grin and closing the door.

After releasing all of the air from my chest and mentally shaking off the entire night, once again, I go back to my original mission to reunite with Emily. As I walk through the dark hallway to the living room, I can't help but feel like someone is watching me; the same feeling I had the first time I stepped foot in this house. It was a feeling of little eyes peering and stalking me, the faint sound of tiny feet inching their way closer to me, the slight breeze of breath and the sense of newly occupied space.

"Where are you?" I whisper, squinting my eyes as I scan my surroundings. I look to my left and see nothing. I look to my right and still nothing but empty space. I quickly turn around, glancing behind me to see Taylor darting straight for me through the hallway with his tongue out ready to strike.

"Ha!" he yells as he sprints at me with his tongue pointing directly at my cheek.

"Not today!" I say and quickly snatch him up before he can lay a single taste bud on me and I hold him at safe distance.

"Haaaa!" he laughs.

"Remember what your mom said? No licking!"

"Ba da ba," he pleads.

"I don't care if it's 'your thing'. It's unsanitary," I tell him, laughing at his weirdness, "besides, what are you doing up? Isn't it a school night?"

"Boo da da," he explains.

"Oh, that's right. You're a baby."

"Ba!" he corrects me.

"Toddler! Sorry! Damn," I roll my eyes and start to carry him back to his room.

"Da da doo?"

"I'm here because I needed your mom's help with something."

"Da?"

"No, not that! I needed help finding someone."

"Ba ba?"

"You don't know her. It's just this girl I'm trying to talk to," I tell him as we make our way into his room.

"Da da doo."

192

"Well, technically, me and your mom aren't together. We're just friends with," I pause, "common interest."

"Da?"

"Trust me, you don't wanna know. Now, go to sleep," I order him as I sat him down on his bed.

"Doo doo da?" he presses.

"I don't know," I sigh, "maybe I could see myself with your mom. I mean, she is pretty amazing and she seems to care about me a lot. Not to mention, she's crazy sexy."

"Ba!"

"My bad! Look, I've had a really long night. So, just go to bed so I can sneak out of here."

"Da."

"I can't stay. I wish I could but there's something I have to do."

"Da doo?" he asks.

"I don't have time to read you a story. So, just go to sleep," I demand before turning around and making my way to the door but stop dead in my tracks to the sound of him whimpering. I look over to see Taylor's eyes watering up while he stared a hole right through me.

"Fine!" I give in, "one story," I walk over to his bookshelf to shuffle through the stories, "Let's see, a lama with abandonment issues, an athletic, attention seeking dog, and a stalker with a food coloring fetish. All of these are garbage."

"Doo doo da?"

"What? I don't know how to make up a story."

"Boo."

"Not that kind of writer! I write songs," I explain and he goes back to his pathetic frowning and whimpering, "oh, my God! Fine! I'll make up a story," I sit down beside his bed as he wiggles and shakes under the covers, getting himself comfortable while staring at me with wide eyes, "Once upon a time, there was, I don't know, a princess and a knight," I pause for a moment to contemplate, "No, wait, it wasn't a knight. It was a jester. Now, this jester was the best entertainer in the whole kingdom. People would come far and wide just to see him perform. He would dance and sing as everyone watched in glee. The king paid the jester in pounds and pounds of gold just to see his show. And the ladies, oh, the ladies loved this guy. But, no matter how many girls threw themselves at him, he didn't care. He didn't want them. All he wanted was the princess. She was the most beautiful princess in the land. She would watch the jester sing and dance every day. And even though he had many fans, she was the only one who really understood him. She knew that just because he would sing and dance and smile and joke around that, deep down, the jester was sad. He was very sad, in fact. So sad that he would drink...um, root beer and pop...candy. It was the only thing that made him forget how sad he was. Then, one day, he decided to stop drinking root beer, stop eating candy and stop entertaining all of these girls so that maybe, just maybe, he could live a life with the princess. So, he runs to Ray's, uh, Tavern where the princess is, but it was too late. She had already fallen for a black knight."

"Ba?"

"No, not black like his skin. I meant he had black armor...also, he's black."

"Da doo."

"How is that racist?!" I snap, "Fine! Then, he was a black knight in white armor. Look, the point is, when he saw that the princess didn't want a jester, that she wanted a knight, he decided to go to the nearest blacksmith and asked for the most shiniest, nicest and most expensive armor he had."

194

"Ba?"

"I don't know, blue?"

"Ba ba?"

"Because it's my...I mean it's HIS favorite color. Now, stop interrupting. So, the jester puts on this shiny new armor and goes back to the princess. When she sees him, she's mesmerized by the fancy armor. She walks up to this brand new knight and grabs the helmet. But when she removes it, she sees the jester's silly hat and goofy face paint. She realizes that he's not a knight and he'll never be a knight. He's just a jester. So, she runs off with the black knight and the jester goes home and drinks root beer and eats candy until he dies," I finish as I stare blankly at the wall.

"Doo."

"Yeah, I guess, that was kinda depressing. Maybe I should have stuck with the books. Look, it's way past your bedtime, anyway," I say, reaching over and tucking the covers under his sides. He looks up at me with his big blue eyes and asks, "Ba doo da?"

"Sure, buddy. I'll come back and make up more stories for you," I answer, giving him a smile, then turn around and make my way through the door.

"Ba lub doo," he mumbles.

"What? I can't understand you," I say.

"I love you, daddy," he replies then rolls over, curling up in his blanket and falls asleep. I stand there in silence, shocked at what he just said. I struggle to find the correct response, but instead, I just look over at this little boy and say, "I love you too, son," then gently close his door behind me.

I stand there in the quiet hallway for a moment to gather myself. I've never had someone say they love me like that before. It was so honest, so sincere, so...unconditional. I stood there puzzled at the idea that this little boy genuinely enjoys my presence enough that he could use such a phrase like love. And on top of that, call me daddy. Not once in my life have I ever considered myself being mature enough to be a dad. I wouldn't even know where to begin. Where would I find an example to lead off of? I have absolutely no viable template to understand what a good dad is like. Yet, here I am, still standing in this house because of the little human beings that live here.

"Hey," I hear a soft voice from behind me. I glance over to see Veronica standing there watching me in my silent contemplation.

"Oh, hey. I was just-" I say but before I can finish, she lunges for me, forcing her lips against mine while pulling me in by my shirt. She turns me and starts to push me toward her room as she kisses deep into my lips. I'm forced to back walk my way into her room as she powers me through the door, never once removing her mouth from mine.

"Wait! Wait!" I stop her, "I have something to say."

"What is it?" she asks and suddenly her complexion changes. She looked to be on the brink of crying as she anxiously waited for my next words.

"Well, this was the best day ever," I say, looking to the ceiling.

"That's what you needed to say?" she ask, raising an eyebrow.

"It's just this thing I do," I reply, staring back at her with a big smile.

.   .   .

.   .

"Chord."

"Ugh," I grunt as I roll over, pulling the blanket over my head.

"Chord!"

"It's too early. The sun is barely up. Give me a few more hours," I plead and Veronica walks over to the blinds and forces them open,

196

"Ahhh! Jesus, you know how I hate the sun," I shout as the ruthless rays pierce my retinas.

"Sun's been up for a while, babe. Maybe you should be too. Come on, I'll cook you something, lazy boy," she insists then reaches over and smacks my ass.

"What are you doing in my house, anyway? Don't you have kids n' stuff. I counted three last time."

"Your house?" she asks and I rub the morning rust away from my eyes to reveal it, in fact, wasn't my house.

"Holy shit," I gasp.

"And here I thought you'd be used to waking up in strange women's beds."

"It's not that. I'm just not used to sleeping that well in strange women's beds."

"Yeah, one more hour and I would have assumed you were dead."

"One more hour and I might have been. I feel like I just woke up from a coma," I change my voice to an old timey movie, *"you, boy in the street, what year is it?"* to which Veronica laughs before pulling the covers off of me.

"Come on, sleepy boy. The kids are asking about you," and on her demand, I leap out of bed and make my way for the door, "Um, Chord," she stops me, pointing at my body. I look down and see that I was only wearing underwear. Her underwear to be exact.

"What is my obsession with wearing women's underwear?!"

"Just like a jester," she replies, crinkling her nose at me.

"Wait, you heard that?!"

197

"I heard enough to know you're the worst story teller ever," she laughs, "Now, change clothes and come to the kitchen. Your queen awaits you."

"Yes, my liege," I reply as she walks out of the room.

Once alone, I rummage around for my clothes that were flung out all over the floor. After replacing my eccentric attire with a more conservative look, I crack every joint in my stiff body and make my way to the kitchen. The crackling of skillet grease and the smell of cooking meat took over my senses as I walked through the hallway. I turn the corner to see all three children sitting at the table while Veronica prepared breakfast on the stovetop.

"I told you he wasn't dead," Ben says.

"Dude, you sleep forever," Valory tells me as I grab a seat.

"Give me a break, I had a long night last night. Pretty sure it's all of your faults," I tell them.

"What do you mean 'all of your faults'? What were you doing last night?" Veronica asks, squinting at me and I quickly look over at Valory who was sealing her lips together, then at Ben who was gesturing me to keep quiet.

"Um, you know, the normal stuff; drinking, getting high...apparently, going through your underwear drawer."

"Her what!?" the kids snap.

"Oh, forget I said that."

"You gotta stop doing that, dude," Ben begs.

Veronica walks over to the table and, one by one, places a plate in front of all of us, "Eat up, guys," she says.

"Hotdogs for breakfast?" I ask, looking down at my plate and at that moment, they all burst into laughter, "I mean, that's cool. I'm always down for new customs. I just thought a balanced meal of eggs,

198

bacon and toast would be better for kids about to head off to school," I say and they burst out laughing again.

"Dude," Ben chimes in, "you really don't know, do you?"

"The nutritional value of a well-balanced breakfast? Apparently, not."

"We just got off of school," Valory finishes.

"Jesus, I didn't know they let kids go to night school. Why couldn't they do that when I was a kid? I'd probably be a rocket scientist by now."

"Babe," Veronica says softly, "it's the middle of the afternoon."

"I slept that long?! Why didn't you wake me?!"

"You looked so cute, all cuddled up in my bed," she answers with a smirk and I look around the table to see even the kids were grinning ear to ear, so I exhale and place a big smile on my own face before taking a big bite out of a hotdog.

"Ba?" Taylor asks me.

"What, you can't cut your own hotdog?" I reply.

"Da da doo," he answers.

"And I don't blame her! I wouldn't trust you with silverware either!" I say then grab his plate and start cutting up his hotdog.

"Wait," Veronica intervenes while shaking her head, "how can you understand him?"

"He's a kid. What's not to understand," I answer, handing the plate back to him.

"Da?"

"Sure, one sec," I tell him and I reach over, grab the ketchup and squirt some on his pile of pork slices.

199

"Doo da."

"You're welcome."

"Wait! I'm confused! How do you-" Veronica attempts but Valory interrupts, "So, Chord, where do you work?" she asks.

"Uh, I don't, actually. Well, I do, just not at a traditional job."

"So, what do you do?" Ben asks.

"I'm a ghost writer."

"Ba ba doo?!"

"Not that kind of ghost! I'm a ghost WRITER."

"What does that mean?" Valory presses.

"It means I write songs, but I don't take credit for them. I just collect my paycheck and shut my mouth."

"Who do you write songs for?" Ben asks.

"Eh, a bunch of spoiled, Silicone Valley offspring," I answer.

"Have you written any songs I would know?" Valory asks.

"Well, I just finished a song called broken," I answer and suddenly all of their eyes light up.

"You wrote broken by Nevaeh?!" she gasps.

"Am I supposed to know who that is?" I ask, chomping into the hotdog and quickly closing my mouth.

"Nevaeh is one of the biggest musicians in the world right now! She's a pop icon!" Valory says.

"That doesn't answer my question," I reply and at that moment Veronica pulls out her phone, clicks around for few seconds before laying it on the table.

"And if you still want this

And if it's still worth it

You've got to believe

You've got to believe

I can be broken

And I can be changed," a young girls voice sings from the phone.

"Hmmm, she actually didn't change any lyrics. Well, she wins a couple points in my book just for that," I admit.

"You're famous!" Valory shouts.

"Infamous," I correct her.

"What does that mean?" Ben ask.

"It means I do all of the work and get none of the fame."

"But don't you want to be famous?" he ask.

"Fu...hell no," I pause, looking over at Veronica, "is 'hell' okay?"

She sighs and answers, "I guess."

"Good. Then, hell no. I hate attention. I'm so antisocial I would probably die if I had people admiring me on that level."

"But, we give you attention, and you spend time with us."

"I guess, you're right, but that's different."

"How?"

"Well, I like you guys," I say, giving him a smile and he gives me one right back.

"Ding! Dong!"

"Now, who could that be?" Veronica asks, getting up and walking to the door.

"Oh, shit," I sigh.

"You were doing so good not cursing, dude," Ben says to me.

"No, trust me. This is the appropriate time for cursing," I reply.

"Why is that?" he ask.

"Just wait," I answer.

"You can't be here right now!" I hear Veronica say at the door, then I look over at Ben and say, "That's why."

"They're my kids too!" a man's voice yells.

"You're drunk! Go home! We'll talk about this later!" she orders.

"This is my home!" he snaps.

I glance over at the back door. It taunted and sirens for me as my primal instincts kicked in and I raise up from my chair and start walking to it. I'm stopped when I look back to see the sorrowful eyes of three little children begging me to stay with their heartbroken glare.

"Fine," I give in and walk back to the table.

"No! You can not come in! Just go away!" Veronica continues to yell.

"Get out of my way!" the man shouts and I hear the sound of shoving. I march my way into the living room.

When I get there, I see Veronica with her hands on a man's chest, trying to prevent him from entering the house any further. He looked to be at least six foot tall with a beer gut, red face and massive bald spot. He stumbles as Veronica shoves him back toward the door. His eyes were glossed over with impairment but when he saw me, he sobered up quickly.

202

"Is this him!? Is this the guy!?" he snarls and stomps in my direction as he tries not to stumble.

"Hmm, apparently, I am famous," I say.

"You're what?" he slurs.

"Oh, we were just talking about how I'm borderline famous."

"So, you been talking to my kids!?"

"I mean, it'd be rude not to."

"Who do you think you are!"

"Well, there goes that fifteen seconds of fame."

"What the hell are you talking about?" he asks.

"Honestly, most of the time, I don't even know," I mutter and he takes his attention off of me and looks over my shoulder.

"Hey, guys," he says softly as he tries to hold himself up. I turn my head and see the kids looking on in terror as they bore witness to all of this, "come here, guys," he says, but instead they run over and hide behind me while peaking around my arms. Suddenly, his complexion changes and his face turns bright red as he stares through my skull, "Who the fuck do you think you are?"

"We've been over this, I'm kinda famous but not really. It's this whole antisocial demeanor of mine. It all really started when I was a child and-"

"-SHUT THE FUCK UP!!!" he yells at me.

"I mean, you asked," I mutter and quickly Veronica wiggles herself in between us.

"You need to leave," she calmly tells him.

"Have you been fuckin him?!" he screams.

"Bob-" she tries but he presses.

"Have you two been fucking! Answer me!"

"Please, stop," she pleads.

"Seriously," I chime, "the kids hate it when I talk about my sex life with their mom."

"I'M GONNA KILL YOU!!!" and he shoves Veronica to the floor then furiously stomps toward me.

"Mom!" the kids cry out as Veronica's body crashes to the hardwood.

"Well," I say as he reaches for me, "like Grandpa always said," then I slap my hands to his shoulders and...

"*Smack!*" I slam my forehead on his nose.

"Ow! Fuck!" I shout, "I never knew that hurt on both ends!"

Bob's head snaps back as he reaches for his face, "You fucking head butted me!"

"Yeah, and I immediately regretted that. Doesn't it hurt like a mother fucker? Maybe I did it wrong," I say.

"What the hell is wrong with you?" he asks, removing his hand and examining it.

"Obviously, no one ever taught me how to fight. Aw! Come on! Are you not even bleeding?"

"You know what," he deviously glares at me before reaching behind his back.

"Other than Grandpa was an absolute bad ass?" I mutter just before he pulls out a gun and points it dead at me.

"What are you doing with a gun?!" Veronica screams.

"This is Tennessee, he probably picked it up on his way here," I say as I push the kids behind me.

"DO YOU EVER SHUT THE FUCK UP!!!" he yells, gun shaking in his hand.

"Pretty sure they give those away in Happy Meals at this point," I say.

"Chord!" Veronica warns me, "shut up!"

At her demand, I pause and look down at the kids who were now quivering behind me then I look back at him and calmly say, "Look, buddy, you're drunk-"

"-I'm drunk?! I'm drunk?! Aren't you the cool guy always popping pills n' shit!"

"Oh, my God! Speaking of," and I reach into my pocket.

"Chord! He's gonna shoot you!" Veronica says.

"Which makes this the perfect time to down a few. Jesus, that's why they call them PAIN killers," I say then pop open the bottle, but before I can take any pills, I see Veronica getting to her feet and staring at me as her eyes begin to flood with tears.

"Chord," she begs, "just go."

"But mom!" Ben tries.

"Ben, stop!" she orders him, "Chord, please, just go."

"But I-"

"You heard her!" Bob groans, "get the hell out of my house!"

I stand there in shock for a moment. I look at the kids again, their faces drowning in tears and fright, Ben holding on to my shirt as he latched on in fear and Valory's arms wrapped around my waist. I look back up at Veronica, "Do you want me to come back later?"

205

"I don't ever want to see your face here again!" Bob demands.

"Please, Chord, just don't come back," she begs one last time.

"Yeah, I guess, I shouldn't come back, huh? I mean, what was I even doing here in the first place," and I try to walk away but the children's grip tightens around me.

"Ben! Valory! Let him go!" Veronica orders them and slowly they release me as I walk away slipping through their fingertips.

"Chord!" they cry, but I ignore it and force my feet to the door. I open the door but before I can leave, I hear, "Ba!!!" Taylor screams as he sprints towards me with his arms out and his eyes drowning.

"Taylor, no!" Veronica shouts and she snatches him up mid-way.

"Baaaaaa!!!" he cries as he reaches for me.

"I have to go, buddy," I explain as my body shook with every step I took away from him.

"BAAAA!!! BAAAAAA!!!" he yells out to me, trying to force himself through his mother's tightening grip.

"I told you, buddy, I can't stay," my face trembled as I walked out of the house, closing the door behind me and through the walls I hear a faint, "Baaa lub doooo! Baaaa lub doooo!!!"

"I love you too, buddy," I whisper before making my way to my car.

.   .   .

   .   .

"Boom!" the sky roars as the dark grey clouds clump together and threaten me with downpour at any moment. I slam on the gas as my Charger twist and turn through the labyrinth back road. The wheels leap up at every hill and the steel body comes crashing down on the

206

hard concrete as I tear through the country veins. My hand rolls over the steering wheel and my knuckles turn white to my tight grip. The points of my teeth crush together until agony shot throughout my jaw. Every muscle in my body flexed at its peak as I shook in misery while my heart pounded hard in my chest, *"SCREECH!"* the tires squeal when I rip through yet another sharp turn. Suddenly, my breathing becomes erratic and uncontrollable as I viciously rock back and forth while forcing the pedal down to the floor.

"Mmmhhh," I ramble, trying to force the pain back down, "don't do it! Don't you fucking do it!" I demand myself and the car starts to sway right and left in the curving, unpredictable road, "Shit! Shit! Shit!" I finally surrender as I jerk the wheel to the side and the giant behemoth skids off road. I slam on the brake causing it to slip and slide on the gravel below. Once at a complete stop, I open the door and completely collapse on the unforgiving ground beneath me, "Ahhhhh!" I scream as the flood water escapes my eyes and spills out on the ground and I'm forced to watch as my weakness seeps into the gravel. I inhale causing my lungs to fill up to my throat and, "Ahhhhh!!!" force the torment out of my body and my vision blurs with tears as I kneel there weeping like a child. I stare through water at my crippled hand before raising it up in the air, looking down at the solid ground of sharp stones, clinching my fingers as hard as I could into my cast and...

"Boom!" the sky screams, flashing a bright light before I can go forward with my assault. I slowly look up with a menacing snarl and yell, "What!? What the hell do you want, huh!?"

"Boooom!" the sky yells back at me as lightening pierces the sky.

"Fuck you! Where the hell were you my whole life? What the fuck have you ever done for me? Nothing! I did everything! I never asked for your help! I never wanted you!!!" I shout to the heavens.

"Boom! Boom!" it roars as lightening cracks and dances across the sky right above me.

"KILL ME YOU SON OF A BITCH! DO IT, YOU FUCKING PUSSY! DO IT!!!"

"*BOOM! BOOM! BOOM!*"

"I HATE YOU!!! I FUCKING HATE YOU!!!" I let out with all of my breath and at that moment, the skies settle, the lightening vanishes and the thunder retreats away into the misty country mountains.

Air rushed through my chest, my body fell numb and my eyes glossed over in shock as I kneeled there on the side of the murky back road. I push off the hard, cold and stony ground, raise to my feet and drag myself back to my car. Once inside, I gently close the door behind me and glance over at the passenger seat. The bottle of pills lay there resting on the vintage leather. For a moment, I glare at the plastic medical prison as my hand trembled at my side until, finally, I reach over and snatch the bottle up, pop open the top and pour half the pills in my throat, swallowing them down hard.

"There's just one more thing I have to do. Just one more thing I have to try," I mutter then I start the car up and dart off into the approaching stormy night.

.   .   .

        .   .

"Bang! Bang! Bang!" I plunge my fist into the door. The clouds had finally broken and the rain was beating down on every surface as the rumbling of thunder echoed through the cold night. I was standing on the front step of a small brick home, maybe two bedroom and one bath. The lights were shining through the blinds as I banged my fist against the door. My legs grew weak as I found it hard to hold myself up and my head felt lighter than air. I had to force my eyelids open as the temptation to pass out became overwhelming. The only thing keeping me conscious was the icy drops of water jabbing at my back and the undying urge to be with Emily that was consuming my existence.

"Bang! Bang! Bang!"

"Uh, can I help you?" a voice behind me asks. I turn around and am shocked at what I see, "Nurse chocolate cake?"

"I thought I told you my name?" she asks, standing in the rain with a bag of groceries and a look of confusion across her face.

"You did, I just like nurse chocolate cake better. Wait, is that racist?" I ask.

"I mean, kinda," she answers.

"I would've went with vanilla cake but, ya know...you're black."

"And now it's racist," she rolls her eyes at me.

"How can I be racist? I had sex with you."

"No, you didn't."

"I meant oral sex."

"And that just gives you a pass to be an asshole?" she ask.

"I mean......"

"Oh, my God. You actually think that gives you a pass to be an asshole."

"What, it was a kind gesture. If you would've blown me then I'd give you a pass on letting a 'white boy' or a 'cracker' slip," I say with a smile.

"You really think we all say 'white boy' and 'cracker'?"

"I mean, I don't know what you people say when we're not around."

"What do you mean 'you people'?" she ask sternly.

"......are you not black?"

"WHAT THE HELL ARE YOU DOING HERE, CHORD!" she snaps.

"I'm here to get my girlfriend back. What the hell are you doing here, nurse...Janice," I ask.

"Okay, first off, I am not your girlfriend-"

"-I wasn't talking about you," I interrupt and immediately the front door swings open, blinding me with a bright light.

"Josh!?" I rub my eyes, temporarily fixing my impaired vision when a beautiful image of a girl with bright green eyes and silky blond hair emerges in front of me.

"Emily!!" I shout.

"Josh!?" she shouts back, standing in the doorway.

"Wait, who is Josh?" Janice ask.

"Oh, my God. Chord," Emily answers, pointing at me.

"Oh, Chord," Janice replies.

"Wait, how do you two know each other?" Emily presses.

"How do you two know each other?" Janice rebuttals.

"NO!" I order.

"...no what?" they ask.

"I'm seriously not doing this again. First time I played this game I almost got jumped by a bartender, a bunch of frat boys and a black guy!"

"Seriously?" Janice groans.

"JESUS CHRIST! AFRICAN AMERICAN!" I correct myself, "the second time, I got my wrist re-broken by a cop!"

"Why did he re-break your hand??" Emily asks.

210

"He pissed him off," Janice answers.

"Of course, he did," Emily grunts while looking at me, "Wait, how do you know this?"

"How do you know this?!" Janice replies.

"NO! I'm serious! Stop!" I demand and suddenly Emily's eyes widen in shock as she stares at me, "What the hell happened to your neck!?" she ask and runs over to examine me.

"He cut himself climbing a barbed wire fence," Janice answers again.

"Will you shut up!" I snap at Janice.

"I told you not to climb that fence," she says, shaking her head.

"Wait," Emily pauses, "why were you two together? And why were you climbing a barbed wire fence?" she asks, punching me in the chest.

"First off, ow! Secondly, to get my car," I answer.

"To get your car?"

"It was stolen."

"It was towed," Janice chimes.

"Why are you still here!?" I yell at her.

"I live here! Now, why are you here?"

"I told you, to get my...wait, you live here?" I ask.

"Yea, with my brother," she answers.

"......oh, shit," I moan.

"Oh, shit?" Emily ask, "Chord, what did you do?"

"Are you fucking my brother's girlfriend?!" Janice snaps.

"Well, not currently but..." I say.

"Why do you care so much?" Emily asks, squinting at Janice.

"Umm," Janice mutters before looking over at me.

"Of course, you had sex with her. Because you just have to have sex with every fucking girl on this planet, don't you?" Emily groans.

"We actually didn't have sex," Janice answers.

"Oh, was your dick too big for her too?" Emily grunts.

"You didn't tell me your dick was that big," Janice says, looking down at my crotch.

"Ugh, it's slightly above average," I say.

"Seriously?" Emily says.

"I said slightly! Come on, you of all people!" I tell her.

"Yeah, yeah, yeah. It is pretty nice," she admits then quickly shakes her head, "wait, so, you didn't have sex with her?"

"......does oral count?" I ask.

"Of course, it counts!" she yells at me.

"That's what I said!" I reply.

"Why do you care, if you're dating my brother?" Janice ask Emily.

"You're dating her brother?" I press.

"I don't know, maybe? I don't know," she rambles.

"So, this must be her, huh?" Janice asks me, "This must be the girl you punched a wall over. The girl you're all heartbroken over. The one you're so madly in love with. The one you've been trying so hard to get back?"

212

"You've been trying to get me back?" Emily asks with a smile.

"Yes, Emily. I've been trying this whole time to talk to you again. My life has been a living hell without you. I love you more than my own existence and I'm ready to change everything about me that you hate just to be with you again," I tell her.

Emily lets out a deep sigh before walking over to me and running her hands up my drenched arms, "Josh, I don't hate you."

"You don't?"

"Of course not. You just really hurt me. And I wasn't sure if you were ever going to change," she explains as she stared up at me with her big, glowing, green eyes.

"I'm ready to change for you, Emily," I say softly.

"Look, guys," Janice intervenes, "this is cute and all, and I love a romance story as much as the next gal but if you guys are together, you need to get out of here before my brother-"

"CHORD!" Murda yells from the doorway.

"Murda!" Emily gasp and steps away from me.

"What the fuck are you doing here, nigga?" he asks me.

"We've established this already. I'm here to get my girlfriend back," I answer.

"Your girlfriend?? Emily is my bitch!" he says.

"Your what?!" Emily snaps.

"You sure know how to pick 'em, don't ya," I snark at Emily.

"You're one to talk, Mr. Pills n' Booze," Janice tells me.

"Hmmmm, is it too late to change my name again?" I ask.

"Wait!" Murda pauses, "how the fuck do you know where I live? Oh, that's right, you some sort of undercover cop or somethin."

"You're an undercover cop?!" Janice ask.

"I don't do that anymore! I'm actually getting a lot better at being more honest," I say.

"You mean like how you're fucking my brothers girlfriend?" Janice snarks at me.

"You fucking my bitch, Chord!" he yells.

"Where did we land on not calling women bitches?" I ask everyone.

"Seriously," Emily agrees, rolling her eyes.

"Have you been fuckin this nigga this whole time!?" he screams.

"So, he can call me nigga but I can't call you Nurse Chocolate Cake?" I ask Janice who was now glaring at me to shut up.

"Why the fuck are you calling my sister Nurse Chocolate Cake!" Murda presses.

"Because she's a nurse and she's attractive......and black," I answer.

"Seriously?" Janice snaps at me.

"Jesus Christ, African American! My bad!" I reply.

"No! I meant, why are you telling him about us?" she asks me.

"About us?! Have you been fucking my sister, nigga!" he yells and stomps in my direction before snatching my collar then raises his fist in the air, "So, you been fucking my girl and my sister!!! Ima fuck you up!!!"

214

"We haven't had sex!" Emily intervenes before Murda can punch me and he stops to glare at me with his knuckles pointing at my face ready to strike.

"You haven't had sex with her?" he asks me with a snarl.

"Well, like I said, not currently but-"

"Josh! Shut the fuck up!" Emily orders me before directing her attention back to Murda, "I swear, we haven't had sex since you and I have been together."

"So, you guys are together?" I ask and Murda's grip tightens around my collar as his face turns red.

"Seriously, Chord, shut up!" Janice also orders, "Murda, I promise you, him and I didn't have sex."

"Is this true, nigga?" he asks staring a hole through my skull as his fist clinches behind him and everyone stopped and watched, waiting anxiously for my next words.

"......does oral count?"

"*Smack!*" Murda's fist clashes against my face and I collapse to the cold, wet ground below.

"*Smack! Smack! Smack!*" he plunges his sharp knuckles into the thin flesh of my cheek as my head jerks back with every strike.

"Josh!!!" I hear Emily scream at the top of her lungs.

"*Smack! Smack! Smack!*" my sight starts to tunnel and the image of Murda savagely beating me grows dimmer and dimmer. The tiny hole that was my vision disappears and I'm left with the faint sound of Emily screaming my name.

"Josh!!" it calls out to me.

When the assault finally stops, my senses return to me only to show me the black sky trickling rain drops into my eyes, "Oh, my God!

Are you okay?" Janice runs to my side, picking my head off of the ground and I look up to see Emily holding Murda away from me.

"Look at me, Chord," Janice frantically says, "do you know where you are?"

"If I ever see you here again, I will kill you, nigga!" he points at me as Emily manages to push him back toward the door.

"Hey, Murda," I mumble as I lay there half unconscious in Janice hands, "if I can't fuck your sister......then, what's your mother doing later on?"

"I'M GONNA FUCKIN KILL YOU!!!" he screams and tries to push through Emily's resistance, but she forces him back into the house.

"Josh!" Emily looks back at me and with tears running down her face she tells me, "please, just go. And don't come back," and I'm forced to watch as she follows Murda back into the house. Janice releases me from her care, gets up and walks back to the door while looking back with a combination of pity and remorse. She overcomes her temptation to tend to me and slowly closes the door as the inside light narrows around my body.

When the door finally shuts, I'm alone outside laying in water and mud on a cold, dark and stormy night. I turn over, submerging my face into a dirt puddle, place my hands flat on the ground and press my knees into the mud as I somehow manage to bring myself to my feet. I slowly let all of the air escape my body as I stand there staring at the house where the love of my life hides away from me. My arms go limp and fall to my sides when I suddenly feel the outline of the bottle of pills in my pocket; the only true constant in my crazy, miserable and unpredictable life. The one thing I can count on when the agony of existing takes over is that the pills will make it all better. My only solace is this accumulation of chemicals in my pocket that cures me of all my suffering. These pills can relieve me of my conscious, my hormones, my hatred and my love. So, one last time, I reach into my pocket and pull out the bottle then raise it above my head and drink the remains,

216

leaving an empty and shallow plastic container before tossing it into the grass and stumbling back to my car.

.

.   .   .

.   .

I burst through my door causing it to swing open and puncture the wall. As I stare down at my feet, I try to guide them through my house, but fail half way do to my circling vision. My body goes crashing against the wall and I hold myself there for a moment to collect my conscious. Oxygen refused to enter my lungs so I had to remind myself to breathe. I've never had to encourage my body to stay alive but after ingesting an entire bottle of pain killers, the once effortless task of living now became an internal battle. My arms and legs fought my every demand to move forward. My heart beat diminished in my chest and my eyes began to fail me as the images surrounding me danced around as if to mock me and my urge to stay alive. I slowly start to inch my way to the living room and when I finally get there, I attempt to release the wall as my crutch but quickly tumble head first into the floor. I try to stand, but at this point my legs were cold and paralyzed as if all the circulation had escaped my lower half. So instead, I post up on my unstable forearms, and with every fiber of my being, I pull myself closer and closer to the kitchen as my motionless legs drag behind me. When I finally get there, I glance up to see three phones hanging on the wall, appearing and disappearing in nauseating fashion. I push off the floor as hard as the numb muscles in my arms would let me onto the wall as I work my way up. The three phones swayed back and forth on the wall as I struggle to pin point which one was real.

"Ring! Ring! Ring!" it shouts in my face.

"Ring! Ring! Ring!" my hand shakes as I slowly reach for the phone in the middle.

"Hel...hel...hello?"

217

"Mother fucker! Man, do you ever call back? I been tryna call you forever now. Listen, I got this bitch down here hounding my ass about getting another song out of ya. Jesus, you would think it's always the time of the month the way they constantly nag. I'm over here drownin' in period blood while you're back in Tennessee cryin' about some Southern cunt," Steve says.

"Mmmfff muhhhh," I try to form words but fail.

"What? The fuck did you just say? Look, whatever man. I don't see why you continue to do this to yourself. I know the South is your home but honestly, what has it done for ya? Every time I talk to you, you're whining about some piece of pussy that broke your heart. You don't talk to your family and I'm your only true friend so I don't see why you don't just move down here with me, baby. You and me would tear this town a new vag-hole. We would fuck this town dry. I'm tellin' ya, the pussy down here is so ripe you'll forget about all of those cunts where you are that are fuckin' with your head n' shit."

"Hel...meh...help...me," I struggle.

"Man, I can't understand a word you're saying. Look, get to work on that song. You were put on this Earth to write, not to love. You're the infamous Chord, baby! You entertain bitches all over this world! So, stop tryna play house and do what you were put in this universe to do; fuck pussy, do drugs, get wasted and, above all, write me that song. Alright, I gotta go. I love you," he says before hanging up.

"Nnn...nnnnooo," I try again, but it was too late.

As I stood there with my body trembling against the wall, I start to contemplate everything he said. Maybe he was right. Maybe I don't have a real purpose in this world. No matter how hard I tried, fate would not allow me the luxury of happiness so I'm damned to suffer forever. I've been searching this whole time for a place in life, and the reason I couldn't find it is the fact that I don't have one. There is not a square inch of this Earth that I belong in. I'm just a mechanism churning out chaos and pain for everyone around me as they're forced to endure my existence. My only application is to entertain people who don't know me so that they can point at me in amusement at my depression.

"AHHHHHH!!!" I scream out, smashing the phone against the wall over and over until there was nothing left but torn wire and shards of plastic hanging down. Unfortunately, that random destruction exhausted my last strength and my body goes fumbling through the kitchen until I finally collapse down on the cold tile. I look around for a ledge, a wall, a counter or something to post myself on but am only granted the trash can next to my head. I desperately reach up and grab it, trying to pull myself up with one last strive but the trash can tips over, spilling garbage across my face. A piece of paper covers my mouth and disrupts my breathing. At this point, I can't afford anymore obstacles holding me back from staying alive so I snatch it up. When I pull it away, I notice there is writing on it. I bring the paper in close and squint hard to try and make out the words. Maybe it was an unfinished song or a letter to Emily or, most likely, just an unpaid bill. When the letters finally settle, I am able to read it.

"The lord himself goes before you and will be with you; he will never leave you nor forsake you. Do not be afraid; do not be discouraged. Deuteronomy 31:8."

"......seriously?" I groan and at that moment, my arms fall to my sides and my chest violently pulsates in and out. Fluid fills my throat and spews out of my mouth as my body viciously convulses and I dig my nails deep into the floor to this torture. Purple and black dots seep into my peripheral, consuming my vision. Finally, every muscle in my body goes limp and my eyes roll to the back of my head as I give in, and let the darkness take over.

.   .   .

    .   .

"I think you're really gonna like this new place," mom says but I ignore her and go back to staring out of the window, "it's got a playground and a place for kids to play football," she tries again with a smile.

Her words didn't even enter my ears. I was too busy watching the town transform as we drove through southern Tennessee. We began our trip in my grandparent's neighborhood where the houses were nice, the streets were clean and the lawns were tended to. But as we drove away from the beautiful suburban sanctuary, the atmosphere began to decay into a concrete nightmare. Cracks started to form on the roads as the pot holes became more and more frequent. The buildings where forgotten businesses once existed were now vacant and covered in plywood and spray paint. Broken bottles paved the side of the streets accompanied by old newspapers and an endless fray of cigarette butts. Any property that wasn't emptied and run down was either a liquor store, a convenience store or a bail bondsman. As we twist and turn our way through this government blind spot, I notice people standing on every corner; not trying to cross, not waiting on someone, just standing there and glancing over their shoulder every few seconds. When we finally pull into what I would be forced to call home, I see that it is surrounded by chain link fence. Once inside, the apartments were made of old, fractured brick with metal bars covering the windows and thick metal doors.

"Well, this is it. What do you think?" she asks with a grin as we park.

"Looks like hell," I groan.

"Hey, watch your language, young man. And besides, it's not that bad. Now, come on. I'll show you the inside," she says with false delight and I cautiously exit the car and follow her across the broken sidewalk.

As we make our way toward the door, I see a man walking down the sidewalk. He was a tall African American man with enormously baggy clothes, consumed in jewelry and his hair was twisted from the roots all the way to the tips where beads held each strand together. As

220

our paths start to cross, I tense up before he looks at me and smiles big, exposing his shiny, golden teeth.

"Sup, lil man?" he says, nodding in my direction then casually goes on with his day.

The door looked to be solid steel and had enough locks to make you think this wasn't a home but a bank vault. Once inside, the floor was a stone cold, cheap and tacky colored tile with some of them missing parts of its tile only to show the concrete and adhesive glue underneath. None of the walls were dry wall; nor were they wood. Instead, every inch from the floor to the ceiling was a hard, abrasive cinder block that was painted white to disguise the fact that they made someone's house out of a cheap sand cement. I try to stare out at the sky but am interrupted by the metal bars fracturing my vision to the outside world. This was not a home; this was a prison.

"It's nice right?" she asks, standing in the middle of this confinement while forcing a grin across her face.

"Why didn't Alexis have to come here?" I ask. She clears her throat to hide the insult to my choice of words before replying, "Alexis is gonna stay with grandma and grandpa."

"Why can't I?" I plead.

"Because, sweetie, there isn't a room for you there," she explains.

"But it's a three bedroom house."

"You know the other room is where they keep Alexis's stuff."

"Cause they need a whole fucking room just for her trophies," I snarkingly reply while rolling my eyes.

"Language!" she demands before calming herself, "besides, I need my special guy with me or else I'd get bored."

221

"When do I get to see dad again?" I ask sternly. She pauses for what seemed like an eternity and stood there looking at the floor as if to contemplate what to say next. It was a simple question and it called for a simple answer. What time frame do I have to wait before I can see my father again? You would think it was a straight forward answer, yet here I was, staring at her as she struggled to form words. As if I'm asking so much of her just to tell me when I can see dad again. Why can't she just answer me and end this torment already? For months my mind has been hostile just wondering when I can see him again. Is she so stupid that she can't form words together in her brain just to answer me?

"Josh," she finally says, breaking the silence, "Mark is not your father."

.   .   .

    .   .

"*Beep! Beep! Beep!*"

"Ugh!"

"*Beep! Beep! Beep!*"

"Will someone turn off that damn answering machine!" I yell in hopes that I wasn't the only one in my house.

"*Beep! Beep! Beep!*"

"God damn it!" I moan before picking up the nearest object and hurl it towards the phone without even bothering to open my eyes.

"Hey! Be careful. That machine is expensive," a female's voice says.

"No, it's cool. I got it at a garage sell for like, ten bucks. Wait, what are you doing in my house?" I ask, laying my heavy head back down on the pillow.

"Your house? Sweetie, you're in the hospital."

222

"What?!?!" I jolt up with my eyes springing open to reveal I was in a hospital room, "what am I doing in the hospital? And why does a hospital room have an answering machine?"

"It's called a heart monitor, and you came here in an ambulance," the nurse tells me as she studies the computer screen next to my bed.

"The last thing I remember was...dying."

"Well, you didn't die. Came close, though. Your heart stopped a few times but we were able to bring you back. Then we had to pump your stomach."

"Pump my stomach?" I ask.

"We had to suck out everything in your tummy," she explains.

"Well then, first off, you owe me a sausage Mcmuffin, and second-"

"-beeeeeeeeeeeep!"

"Hey! Put that back on!" she orders me as I toss the finger clip to the side.

"Why? We obviously know I'm alive. No need in keeping that headache going."

"You're starting to become a headache, yourself," she sighs.

"Oh, my God. You should see my other doctor's office. They like, hate me," I laugh.

"Can't say that I blame them."

"Well, good job on keeping me alive. Now, goodbye," I say before raising off the bed and ripping off various sticky monitors.

"You should not be walking around right now!"

"Uh, it's not that hard. One foot in front of the other, sweetheart. Just because I died doesn't mean I was born yesterday," I tell her as I take off my gown.

"Excuse me, sir!" she gasp in offense to my sudden nudity.

"Seriously? You guys were the ones that got me naked in the first place. Act like you've never seen a dick before. You're a nurse, you probably examined ten clap ridden, teenage dicks before even coming to my room."

"How dare you!"

"What? I didn't say you gave them the clap. Although, being around that many infected wieners can't help, either."

"I'll have you know-"

"-which one of these drawers my clothes are in? Thank you," I interrupt as I tug on different handles, "hey, all of these are locked."

"It's to prevent people from stealing."

"Stealing what? My own clothes?!"

"The keys are at the front desk," she answers, picking up my gown to hand to me.

"Well, now this is happening," then I walk past her toward the door.

"Sir! You can not go out there!" she yells.

"Now, you say that buuuuuuuuuut," and I open the door and begin to walk my naked ass down the hospital.

As I make my way through the fluorescently lit hallway, private parts dangling below, I pass by several different patients as they stop and stare at my manhood on display. When I finally come across a white coat staring into a clipboard, I try to get her attention.

"Hey, do you know where the front desk is?" I ask and she doesn't even bother looking up from her files.

"It's right down the hall, to the left," she pauses when she finally looks up at me, "Do you wanna tell me why you're butt naked in my hospital?"

"Do you wanna tell me why you drug grown men unconscious, then dress them up in gowns?" I reply.

"You must be Mr. Chord," she rolls her eyes.

"Wow, I've really become famous amongst you doctors. You must know my other doctor, he hates me too," I say as a group of nurses walk by, staring at my naked body.

"No, but your girlfriend warned me you'd be a gigantic pain in the ass," she groans.

"And by gigantic, do you mean......wait, my girlfriend?!" I ask in shock and at that moment I hear a voice call out from behind me, "Josh!" I turn to see Emily down the hall with wide eyes staring at me. It looked as if she'd been talking to a nurse but stopped right when she saw me, "Why the fuck are you naked?!"

"This jerk stole my clothes," I say, pointing to the doctor.

"Why did you steal his clothes?" Emily asks the doctor as she walks up next to me.

"I didn't STEAL anything. We lock the clothes in a drawer to prevent stealing," she explains.

"Which begs the questions; how can I steal what is already mine?"

"It's not for you!" she snaps, "it's for the nurses, and it's just a precaution."

"So, you drug me, put me in a dress then have the nurses pick-pocket through my clothes?"

"We didn't drug you! You came in drugged!" she replies while attempting to contain herself.

"Seriously, Josh," Emily says, "your heart stopped twice. They brought you back each time."

"Seriously?" I ask the doctor.

"Yes, Mr. Chord, the ambulance brought you in. You had enough pills in your system to kill ten people, but somehow we were able to keep you alive before pumping your stomach-"

"-Sausage Mcmuffin."

"-Shut up!" she orders before turning her attention to Emily, "and I will get his key. Now, will you please direct your man-child boyfriend back to his room?"

"Oh, he's not my," Emily stops to look over at my bruised, scared and naked body then around at the on looking patients and nurses, "Ugh, fine. Come on, man-child."

"You forgot the other part," I say with a grin as she escorts me back.

"No."

"No what?"

"I'm not saying it."

"But you were thinking it."

"Ugh!" she loudly grunts, "will you hurry up!"

Once back in the room with the key, I finally release my clothes from captivity, "What the hell did they spill on them?" I ask, staring down at my stained shirt.

"They didn't," Emily answers, "you threw up all over yourself trying to get the pills out of your system."

226

"Well, guess I'm going shirtless," I throw the shirt in the trash and put the rest of my clothes on when I look over to see Emily sobbing in the corner.

"Josh, what the hell?" she asks me.

"What, you expect me to walk around with a puke stained shirt? Hell, I was all ready to prance around nude if they'd let me. I don't see why we all don't just-"

"-Not that! I meant why did you do it?"

"I told you, I don't like wearing gowns," I answer. At that moment, Emily's face began to tremble as she fought back tears, "Will you please, for once in your life, take something seriously?"

"I mean it. I seriously don't like gowns," I reply with a smile but she wasn't entertained. Instead, she burst into tears before running into my body and wraps her arms around my sides, "You could've died, Josh."

"Aw, come on. You can't get rid of me that easy."

"I don't want to get rid of you, asshole!" she says, pushing me off and punching me in the chest.

"Okay, ow! Did you not hear the doctor? My heart stopped...twice!"

"Just tryna keep it going," she replies with a smile while running her hand over my bare chest.

"You were always able to get my heart beating," I wink at her.

"Oh, my God. Let's go home, stud," she grabs my hand and guides me out of the room.

"Wait, how did you know I was here?" I ask as we walk.

"Does this look familiar," she answers by reaching into her pocket, pulling out an empty pill bottle and tossing it to me, "after Murda kicked your ass-"

"-I wouldn't say he *kicked my ass*."

"No, he definitely kicked your ass."

"Unfair advantage, I was stoned out of my mind."

"Anyways!" she snaps, "after that, I pushed him back inside, calmed him down and left the house to check on you. Which, is when I saw an empty bottle of pills laying on the grass."

"The real crime here is littering."

"When I saw the bottle, I rushed to your house. When I got there," she pauses to let the tears fall down her face, "you were laying there motionless in vomit and trash. You were so cold, Josh. I was so scared."

"And you didn't bother to grab me a clean shirt?"

"Ugh!" she punches my arm.

"Again, ow!"

"I thought you were dead, asshole! The doctor said if I had shown up any later you would have died," she says as said doctor approaches us in the hallway.

"Where is your shirt?!" the doctor asks, shaking her head, "you know what, forget it. Just sign here so you can get out of my hospital."

"And here I thought you would have kept me around just to rack up my medical bill; pumping me full of unnecessary meds, only using one pair of latex gloves, but making me pay for an entire box, charging me for cable so you can binge a couple episodes of House while you operate on me."

"Just sign the damn paper!" she yells.

228

"Hey, wait," Emily intervenes, "let me see that pen," and I hand it to her when she grabs my bad wrist and starts writing on it.

"What are you doing?"

"I never got to sign your cast," she answers.

"Probably had something to do with the fact that you WEREN'T TALKING TO ME!"

"Oh, hush," she says when she finishes her signature. I look down to reveal the word *asshole* written across my cast in big, bold letters.

"Well, that's definitely your signature," I say and we both burst out laughing.

"If you two are done, can you both please leave," the doctor pleads and we finally make our way to the main entrance.

The lobby before the entrance (unlike the rest of the hospital) was actually quite pleasant. The bland fluorescent lighting was replaced with soothing yellow light fixtures that calmed the atmosphere. Instead of tile, there was a thick, yet soft carpet below. The walls were painted an egg white but expressed the same yellow glow as the fixtures above and, in the corner of it all, stood a piano.

"Why's there a piano in a hospital?" I ask, making my way toward it.

"It's probably just for decoration," Emily answers and she turns her head to see me sitting at the beautiful instrument, "Josh, we don't have time for this."

"I almost died. All I have is time," I position myself over the keys.

"Seriously, Josh. I have to-"

"-I wrote a song for you," I interrupt and she lets out a sigh before replying, "Of course, you did."

"You told me to."

"That was a long time ago," she says and crosses her arms in protest of my potential musical display.

"Okay, maybe I'm a procrastinator. But in my hectic, unpredictable and dangerous life, I still always thought of you. Enough to write a song. You've always been the first to hear my work, so please, let me play this for you," I beg.

"Fine," she gives in, sitting down next to me.

"Think back to hell again could

  We ever understand what

  We could have had or could have been

  Love aint no friend of me so

  Here's to our enemies, who

  They only want to see us down

  And in the distance I see

  A universe where we

  Have no pain and have no end

  Across the stars I'll meet you

  Don't let your heart defeat you

  Cause only we can stop us now

But you know I love it when you say

Maybe I think I'll stay here

This time I'll love

This time I'll try

This time I'll think before saying goodbye

This time I'll hurt

This time I'll cry

And when I think of the years gone by

This time I'll learn

This time I'll learn

Lost in a second chance we

Kiss then we make up only

To see our kingdom crumble down

And in the wreckage we know

There comes a fork in the road

And I'm forced to let you go

But in the darkest hour

We are the only ones

We are broken but we are young

And you know I love it when you say

Baby, I think I'll stay here

This time I'll love

This time I'll try

This time I'll think before saying goodbye

This time I'll hurt

This time I'll cry

And when I think of the years gone by

This time I'll learn

This time I'll learn"

"Josh, that was beautiful but..." she struggles.

"But what?" I press on.

"What am I supposed to say to that?"

"Say you love me. Tell me that you feel the same way that I feel inside about you. And that every minute we're apart, you think of me as much as I think of you. Tell me that we can leave this all behind and be together. Emily, when you're gone, all I do is punish myself. I numb myself of the pain I feel when I'm away from you until the moment I get to see you again and all of the addictions fade away. I know I've messed up in the past. I know I have my demons. But I also know, that if we're together, I promise I will spend every waking minute of my life becoming the man that you deserve to have, if you just tell me you love me."

She stares at me in silence, taking in every word that I just dropped on her. Then, she looks down at the piano keys as if the sight of me was unbearable with what she was about to say.

"Josh," she says softly.

"Emily, I want you to marry me," I say as I look deep into her bright green eyes. She sat there in shock of my proposal. She opens her mouth but words didn't follow.

"I know it sounds crazy," I tell her, "but it's the only thing that makes sense to me right now. I've never been more sure of anything in my life. If you give me a chance, I will change for you. Emily, I want to spend the rest of my life with you," a big goofy smile comes across my face in delight of my new confession.

"Josh......I can't," she painfully answers and my heart turns in my chest. The smile faded as the delight decayed into sorrow.

"Why not? I mean, you rushed to my house. You showed up here while I was dying. That must mean that you-"

"-that means that I care about you, Josh," she intervenes, "and I always will. But...I can't love you anymore."

"What do you mean you can't?" I ask confused. She raises from the piano bench, grabs me by the hands and, with tears falling from her eyes, explains, "I wanted to tell you, but I was so mad at you. Then, we weren't talking for weeks and when I did see you, I hear about all these girls and just...Josh, I'm leaving."

"Leaving where?"

"They gave me an offer to fly out to the Middle East where they're gonna train me to be a military doctor. They said when my training is done, I could come back and work on getting a degree. They're gonna pay for it all. All my hard work is finally paying off."

"That's great!" I say as the joy comes back to me, "Hell, I'll buy a ticket and go with you. So, where are we going? Iraq? Pakistan?

Iraqistan? Should I bring one of those turban things, or just buy one when I get there? And also...what is a turban?"

"You're not listening!" she snaps before calming herself, "you can't come with me."

"What? Of course I can. I can afford any ticket to anywhere on this big planet of ours. Hell, I'll even have us flying first class. Bet the military isn't that accommodating."

"You can't come cause I don't want you to!" she yells at me.

"What do you mean? You don't want me to?"

"My life is finally taking off in the right direction. I finally have clarity on my future and I just don't think you should be in it. I mean, I care about you and I swear I always will but, Josh, you're bad for me. You said it yourself; your life is crazy and hectic and wild, and that's fine cause it's who you are and what you do. I'm done trying to change you. You are who you are. You're the infamous Chord," the flesh of her hands began to trace mine as she walks away and slips out of my fingertips. I had finally run out of words to say. There were no clever one-liners, no excuses, no jokes and no more pity speeches left. I knew even if I tried to chase after her that she would stop me with more words that pierced through me like knives. So instead, I sat there and watched, for the final time, as Emily walked away, leaving me alone once again. Alone, next to the very instrument of my demise. The one device where I reflect my every being onto the world. And in return, it gave me money, fame and sex. But ultimately, I couldn't handle the responsibility that came with this lifestyle. I could not tame this monster I had created and it finally consumed me, leaving no trace of who I once was. All that was left was who I had become. I am the infamous Chord.

.   .   .

.   .

"What do you mean he's not my father?" I ask her and she pauses for a moment to collect herself.

"Everyone told me to wait until you were older, but you deserve to know. It was a long time ago. Mark and I were going through a rough patch and I just got confused."

"Confused?"

"Before I met Mark, I was on tour with this band. We were traveling all around the country from city to city. I was having the time of my life. I mean, here I was traveling with my favorite rock band, partying every night and sleeping all day. We were in a different state every single week. I was seeing new places, meeting new people and doing things most people only dream about. But eventually, that lifestyle started to wear down on me. I started to wonder where I was going and what I was doing with my life. It was fun at first but it slowly became obvious that I couldn't do this forever. After being on tour for years, I suddenly felt trapped, like I couldn't escape this lifestyle. Then, the road manager told me that we were doing a gig in Nashville. I was so happy that I was going to be back home and see my family and friends again. I was torn between staying home and being with my parents or staying with my favorite band and continuing this crazy party life. That's when I met Mark. We met at the show. We were both really young and really high. It was the eighties, after all. He was this nice country boy that looked like he had just got off of work and went to a concert with his friends. We couldn't have been more opposites but somehow, we fell for each other and he convinced me to stay. Not long after that, we found out I was pregnant with Alexis. Being the traditionalist that he is, Mark proposed while I still had the pregnancy test in hand. Nine months later your sister was born. That's when things just started to change. For some reason, Mark and I grew apart. I mean, we were so young when we met, and having your sister was a blessing but it was just too soon for us. We decided it was best for everyone if we separated. Alexis and I went to go stay with Grandma and Grandpa while he stayed at his house. Then, one day I got a call," she lets out a deep sigh, "it was the lead singer of the band. It was officially the nineties and hairbands were out and grunge was now in. Apparently, it was getting harder and harder to fill arenas. The record label finally decided to pull the plug and he was left all alone in his mansion with millions of dollars but, for some reason, he thought of me. I left Alexis with my parents and flew out to see him. It was only supposed to be for a few days, but that changed. When I got there, it wasn't the same life I had left behind. There was no music, no partying, no traveling, no fame, and no passion. All that was left were the drugs. I don't remember a lot from there on. That part of my life is too blurry. I do remember getting a call from your grandmother asking where I was. I told her to relax and that it had only been a week. That's when she dropped it on me that it had actually been months since I had been home. I snuck out, not even saying goodbye, and took the first bus home. When I finally got back, Mark was furious. We screamed at each other for what seemed like days, but when it was all over, for some reason, we made up. Something about being apart from each other made us realize how much we truly missed one another. I promised to leave that life behind if he promised to give me a chance and not distance himself. The family was going great. That's when it happened. We found out I was pregnant again. Unfortunately, the time frames didn't add up for him. I begged and pleaded to him and he finally agreed to stay in our lives knowing that you weren't his son. The day you were born he seemed so happy. I thought maybe this could work. But as time went by, he just became more and more distant. I don't think," her eyes began to flood with tears, "I don't think he ever really forgave me for having someone else's child."

"So," I pause, "I was a mistake?"

"Sweetie, no!" she runs over and places her hands on my shoulders, "you and Alexis are the greatest things to happen to my life. I swear, even if I could go back, I wouldn't change a thing. It doesn't matter who your father is. You'll always be my boy."

"Who is he?"

"What?"

"Who is he! Who is my father!" I raise my voice at her.

"Sweetheart, please."

"No! I wanna know! Who is my father! You lied to me this whole time! Tell me the truth!" I scream in her face as she cries.

"Please, Josh," she begs me.

"You're nothing but a liar! Tell me! Tell me who he is!" I jerk my body out from her grip hard enough for her to fall to the floor and she sits there sobbing.

"I don't know," she answers softly, "I don't know who your real father is. All I know," she wipes the tears out of her eyes, "I conceived you when I was in Los Angeles."

"I hate you!!!" I yell at the top of my lungs.

"No! Josh, please!"

"NO! YOU'RE A LIAR AND I WILL ALWAYS HATE YOU!!!" I launch myself forward and shove her down before darting off into one of the random rooms in this cement prison. I slam the door hard, locking it behind me then falling to my knees as my blood boils in my veins and my vessels poke through my skin. My body tenses to the point of agony when I run to the corner and crouch down with my back against the wall and my knees to my chest as I fight back tears.

"Josh, please open the door," mom cries outside of the room. I start to bang the back of my head hard into the cinder block wall behind me over and over again.

"Open the door," she begs me but I ignore her and continue bashing the back of my head into the wall harder and harder until I felt dizzy. I stop when I hear silence on the other side of the door. For a moment, it was quiet and still. My skull ached from my self-abuse, and I began to think mom had given up when I hear her say, "I'm sorry, Josh. I'm sorry that this is all happening to you. You didn't deserve what happened to you and I need you to know that this is not your fault. You can blame me if you want just, please, open the door. I need you now more than ever cause I don't think I can do this on my own. I'm afraid too, Josh. Please, give me a chance."

I sit there for a second, shaking in my own arms when my conscious finally comes back to me. My blood settled as my veins retreat back into my skin. The pain reseeded, the guilt left me and the confusion was gone. All that was left was my mother and I. So, I raise to my feet, walk to the door and reach for the knob, opening it and letting my mother in.

.   .   .

      .   .

"Hey, you!" I say, pointing to a man sitting next to the wall. He was a middle aged man with dirty, torn clothes from his jacket to his old, worn down shoes. His hair was long, frizzy and brown from not washing it. His beard reached down his chest and his teeth were various shades of yellow. He looked up from his blanket to see me quickly approaching.

"Hey, man! I don't want no trouble," he trembles.

"Stand up," I demand him.

"Look, pal, I aint got nothing to my name. What could you possible want from me?" he shakes in fear.

"Will you stand the fuck up? I don't have all day!" I yell and on my order he raises to his feet, shaking against the buildings wall.

"You see this?" I ask, taking a green sheet of paper out of my back pocket.

"Uh, yeah."

"You know what this is?"

"Uh, yeah. It looks like a car title. But what does that have to do with-"

"-Here," I interrupt him as I pull out a pen and start writing across the paper, "you see that Dodge Charger right there?"

"Yea, man. Is, is that yours?"

238

"Not anymore it isn't," and I hand over the title to him as he stares at me with a combination of confusion and delight.

"Hey, wait!" he snaps, "it's all beat up. The front is smashed in, the windows are cracked and there's a scratch going from the fender to the door!"

"Seriously! You're gonna complain about a free car?!" I yell at him.

"I'm just saying, you coulda takin' better care of it, is all," he shrugs his shoulders and I let out a hard sigh before replying, "Look in the glove compartment. There's a UT shirt signed by some famous football player. Don't ask me which one cause I don't remember. It should help pay for the damages. And also," I look back at my big, sexy, beautiful, black machine one last time, "treat him better than I did, okay?"

"You call it a boy?"

"YES! I CALL IT A BOY!" I scream, "Jesus, this was supposed to be a sentimental moment!"

The poor man pauses for a moment to glance over at the Charger. His face quickly changed to express gratitude for this random gift. He stared at the car as if it wasn't just a car. It was a place to sleep. It was transportation to a potential job. He looked at it as if it was a second chance.

"Thank you," he says softly and I continue my march toward the building.

As I make my way to a set of revolving glass doors, I see an entire spectrum of people coming and going through the turning entrance/exit. Some people leaving, some people possibly returning home. Happy families and young men and women, all with their own unique story to tell. I doubt any of their stories are quite as crazy as mine, though. I was born and raised in this beautiful southern jungle we call Tennessee and over the years it's treated me with both pleasure and

239

pain. I've been spanked, beaten, broken, abused, punched, sliced, crippled, had guns pointed at me and had my heart shattered into shards. I gave this wonderful state everything I had to give from my body to my soul. The people I've come across gave me experiences that I will never forget. Whether it be the southern girls just looking for a soulmate, a perverted ginger nympho, a single mother and her amazing children looking for a friend, a nerdy but sexy nurse with social anxiety or the love of my life, Emily; all of the women in my life have left an everlasting impression on me. Every woman I've ever met has changed me in some way. Regardless if I can call them good times or bad, I somehow came out of every encounter a better man. Each woman managed to point out a fracture in my being, forcing me to mend the gaps until I was whole. They made me smarter, stronger, powerful and, above all, self-aware. They forced me to examine myself as they relentlessly amplified my flaws into my own eyes until I was forced to surrender my narcissism and give in to change. For that, I am eternally grateful. But I can't stay here any longer. My journey has ended in this wasteland of liquor, drugs, sex and heartache. It's time for me to move on. It's time for me to open the door to my future and face the new challenges that lay ahead. This entire time I've been inserting myself into roles where I don't belong. I'm not a boyfriend. I'm not a husband. I'm not a father. I am a ghost writer named Chord.

"Hello, sir" the young woman says from behind the desk, "how can I help you today?"

"I need the first ticket to L.A." I tell her and she proceeds to tap on her keyboard while scanning her eyes over the computer screen.

"And what's your name?"

"Chord."

"What kinda name is Chord?" she ask.

I grin and reply with, "it's just who I am."

"Well, it'll just take one moment for me to pull up your options, Chord. So, what's your reason for leaving the south? Business or pleasure?" she casually ask me.

"Escape...I just need to escape."

.   .   .

.   .

How To Escape The South

www.ingramcontent.com/pod-product-compliance
Lightning Source LLC
Chambersburg PA
CBHW050926120626
46552CB00001B/63